young
love

Have you ever wondered how books are made?

UCLan Publishing is an award-winning independent publisher. Situated at The University of Central Lancashire, this Preston-based publisher teaches MA Publishing students how to become industry professionals using the content and resources from its business; students are included at every stage of the publishing process and credited for the work that they contribute.

The business doesn't just help publishing students though. UCLan Publishing has supported the employability and real-life work skills for the University's Illustration, Acting, Translation, Animation, Photography, Film & TV students and many more. This is the beauty of books and stories; they fuel many other creative industries! The MA Publishing students are able to get involved from day one with the business and they acquire a behind the scenes experience of what it is like to work for a such a reputable independent.

The MA course was awarded a Times Higher Award (2018) for Innovation in the Arts and the business, UCLan Publishing, was awarded Best Newcomer at the Independent Publishing Guild (2019) for the ethos of teaching publishing using a commercial publishing house. As the business continues to grow, so too does the student experience upon entering this dynamic Masters course.

www.uclanpublishing.com
www.uclanpublishing.com/courses/
uclanpublishing@uclan.ac.uk

Young Love is a uclanpublishing book

First published in Great Britain in 2025 by
uclanpublishing
University of Central Lancashire
Preston, PR1 2HE, UK

978-1-916747-35-7

1 3 5 7 9 10 8 6 4 2

Text design by Becky Chilcott.
Set in Kingfisher.

A CIP catalogue record for this book is available from the British Library.

Printed and bound in Great Britain by Clays Ltd, Elcograf S.p.A.

suzanne ewart

young love

uclanpublishing

To Max and Sophie

I'll be waiting on a table, chatting politely to a customer while they put their pin number into the card machine and decide how much they'd like to tip me. They'll say something funny, and I'll throw my head back – a little too dramatically, perhaps, but it's nice they're making my shift better by cracking jokes. I'll feel a tap on my shoulder and will turn round to find him standing there, that almost too large smile on his face. I'll be laughing because of the customer's joke, and then I'll be laughing at this – at how typical it is of him to show up in the middle of my shift without any warning. It's only once our eyes lock that my laughter will fade, as the significance of this takes hold.

"You came back," I'll say, once I've found my voice.

"I came back," he'll agree, before we kiss to applause from the diners around us.

Or I'll be outside the restaurant, and it'll start raining – an unexpected burst that falls on me like a shower. I won't be wearing a coat, having only come out for a breath of fresh air before returning to finish my shift. I'll point my face up to the droplets, letting the cool rain fall over my cheeks and down my neck.

"Would you like to come under?" he'll say, startling me.

I'll know the voice instantly, but I won't be able to look straight at him. Instead, I'll focus on the underside of the black golf umbrella that's now protecting us both. I'll find myself wondering what made him decide to make the upgrade from the putting-his-hood-up-and-legging-it technique of keeping dry he favoured when he was last here. He'll give me the moment before gently pressing his palm against my cheek, turning my face until I'm looking into his deep, hazel eyes.

"You came back," I'll say, the leftover rain on my face merging prettily with my tears.

"I came back," he'll agree, before leaning forwards and softly kissing my lips.

Or I'll be in the cramped staff room, polishing the cutlery ahead of a shift, and Tom will come in. He'll hold the door open because there will be someone with him who is waiting to be introduced.

"Kelsey," he'll say. "We've a new waiter starting today. As my most trusted waitress, I'd like you to train him up." There'll be a distinct note of mirth in Tom's voice, but I'll choose not to comment.

"No problem," I'll say, and stand to greet my new trainee. Tom will stand to the side, and I'll fall back into the chair as soon as I see him. Tom will wink at me before leaving us alone.

I'll want to rush to him but the shock of him in front of me won't let me move. Not caring how dusty the floor is, he'll come forward and kneel before me. I'll trace the contours of his face with my fingers, the face I've seen every night in my dreams since he left.

"You came back," I'll say.

He'll lean forwards, closing the inches between us, and he'll kiss me passionately, making up for the year since we last did that. When he finally stops, he'll breathlessly whisper, "I came back."

one

Kelsey

I OPEN MY EYES AND REACQUAINT MYSELF WITH REALITY. Toilet cubicle, the smell of recently poured pine-scented bleach, the blinking light that's never been fixed in the five months I've worked here, Dessie on the other side of the door getting ready for our shift to begin.

I look at my watch. Six forty. *Shit*.

"Jesus, Kelsey," Dessie says. "You planning on hiding in there all night?"

"Coming now."

Stop, I tell myself, the internal lecture my brief digression has earnt as familiar as the chorus of a pop song or a children's nursery rhyme. *Stop fantasising about him. Get on with the day and stop wasting it wishing for things that aren't going to happen.*

I breathe out slowly in the same way I see customers exhale when they've successfully ordered a Diet Coke instead of a glass of wine or have turned down an offer to go outside for a fag. Now my willpower's kicked in, I'm ready to step out and join Dessie in front of the mirror.

Under the excellent glaring lighting the ladies' toilets provides, I make sure my white shirt is tucked neatly into my black apron, that my make-up is still as flawless as it was when I put it on. Once I've checked my name badge is straight and on display, not hidden under the long extensions of black hair I curled before I left my bedroom, I'm ready.

Next to me, Dessie pulls her ponytail tighter, flattens a few loose strands around her hairline and puts a finger to her full lips to rub the clear lip gloss in a little more. It's the only make-up she ever wears, and she doesn't need it. It's hard to understand how she's here, working another Saturday shift with me at Ilk, a distinctly average mediterranean restaurant, albeit with a great setting by the water at Liverpool's Albert Docks. It's hard to understand how she is still struggling to earn enough from the odd extra job on TV instead of being a household name. A drama school graduate, she's talented *and* beautiful – and yet she is still here. Standing side by side, we're almost opposites: her tall and effortless, me petite and with the full face of make-up I always wear to work.

"Have you seen how busy it is outside?" she asks. "And Noah's just called in sick. We're going to be earning our tips tonight, ladies."

"If we get any tips," Joy says from inside the cubicle where I can hear her having a wee. "The state of most of them, we're going to struggle to get them to remember to pay the bill, let alone to tip us."

"Bloody heatwave," Dessie moans. "Brings out the knobhead in everyone."

Joy flushes the toilet and comes out, walking towards the

4

immaculately clean row of sinks. Joy never lingers in front of the mirror. She doesn't care what she looks like, doesn't worry one bit how straight her name tag is, how neat her uniform is. In a few short months, Joy will have finally finished her PhD in Medieval History and will be embarking on a career in academia. If an Oxbridge professor with an opening in their department happened to call in and start up a conversation about the socioeconomic consequences of the Black Death after ordering their garlic bread, I'm sure Joy would find it in her to be a wonderful waitress, but given that's not likely, a curt smile and an effort not to roll her eyes at the customers is the best she can offer. It's no secret that she's just here for a bit of money.

And for Dessie and me. She sticks it out because of us, too. As a trio of friends, we're an unlikely match but we've been together for months now. We work.

Before Joy moves off after washing her hands, we exchange a look which Dessie catches in the reflection.

"What?"

"Oh, come on," Joy says. "You might be right about the weather, but you're only jealous you have to serve customers all night instead of getting pissed with them."

"I am not," Dessie protests. Then she smiles. "OK, I am. Completely jealous. But it's all right, girls. Instead of sitting in the sun, we get to fetch their drinks and put up with six hours of bad flirting."

"Kelsey doesn't," Joy says. "You've got the dining room tonight, Kels. Hen party of twenty coming in at seven."

"Sorry," Dessie commiserates.

The dining room, a partitioned area at the back of Ilk available for private hire, with a back wall covered in fairy lights and champagne coloured velvet seats around a long black gloss table, is meant to be seen as a golden ticket for waiting staff due to the tips. The reality is hours of hard work with demanding customers, their cloying Prosecco breath all over us as they ask for way more than the extra tenner they throw in warrants. Unless we're in desperate need of more cash, Dessie, Joy and I try to avoid it.

"OK," I say, absently.

"OK? You'd normally be begging us to swap with you," Joy says. "What's up?"

"Nothing."

"I'd already prepared an excuse for why I couldn't trade places with you. Seriously, are you all right?"

I hover between insisting I'm fine and giving them the truth before the decision is taken out of my hands. A rush of words fills my mouth, desperate to be let out. "If you must know, today is exactly one year since Lewis left. I wouldn't mind the distraction of a night rushed off my feet."

"Oh, right. Sorry?" Dessie offers, and I understand the uncertainty in her voice. A year since my best friend left to go and work in New York is hardly an anniversary to be mourning.

"I know it's no big deal, it's just that Lewis is so obsessed with dates and symmetry, I can't help wondering if it might mean something to *him*. When we were teenagers, I struggled remembering my college timetable, but he would constantly be

6

like, 'Do you know it's been six months since we spent that day in Blackpool and you lost your flip-flop on The Big One?', or, 'It's coming up to the one year anniversary of us sneaking into The Forresters and getting pissed – shall we go back to mark it?' And . . . one *year*. It's a long time to be gone."

Dessie perches on the sink next to me. "Yeah, if you were girlfriend and boyfriend, I suppose it would be. But you're not. Or rather, not yet – but who knows in the future?" She backtracks when she sees her words have hit me like an accusation.

"I know," I sigh. "And I know it shouldn't matter how long he's stayed away. If he's happy, I'm happy and all that, but . . ." It's hard to tell them how upset I am that he's still not home, how the anniversary of him leaving has knocked me so much.

"But it does bother you," Joy finishes for me.

I shake my head at my reflection. "I'm trying really hard for it not to."

"I get it," Dessie says. "Before he left, it looked like you were becoming more, and it never happened. Even if you've managed to keep the friendship, that's tough."

"We already *were* more, and it already *had* happened, before him moving to a different continent forced us back to being friends," I correct her, images of the last time I saw Lewis pushing into my thoughts, his whole body pressed tightly against me as his lips explored mine. "And I've made my peace with that, for the most part." Dessie opens her mouth to object. "I have! It's just today. I can't help thinking about this time last year and how happy I thought we were."

Before Joy can pull me into one of her hugs, before Dessie can catch me with that pitying expression of hers, I leave them to finish getting ready. I've a sudden urge to go home and crawl into bed, the shift ahead stretching longer than it did a few minutes ago. I wish I hadn't brought any of this up. I've wasted months daydreaming about him coming back, instead of moving on like I should. I'm not meant to be doing this any more.

I take the steep stairs up to the restaurant floor, hoping that no one is going to fall down them this evening – especially any of my hen party. It was only two weeks ago I spent an hour bandaging up a woman's leg and waiting in the back with her for an ambulance. The paperwork those tumbles cause is the last thing I want tonight.

I try to push down the feeling that stepping into the private dining room is like getting into a cage and start arranging the table for twenty, laying out the A1-sized paper menus over neatly lined-up cutlery.

The next few hours go as expected. The bride-to-be is an accountant from Cheshire who admits to me in between courses that she was hoping her sister would organise a spa day rather than a drinking session. I feel sorry for her when she finds out that next on the agenda is a stripper in a function room at the back of Revolution. Still, it means that by just gone ten the dining room is tidied, and I'm free to step back into the main restaurant.

"Where do you want me, Tom?" I ask, but he's too busy in schmoozing mode with a table of six in the corner to give the matter any thought and dismisses me with a bat of his hand. The restaurant is almost empty. Dessie and Joy are leaning against the bar, looking wistfully out of the glass front at the busy outdoor seating area overlooking the water.

"How's it been in here?" I ask them.

"Hot and dead. Tom said he didn't need us outside, but, of course, that's where everyone has wanted to be all night. We've hardly earnt any tips stuck in here. To think, I've missed out on one of Professor Drake's wine and cheese nights for this," Joy laments. "Damn needing to be able to afford food and rent."

"To think, I could have been two bottles of wine in by now with some of the cast of Hollyoaks," Dessie adds. "Damn not being rich and famous yet."

They both turn to me with expectant looks on their faces. If I wasn't here, I'd be home with my grandparents in front of the TV.

"Come on," I say instead. "Let's not worry about what we wish we could have been doing tonight, but what we still can," I say, offering up the advice I've been trying to get myself to listen to for the last year. "If we get this lot paid up quickly, we can still make it in time to sit out and have a drink. The night's not over yet!"

two

Kelsey

THE RINGTONE I'VE SET FOR LEWIS'S MESSAGES PULLS ME from a night of crap sleep just before eleven.

I find my phone tangled in the duvet at the bottom of my bed and open WhatsApp, to a message sent all the way from New York.

LEWIS: You alive?

I sit up in bed, regretting the amount of wine we ended up drinking last night as I do, and work out what I'm going to write.

KELSEY: Yeah. Only just. Drank too much last night and this heat is insufferable. Insufferable!!

I grimace when the two blue ticks arrive. I tell myself to act normal, otherwise he'll know something's up. *Be cool, Kelsey.*

LEWIS: Please. You should try a heatwave in New York. The sweat! The smells! Take it you're still in bed then?

I look around my tiny bedroom; a room that's not designed to be a bedroom at all. In the other bungalows on our road, this room is used as a TV room, or a study, or a plush dressing room with a mirrored wall in the case of Mrs Delaney, three doors down. Gran and Gramps haven't had the luxury of using it as a spare room for themselves, as when they bought their retirement home it came with one granddaughter to house too.

The room fits a single bed and a small wardrobe. I've added to it over the years – there's a TV on the wall and fairy lights across the headboard that jazz it up a bit – but, even so, it's a world away from the king-sized bed, floor-to-ceiling window and charcoal fitted wardrobes Lewis has told me all about in his bedroom. That's how being twenty-five should look.

KELSEY: Yep. Where are you?

LEWIS: Just got up. Going to the gym in a bit and then working.

KELSEY: Gross. It's a Sunday, and isn't it 6 a.m. over there? Why aren't you hungover like a normal person?

LEWIS: Healthy body, healthy mind, and all that. So . . . what's on the menu this morning?

KELSEY: Good question. Will check and report back.

I let my phone fall on to my bed and get up, the craving of an ice-cold coffee far stronger than the craving of more sleep.

Gramps is already clattering in the kitchen next to my bedroom. We've had words about this. With my late shifts, he's promised to hold off on his baking until he's seen me surface and I've given him the thumbs up, to tell him I'm in a fit state for the whir of his cake mixer.

"Morning, Gramps," I say from the kitchen door, taking in the mess before going over to kiss him on his cheek. "What is it today?"

"Vanilla slices. I woke up last night with a craving for them. You know, I don't think I've made them in fifteen years. Did I wake you? I thought, given the time you crawled in last night, you'd have been out for the count."

"Nah, it's too hot to sleep."

"Iced coffee, then?"

"It's OK. I'll make it."

Gramps moves to sit on his stool by the back door, where the Sunday papers are already sprawled over the breakfast bar. Most mornings he folds himself over them, the MDF worktop cutting his stomach in two. But on Sunday mornings, he studies me. Running clothes on when I emerge from my room – I've had a sensible night. Fluffy slippers and straight to the frying pan to make a bacon butty – I'm rough as hell.

"We ended up sitting outside the restaurant last night after we shut up," I tell him, giving him the information he's after. "Even at two in the morning, it was still warm. We had too much wine to be honest, but we couldn't stop Tom bringing out more rosé and pretending he was in Ibiza. It was fun," I say, in an attempt to remove at least one of the wrinkles of worry from his pink, weathered face.

"Well, now, that sounds lovely. I'm pleased you had such a nice night."

"Yeah, I did," I tell him, and he returns to his papers with a smile.

"How about you?' I ask. "Did you sit out?"

"We did. Half twelve, it was, when we went to bed. It was so pleasant we didn't want to come in."

I smile at the thought of Gran and Gramps sitting next to each other on their beloved patio furniture enjoying the warmth. "Gran still in bed, then?"

"No, she's been up for hours. She's next door, looking after Emma's two little ones for an hour or so."

"In that case, why don't you get going with these vanilla slices? They'll be a nice treat for her when she returns."

I take my coffee and move away from the work surface. Gramps slides himself off the bar stool and eagerly returns back to his ingredients and beloved Magimix, and I head to the lounge at the front of the bungalow.

With its gold sofas, ornaments lining the windowsill and fireplace, and the boxy, very non-smart TV in the corner with the lamp on top, this is markedly Gramps and Gran's domain. Usually, I'll find Gran in here and sit with her to watch whatever daytime TV programme she's chosen, but today I'm free to pick up the heavy remote and flick through the channels myself.

I sip my coffee on the sofa, not fully relaxing back into the cushions to minimise the risk of spillage. I settle on a dating cookery show on the beach on Channel 4 but am disappointed by it immediately. The dish of scrambled eggs and avocado the bare-chested chef prepares for his bikini-clad date fails to excite anyone. He didn't use any seasoning.

I don't bother to turn it over. Leaving it on as background noise, I pick up my phone.

KELSEY: *Vanilla slices.*

LEWIS: *Nice. Send me one, will you?*

KELSEY: *Sure. I believe vanilla slices travel very well internationally.*

There's a pause before his next reply.

LEWIS: God, I miss your Gramps's baking.

KELSEY: Believe me, Gramps misses you eating it. He used to go pink with glee when you made a show of enjoying something he'd made.

LEWIS: Seems so long ago since I was with you all. I used to love Sunday mornings at yours.

KELSEY: Me too.

LEWIS: What's the plan today, then?

The plan today is to watch TV and maybe sit in the garden if I can be bothered with the heat. It's the plan for tomorrow, too. But I don't tell Lewis that. One thing I've learnt about having a long-distance friendship is that it's quite easy not to be honest. Lewis likes the idea of me having a full life without him. I've been taught time and time again that we chat so much easier, we fall back to being us so much better, when he thinks I'm doing just fine without him.

That's what I try to be. Fine without him. And these last five months, with starting the new job and meeting Dessie and Joy and Tom, I've been almost successful. Today, though, I feel flat, the thought of an empty day to fill making me long for the hours to disappear.

KELSEY: I'm not sure. Joy wants me to go back out for more drinks this afternoon with a few of her course mates (one in particular who she keeps talking about setting me up with) and there's talk of a few of the Ilk lot going down to Crosby for a beach day, but I don't think I can face it. There's that new Marvel film out, so I might shun the lovely weather and see if anyone fancies an afternoon of crap food in a dark room.

14

LEWIS: Don't do the cinema. Put on your sunglasses and get out. There's nothing like a British summer, you know.

KELSEY: I think you might be forgetting British summers. It's not all picnics and floral dresses. It's topless men and hay fever.

LEWIS: True, but go out and enjoy it all the same. You should meet Joy's course mate. You never know . . .

KELSEY: Actually, I do know. He came into the restaurant a few weeks ago. Very much not my type.

LEWIS: Shame, but you should still go! Best get moving. Speak later, OK? x

KELSEY: OK Xx

I put my phone down and lie back on the sofa, disappointed that's all I'm getting from him. It's still so early. Hours and hours ahead. That's the thing about Sundays: they're haunted days, the spaces in them filled with memories of the past. When I close my eyes, I'm met with my parents, taking me to the beach when I was young, or to the shops or bowling when I was older. I'm reminded of roast dinners at pubs and films in the lounge, Dad having moved the sofa in front of the TV so it felt more like a cinema, much to Mum's annoyance.

In the future, I'm going to fill my Sundays to the brim, so there's no space for ghosts. Every hour will be allocated with walks and lunches and day trips, so that when I fall into bed, I'll be so tired I'll barely have the energy to look forward to the week ahead, let alone back into the past.

As it is, though, the best thing for it now is to go back to bed.

Before I move, I read through today's exchange of messages

15

again to remind myself that I'm not wrong, that I've not imagined the change these last few weeks. It's not just the fact it's been a year now – it's his messages, too.

Since moving to New York, since re-establishing us as friends and nothing else, Lewis has mentioned a number of girls. No one serious, but certainly enough dates over the last year to keep him busy. It's not like I haven't done the same. In a bid not to sit on my own pining for him, I've made myself date – and they haven't all been bad, but none of them have been close to serious. It always felt like that was the way it should be – an unspoken agreement between us. Until Chloe.

When Chloe came into his life, she took up so much of his time, I worried she was on her way to becoming his girlfriend. He threw himself into dating her with sickening speed. I endured weeks of hearing about walks in Central Park, quirky restaurants they'd discovered in Hell's Kitchen, parties at Chloe's shared apartment in the Lower East Side. Eventually, he simply ceased to be an individual and became a plural. It was painful to open his messages and see him entwined with someone else, when for so long it had been our lives wrapped together.

But Chloe is now completely absent from his messages, and there's been no mention of anyone else since. Today he asked for one vanilla slice, not two. It's always been a worry that Lewis would meet someone in New York, fall in love and never come back. But not only is Lewis seemingly single now, we're texting more than ever – he's talking more of home, of the things he misses – and I can't help feeling that there's something shifting,

16

that Lewis's time in New York is coming to an end.

The idea that Lewis could be back soon takes away any tiredness from last night. I return to the kitchen, where Gramps is lining up his ingredients in a neat row.

"Mind if I help?"

"Thank God for that," he says. "I don't have a bloody clue what I'm doing."

I'm given the job of making the custard filling. It takes two attempts and comes out a bit too runny but still trumps Gramps's homemade puff pastry, which has a distinct lack of puff. We fall into our favourite routine of pretending we're contestants on *Bake Off*, with Gramps doing Noel Fielding's voice at regular intervals.

"Bakers, you have ten minutes left!"

It's fun, and it whittles the day away nicely. As we work, Gramps tells the familiar story about how much I used to love helping him in the kitchen when I was a little girl. How I would stand on a chair next to him and stick out my tongue with concentration when weighing out the flour. I remember those times, too, but my clearest memories of standing next to him, feeling the weight lift off my shoulders as I mixed ingredients and listened to his gentle instructions, date back to when I first moved in here at sixteen. Gramps and Gran moved back to Liverpool from Morecambe for my sake, and it was agreed I would live with them. He'd coax me out of my room with recipes he'd found or silly decorations he'd bought for us to use on cupcakes. Back then, we wouldn't talk about anything but the baking, and it's a rule we've stuck to ever since.

Once we've sampled our goods and agreed neither of us would be winning star baker for our attempts, Gramps sets his sights on the washing up and I return to the lounge to check my phone. There's a message from Lewis waiting for me. My heart is racing as I read the words on my screen again and again.

LEWIS: There's something I need to talk to you about. Can I call you?

I've waited a whole year for this message.

three

Lewis

FIFTEEN YEARS OLD

THE WAY HE'D GREETED HER WHEN SHE ARRIVED AT HIS house tormented him for months afterwards.

Rather than giving him any advanced warning, his mum had shouted up the stairs that she was going out for a bit and the door had slammed straight after. 'Going out for a bit' on a Tuesday evening normally meant a trip to the Co-op on a chocolate run, or to put petrol in the car ready for the next day. It did not mean going to collect the girl Lewis had a huge crush on from her house, in order to bring her round to stay with them.

As it was, when Lewis heard the door open an hour after his mum had left and was summoned downstairs by her, he left his room with no consideration at all to how he looked – and he looked a mess. He stopped short at the top of the stairs when he saw not only his mum looking up at him, but Kelsey Bright. If he could have run back to his room, shut the door and changed out of his loose T-shirt and baggy tracksuit bottoms, and put his hair back up into the careful quiff he worked at every morning before school, he would have done – but there was no chance. She was staring right at him, her eyes wider and more red-rimmed than he had ever seen them.

"Kelsey's coming to stay with us for a night or two, aren't you, love?" his mum said, giving Kelsey's arm a squeeze. "Come down and help me with the bedding, will you?"

He noticed the rucksack she was gripping on to then, how the material bagged at the top. His crushing embarrassment lessened as he imagined her packing to come here, putting her possessions into that bag and not managing to fill it.

"OK," he said, stopping by his mum's side at the bottom of the stairs where there was a wooden chest filled with bedding for the sofa bed. She stacked up sheets and pillows and a duvet in his arms and instructed him to go to the front room and make up the bed for Kelsey. At least he wasn't being made to give up his bedroom. He couldn't have beared it if Kelsey had gone upstairs to see his display of dirty dishes, clothes over the floor and his childhood teddy that his mum still put on his bed every morning when she made it.

As he passed her with his arms full, he said, "Hi," and cursed his voice for coming out at such a high pitch.

She looked down at her feet. "Hi."

In the lounge, he struggled pulling the sofa bed out and struggled even more with getting the fitted sheet on, but he didn't ask his mum for help like he might have done if they were alone.

He told himself it was going to be fine. Yes, Kelsey was the most popular girl in the year, the one he and most of his friends fancied. But that wasn't all she was. Lewis and Kelsey had history; they had been linked to each other since they were babies, when their mums bonded in a baby group about how knackered they were and became friends. Before Kelsey's dad became unwell at the end of primary school, there had been countless nights at each other's houses, and trips to the Lake District when they'd spent hours playing board games inside tents while their parents waited for the rain to stop. But in all that time, they'd never been friends. Lewis didn't think about Kelsey much as a child; he never went to the effort of getting to know her. She was just someone who was there.

When they found themselves at the same secondary school, they would smile at each other if they passed on the corridor – if there was no one around they might have even said "hi" – but for the most part they might as well have been strangers. It was only when year eight hit and Kelsey became the girl his friends would spend their lunchtimes talking about that Lewis began to notice Kelsey in a different way. It was impossible to listen to Connor and Joel talking about how pretty she was and how funny she could be without altering his view of her. Everything they said was right. At thirteen, Lewis had learnt the girl he had grown up with was beautiful – and he'd been awkward around her ever since.

But that night, his crush didn't matter quite as much as normal. As he pictured her standing in his hallway with her bag, his heart hurt for her. Kelsey was here because his mum and her mum were friends; because her mum was struggling so much to cope after

Kelsey's dad died that Kelsey had to leave her home to come to his. He'd seen the pain etched on her face as she'd looked up at him, and he knew the last thing she needed was him making her feel awkward because he couldn't manage his own feelings. What she needed was a friend, and he was determined that as long as she stayed here, that's exactly what he'd be.

Once he'd made the bed, he emerged from the lounge and, trying the best he could to keep his voice causal, said, "Hey, Kels, do you like *Family Guy*?"

They perched on the end of the sofa bed and watched five episodes together. During the first two, Lewis frantically tried to come up with things to say to her – something that might make her feel better. But, by the third episode, when she'd shuffled back so she was stretched out, he wondered if maybe not saying anything was helping more. Maybe watching *Family Guy* together in silence was just what she needed from him right now.

Melissa came in and brought them both cups of weak, low-calorie hot chocolate before she went to bed, and Lewis made a show of grimacing after his first mouthful.

"Best thing is to close your eyes and think of a decent hot chocolate with whipped cream and marshmallows. Makes it taste better," he told her.

Kelsey didn't laugh at his attempt at humour, but she did smile for the first time since she'd arrived.

At half twelve, Lewis stretched out and made a show of yawning. "I'll leave you to it," he said. "Do you need anything?"

"No. I'm fine," Kelsey said, her voice tired.

"OK. Goodnight."

As he was about to shut the door behind him, he heard her say, "Night, Lewis. Thanks."

When Lewis came down the next morning and saw Kelsey in his kitchen, he poured them both cereal and they sat down together to eat breakfast. As they would every day for the next month.

four

Kelsey

ON TUESDAY MORNING, I LEAVE THE BUNGALOW EARLY TO line up at the bus stop, my freshly pressed uniform on, denim jacket back in place over my shirt now the clouds have regained the sky.

The bus, when it arrives three minutes late, is more crowded than I'm used to. It stops at every one of the twelve stops into Liverpool city centre, filling up to the point that a man ends up sitting on the seat next to me, close enough that I can smell the tea on his breath. As Ilk only opens at twelve, I would normally catch my bus later than this, when the commuters have long gone, but today I've errands to run for Gramps.

When he handed me his prescription this morning, with instructions to go to the busy pharmacy near the University of Liverpool, I don't think he was expecting the ready acceptance and kiss on his cheek he received. Nothing, not even picking up a prescription for his IBS medicine, is going to dampen my mood today.

I smile to myself and take out my phone, re-reading the last message from Lewis.

LEWIS: Speak to you at 8 x

At eight o'clock tonight, Lewis is going to phone me. Not a message, but an actual phone call.

In the year since he's been gone, Lewis and I have talked on the phone twice. We've not video called once. He hates video calls, the idea of it being awkward, or us spending the time talking about dodgy phone connections or how close we're getting to our forty minutes free time being used up. When he asked to call me, I knew the significance of that phone call at once.

He's calling to tell me he's coming home.

With Chloe gone, the growing sense I'd had the last few weeks that he was becoming more homesick, that he was careering towards an ending – it *has* to be leading to this. Finally, he's ready to come back.

The bus stops outside the university's Students' Union, and I get off along with most of the other passengers. Turning away from the campus, I begin to walk down Mount Pleasant towards the chemist but take a detour into a funky little cafe that I haven't noticed before and certainly wasn't here during my brief stint as a student at the university. I order a flat white and a flaky Danish pastry and sit at a table by the window. As everyone else in here is staring at their phones, I figure I may as well join them and read over our messages again.

My blissful relaxation is swept away by panic when I finally glance at the time on my screen. I reckon I'll just be able to make it to the chemist before racing to Ilk, but when I open the door to Chemist Cares, I see I've made a mistake. A long queue fills the shop floor, and behind the counter the half-a-dozen pharmacy employees are working flat out in stressed silence.

I deliberate whether to stay. Tom hates his staff being late but has such a soft spot for Gramps I can't imagine he'll begrudge me getting him his medicine – especially given that Gramps has spoken at length to Tom about what a martyr he is to his bowels.

While waiting, I marvel at the wonderfully random array of items available to buy in the pharmacy. The pharmacist shouts out the names of people to come and collect their prescriptions and the queue shuffles slowly forward. I have just put down the three-pack of glittery scrunchies I really don't need to buy when another name is called out.

At first, I think I must have imagined it – that my brain has played a trick by transferring my thoughts outside my head. But then it happens again.

"Lewis Gardner."

I stand on my tiptoes to get a look at whoever this person is who shares a name with Lewis – how bizarre that someone else has the exact name of the person who has been on my mind all morning! There's a tall man in front of me and too many people in front of him, so I turn to the side of the queue to catch a look at him when he comes out. I want to have a good description so I can tell Lewis all about his namesake tonight, make a joke that he doesn't need to come back now because there's another Lewis Gardner in town.

But the person who passes me a few moments later isn't a man. She looks smaller than I remember her – her hair shorter, her face much older than a year of aging should have left it. She's carrying a huge bag of medicine, and when she sees me staring at her, the little colour remaining in her face drains away.

five

Kelsey

"MELISSA, WAIT!" I SHOUT AS SHE RUSHES OUT OF THE pharmacy, colliding with a woman and toddler opening the door in her haste to be out.

I give up my place in the queue and follow after her. Lectures must have finished not long ago, as the street is filled with groups of students clogging up the pavements and it takes me a few seconds to spot Lewis's mum weaving through them. The way she glances over her shoulder and hurries away makes it look like she's on the run from the police, not her son's best friend.

"Melissa, it's me," I shout after her, but she's managed to get to the pedestrian crossing and is darting across the road as the traffic lights turn to amber. By the time I get there, they are on green and a steady stream of cars pass by me making it impossible to cross. She turns to look at me one last time before disappearing down the street that leads to an NCP car park.

I hesitate, wanting to catch up with her but knowing I don't have the time to keep going. Disappointed, I return to the pharmacy, but the line is even longer now. I'd be too late for work if I joined it again. Promising myself I'll come back after my shift, I start to walk down Mount Pleasant, towards the docks, and take out my phone.

KELSEY: Hey, the strangest thing. I just saw your mum and she literally ran away from me! I was in the pharmacy, and your name was called out. Then I saw your mum coming out and she bolted. Is everything OK?

Knowing Lewis will be at work, I put my phone back in my bag.

Melissa and I used to be close. When I was a teenager, she was the only adult I chose to open up to, and she always said I was the daughter she wished she'd had. She took me in, offering me the support I never knew I needed, and I was always grateful for that. After Lewis left for New York, we met up a few times, but it felt strange without him there too. Sharing dough balls in Pizza Express didn't have the shine it once did, and it was clear Melissa found it uncomfortable. Eventually, I let it go. It made sense, I suppose – as an adult who didn't need to rely on others taking me in, Lewis had become the link that held us together. When our link moved to New York, it seemed inevitable that we'd drift apart.

I always thought our dwindling texts and the relegation of our relationship to one of sending birthday cards came as a relief for her. I can see that us bumping into each other might have felt a little awkward for her, perhaps littered with uncomfortable small talk, but her reaction today was so strange. Why would you look horrified to see someone who had meant so much to you? Who, the last time you met, you had given a huge hug to and told them you thought the world of them?

And then there's the prescription. Why was Lewis's name

called out in the first place? I'm pretty sure America isn't all that keen on having prescription drugs posted into the country. I've no idea how that bag is going to make its way to him.

Suddenly, my mind goes into freefall. Lewis is calling me tonight, and I'm sure he's calling to say he's coming back. What if he's ill? What if that's why he needs to come back? Not because he wants to give us a try, but because something catastrophic has happened that's made him have to give up on his new life in New York.

My pulse is thudding in my neck, my stomach churning, the ground unsteady beneath my feet before my brain puts on the brakes. I tell myself that can't be it. If it's something new and terrible, surely Melissa wouldn't be able to get him drugs without him actually being in the country. He'd need to see a doctor here first, and he's still in New York.

But if the drugs aren't for Lewis . . . then who are they for?

* * *

"You're late, Kelsey." When I arrive at Ilk a few minutes after my shift has started, Tom doesn't even look up from the laptop at the front desk to greet me.

This is the thing about Tom. One shift he's your best friend, opening bottle after bottle of house wine after hours, giggling so much he ends up spraying mouthfuls of the stuff over himself. The next, he'll go out of his way to remind you of the chain of command, even though pissed Tom has already admitted his hourly rate is only two pounds more than the waiting staff.

"I know, I know. I'm sorry. I had to go to the chemist to get Gramps's medicine."

"Right. Go on then, get to it."

"Yes, boss. And when we've a spare minute, you can tell me all about your date with *Luca*." I make sure to say 'Luca' in an Italian accent, and it works as expected. A grin cracks Tom's stern face, as my friend returns to me.

"Let's sneak in a break once Joy comes in, and I'll reveal all."

"Ooh, can't wait," I tell him, before heading downstairs to put on my apron.

I quickly check my phone, and, as expected, Lewis hasn't replied. I send off another message before I try to put Melissa out of my mind for the next six hours.

KELSEY: Your mum had a bag of medicine, which she got in your name. I don't want to worry you, but something didn't feel right today. Will speak to you tonight about it, and we'll figure out what to do. OK?

It's a good job he's coming home. The last few days, I've only considered what Lewis coming home means to me. I've let hope in again, that it will finally be the right time for us to become more than friends. I've imagined long walks, our legs aching but neither of us wanting to stop, meals out where we're the last to leave the restaurant but the waitresses don't want to disturb us. I've imagined days cocooned in my room exploring each other.

But that's not reality. Lewis is coming back to his life, not just me. He'll need to work, to see if he can fall back in with his old college friends, to deal with whatever's going on with his mum, and he's going to need me to be there for him. That's more important than these fantasies I keep having – it's what I want, too. When we speak tonight, I'll make it clear we'll handle whatever might be going on with Melissa together.

Buoyed by my new determination, I head upstairs to start my shift, hoping that it will pass quickly so I can go home and get ready to speak to Lewis.

The restaurant is quiet now the sun has disappeared, and Tom announces it's time for a break twenty minutes after I've started work. Leaving the new waitress, Yasmine, in charge, Tom, Joy and I walk through the kitchen and out of the fire escape to a small deliveries yard.

"So, Luca?" I ask, once we're sat in a line on the wall.

Tom laughs. "Luca? We've got five minutes before we need to rescue the new girl. Believe me, I could tell you *a lot* about Luca. You'll need to be more specific than that."

Joy and I look at each other and nod. "Is he good in bed?" Joy asks.

"Excuse me, how do you know we've slept together?"

"Your face," Joy and I say together, before bursting into laughter.

"You only ever get giddy about someone after you've slept with them. Your little pink cheeks tell us all we need to know," I add.

"Fine," Tom relents. "We did sleep together, and it was bloody fantastic."

"Details," Joy orders, and Tom abides. At length.

I smile along in all the right places and wince at an awkward moment about Tom's shirt buttons. But I struggle to maintain total focus. I've left my phone in my bag downstairs, and I wish I could use the break to check it in case Lewis has replied about Melissa.

"Hello? Kelsey? Tom's sharing *all* the details over here and you're miles away. What's with you today?"

"Sorry, sorry. Carry on." Tom loves telling us stories about his dating life. I've just encouraged him to do so, and I know I should be all over this instead of worrying about my own stuff.

"God, please don't," Joy says. "Seriously, Kels. You were staring into space. What are you thinking about?"

"Lewis," I say reluctantly.

"No surprise there," Tom replies sulkily.

"Sorry, Tom. He's ringing me tonight, and I'm sure he's going to tell me he's coming back."

"Oh, Kels," Joy says, putting her hand on my knee and looking at me with a scrunched-up face full of sympathy. "You've been here before. Remember last Christmas Eve when he asked if you could make yourself free to message him with no distractions and you thought he was going to say he was coming back then, and it turned out to be nothing? Or when he didn't send you anything on your birthday, you were sure it meant he was going to arrive as your present? Please don't get your hopes up too much."

"First of all," I start, preparing again to explain how our relationship works, "Christmas Eve wasn't nothing; it was a chat to remember the Christmases we'd spent together, and it was lovely. Secondly, he was in the middle of a huge project when it was my birthday and the flowers he sent me the day after to apologise more than made up for it. And anyway, it's different this time. I know it is. How about this for a sign – I haven't seen Lewis's mum for nearly six months and today, on the way into work, I run into her. It's like the universe is realigning us, ready for Lewis to come back."

"I think you're absolutely right," Tom says, nodding sagely. If there's one thing Tom believes in, it's the power of the universe in shaping our lives.

"No, she's not!" Joy objects, the mystical power of the universe having no effect whatsoever on her fact-driven historian's brain. "If you want to bring the universe into this, fine, but at least be honest. The only change in the universe happened twelve months ago when he upped and left to go to New York straight after you kissed. All this time, that's been the only sign you needed to pay attention to, and you were finally getting it. You've been on two dates in a row with barman Jamie, and you said yourself he's nice and makes you laugh. I can't believe you're going to backtrack on everything now."

There's only concern in Joy's expression and I know it's not fair to expect her to understand, as she's never met Lewis. But it's still painful to hear her talk of him, of us, as though it's all so black and white.

"I'm not backtracking. Jamie might be nice, and I suppose he can be quite funny, but he doesn't mean anything to me. Lewis does. And yeah, there's a chance I might be wrong about what this phone call means, but the truth is I miss him and want him to be back and, more than anything, I need to know what's going to happen between us."

"I know you do," Joy says, softening. "And I want him to give you your happy ever after. I'm just not sure it works that way, that it should be all down to him and what he does or doesn't do."

"I'm not expecting that," I try to reassure her. "Once he's back, we're going to have to decide what happens together. Him moving away was like him pressing pause on us, but he didn't press stop. Maybe when we un-pause we'll realise it's too late, that our chance got on the plane and left with him, or maybe the time apart will have made us stronger than ever. I just want to find that out."

"I get that," Joy says. "But promise me you'll be careful, OK? I know Lewis means the world to you, but what you want and need is just as important, too."

"She knows that," declares Tom, standing up and reaching for my hands to pull me up too. "But it's all going to work out just as it's meant to, I'm sure of it. Now, come on. Seeing we're not dissecting my date with Luca as promised, we really should rescue Yasmine. I can't have another waitress quitting."

The rest of the shift passes quickly, with Tom asking me to train Yasmine up on the till. I put Joy's concerns out of my mind and before I know it, I'm back outside, retracing my steps to the pharmacy where I pick up Gramps's prescription before getting the bus back home and making tea. It's a Tuesday and my night to cook. Lewis hasn't replied to my texts, but by the time I've cleaned up after making my speciality – breaded chicken and chips – it's only an hour until he's going to call.

I go to my room to get ready to speak to him. I brush through my hair and put more concealer and blusher on. I spray the Jean

Paul Gautier perfume he used to like so much and sit on my bed waiting for him. I hope to remember this night for the rest of my life, and even though he won't be able to see me, I want to hold these finer details in my mind. How nice I looked wearing my pale blue dress with baby pink flowers, how my hair flowed over my shoulders, how my face lit up when I heard his voice telling me he was coming back.

I'm ready at eight with my heart thumping and my phone on in my hand. But eight o'clock comes and goes. Nine o'clock does the same. At half nine, I call him. There's no answer.

I text and I phone again, and I wait, sitting cross-legged on my bed until two in the morning. Then I put my phone back on the bedside table, curl up on my bed and begin to cry.

six

Kelsey

KELSEY: WHAT'S GOING ON, LEWIS? ARE YOU OK?

    KELSEY: Please tell me why you aren't replying.

    KELSEY: Lewis?

    KELSEY: LEWIS?

    KELSEY: Whatever's going on, you know you can talk to me.

Days pass without hearing anything from him. My messages go unread, and his phone goes straight to an automated answerphone message. I lie for him when Joy and Tom ask me about the phone call and tell them he's lost his voice so is ringing later in the week when he can speak properly. They don't buy it, but are good enough not to say so. The hurt tattooed across my face and my insistence on taking care of the largest tables to keep busy does the job of repelling any further conversations. I go through the week on autopilot, getting through my shifts with hardly any tips at the end of them, watching too much TV and eating far too much cake with Gran and Gramps. And I never stop thinking about him.

Something has gone wrong. In between his last message and

the time he was meant to call, there's been an event, an occurrence, a moment that has taken him off course, and all I can do is try to guess what it might be. I sway between him having been in an accident and ending up in hospital, to him having been pulled on to an important project at work that needs all his attention until the deadline. After two days of not hearing from him, I considered texting Melissa, but I reasoned she wouldn't be likely to know what Lewis was thinking not ringing me.

If it were anyone else on the planet, I'd concede it looked very much like they'd simply let me down. That's what Joy and Dessie would tell me, which is why I don't want them to know. But this is Lewis. Lewis doesn't do that. Lewis is there for me. He always has been. After Dad died, and my small happy family triangle was ripped apart, Lewis stepped into the huge gap Dad's absence had caused and made my life more bearable. He saw my broken heart and made it his mission to care for it and to soothe my pain when he could.

That person would never, ever, hurt me deliberately. Accidentally, perhaps, but never on purpose.

When he first moved to New York, there were two whole weeks when he didn't get in touch. I didn't know where he was, and he didn't pick up his phone or send a message. I was left to try and work out what had happened – how we could have gone from our first kiss, from him pulling himself away from me to go on his work's night out, leaving me with my lips tingling, to the absolute hell of silence. When he finally got in touch, he begged my forgiveness. He'd been swept up in the excitement of the surprise

38

job offer, the speed in which he had to move, the focus he had to put into setting up a new life while getting to grips with a new job in a new country.

He swore he would never leave me in the dark again. I believed him then, and I believe him now. He'll be in touch. I just need to be patient.

* * *

I'm not in work on Friday and I contemplate ringing Tom to see if there's an extra shift going. Anything to whittle the time away until I hear from Lewis. My phone is in my hand and I'm about to call Ilk's number when I remember Joy and Dessie aren't working today either. They'd both asked earlier this week if I was free to go with them to pick up a costume for a play Dessie is in. I'd turned them down, thinking I'd have heard from Lewis and would probably be busy preparing for him to come home, but spending a fun afternoon with them to distract me now sounds ideal.

A few hours after texting Dessie to say I can come along after all, I'm waiting by a warehouse on a run-down industrial site in Wavertree, wondering if she has given me the wrong address. I breathe out with relief when I spot Joy's unmistakable sweep of beautiful red hair, down and fanning her face for once.

"I'm so glad you're here," she says, bounding up to me, her cheeks pink from her quick pace. "You've saved me from a full afternoon of doing nothing but following Dessie around while she takes an age to make up her mind about her costume."

"You're welcome," I say, smiling at how genuinely pleased she seems to see me. "I'm so excited for this."

"Don't be," she says, rolling her eyes. "I've been before and it's musty and it's boring and the guy who owns the place will only let Dessie try on the dresses."

I shrug. "I don't mind. Beats being at home."

"Waiting for Lewis to decide whether or not he's going to call you and put you out of your misery?"

"Something like that," I say, unwilling to let Joy know quite how on the money she is.

"Well, seeing as you are here, promise me you'll think about something else for a few hours?"

"I'll try," I say honestly, knowing I can't keep obsessing about him like I have been.

Dessie arrives ten minutes later. She pretends to soberly take the earful she gets from Joy about being the last to arrive despite being the only one who drives, but I can see she's brimming with excitement.

"Finished?" she asks Joy. "Let's go. Dan will be wondering where I've got to. You're going to love it, Kels," she says, linking my arm. "They have everything in here, from Las Vegas showgirl outfits to army uniforms to the gowns of Marie Anntoinette."

"Historically inaccurate gowns," Joy corrects.

"Amazing," I say, ignoring Joy's interjection. "What costume are you getting?"

"Victorian meat pie bakery owner."

"Right . . ."

Dessie smiles. "I'm playing Mrs Lovett in Sweeny Todd. It's a poor-as-piss production, which is why I'm having to get my own costume, but rehearsals are going well. You are coming, aren't you?"

"Of course I am," I say.

After Dan has greeted Dessie with open arms and told Joy and I to look and not touch, we're left to explore the huge space, packed with rack upon rack of clothes of every variety. Joy pretends to grumble as we immediately ignore our orders, following Dessie round the costume warehouse, holding beautiful sparkly gowns against our bodies, laughing at hideous dresses, putting on full-length 1920s style velvet coats and trying on hats with distinctly funky odours – but I know she's enjoying herself as much as I am playing dress up.

When Dessie shows us the moth-eaten black corseted dress she's chosen to wear, I tell her what a shame it is that she hasn't been cast in a more glamourous role, and Joy tells her, amateur dramatics or not, it's ridiculous she has to be the one paying for such a shoddy outfit. But when she emerges from the changing room, the shoddy outfit actually looks amazing on her and she beams as we tell her how perfect it is.

It's a lovely afternoon, topped off with a trip to Starbucks, and I'm surprised when Dessie announces that it's half four and she needs to get to a rehearsal. Joy says she can't justify not doing any work on her day off, so leaves us to get the bus to the library.

Dessie drops me off at home and before I get out of the car, I tell her to make sure she gets me a ticket for opening night. I'm smiling as I watch her drive away. Today has been exactly what I needed, and I wish it could have lasted longer. I've not entirely managed to stop thinking about Lewis, but I've not checked my phone once.

"You joining me, love?" Gran asks when I let myself in. I can hear the jingling musical notes from one of her gameshows starting.

"I'm OK, thanks," I say from the hallway.

"All right. Good day?" she asks.

"Yeah," I tell her. "Surprisingly so. You?"

"Lovely day," she says, as always, before laughing at something the presenter has said.

I go my room to pull on my hoody and then to the kitchen to get a snack. I make myself wait until I've done everything I would ordinarily do when coming back home before I take my phone out of my bag.

I feel sure a day of good behaviour, of getting out and not sitting in my room watching my phone, has surely earnt me a reply. But any hope I had is crushed when I check our chat and see the last message there is from me, and it's still unread.

seven

Lewis

FIFTEEN YEARS OLD

LEWIS STARTED SETTING HIS ALARM HALF AN HOUR EARLIER.

A few nights of Kelsey staying at his house had turned into a
month, and even though he was growing more comfortable with
her being there every day, this was still a girl living with him, and
he still had his standards.

Gone were the days of him stumbling out of his room in his
too-tight dressing gown in search of food before taking it back
up to eat in bed, the days of him spraying himself with Lynx
instead of taking a shower. Now he made sure that before he went
downstairs, he was ready for the day – hair done, teeth cleaned –
and there wasn't a hint of laziness about him.

Kelsey didn't always follow suit. She would often emerge in
pyjamas, her hair scraped back, and she would stand by the kettle
rubbing sleep from her eyes as she made a cup of tea before she
started the mad dash to get ready in time for the school bus.
But it was different for Kelsey. Lewis thought she never looked

more beautiful than in the opening minutes of her day.

Lewis saw Melissa shooting him looks in the mornings, the change in him not having gone undetected. The amused smile on her face suggested she knew exactly what it was due to, as well. He wondered if Kelsey noticed too, if she compared the new slick Lewis to the scruffy one she'd seen the first night she came to stay. He wasn't sure if he wanted her to or not.

One Saturday morning, he was surprised by a knock on his door, six minutes before his nine o'clock alarm was about to go off. He cursed himself for thinking Kelsey would want to lie in and not setting it earlier, and shouted, "Won't be a minute!"

It wasn't the first time she'd been in his bedroom, but it was the first time he'd been unprepared. He charged around his room as quickly as possible, pulling on clothes, opening his windows as wide as they would go, making his bed, flattening his hair.

When she came in, she sat on his bed, without looking round the room or at him.

"I need to go home," she said.

"Really?" Lewis asked, surprised. "But I thought you and your mum agreed you were staying another week or so."

"No, *she* said I was staying another week. I didn't agree to any of this. That's not what I mean though. I am staying – that's why I need to go home and get some more stuff. Will you come with me?"

Lewis hesitated, frightened by the depths of her mum's grief and the possibility he'd be confronted by it if he went to her house. Lewis hadn't known grief. His only loss had been his father – but that was when he was a baby, because his dad was undependable and unloving, and so his mum had left him. Lewis knew Kelsey was grieving, but she tried so hard to hide it from him – he saw little else but the red eyes, the pale skin, the distracted stares into space when they were supposed to be watching a film together. He imagined her mum's grief to be entirely different. Loud and inescapable.

"Lewis?" Kelsey asked.

"Sure," he said. "When do you want to go?"

They agreed they'd get it over and done with and head into the city centre afterwards for a mill about the shops. Showered and ready, Lewis found her in the kitchen where she handed him a diet hot chocolate before they set off.

Lewis felt Kelsey's nerves building the closer they got to her house. By the time they turned onto her road, a road not too dissimilar to his, they were in silence, and Kelsey's lip was bright pink from where she'd been biting at it.

"Hello?" Kelsey called out once inside the house, but there was no answer. She let out a long breath and told Lewis to take off his shoes before she led him into the lounge.

"It's looking nice in here," Lewis said, and he meant it. The room was immaculate. Cushions were lined up neatly on the two huge grey velvet sofas, and the carpet had been recently hoovered. He'd imagined finding chaos – the mess of someone who wasn't coping, who couldn't look after her daughter properly – but he found the opposite.

"Yeah."

Kelsey went to the TV unit in the corner and started to rifle through a substantial DVD collection, taking out a dozen or so and piling them up. Lewis let his eyes wander to a photo on a side table by the window. In it, a much younger Kelsey was nestled between her parents. They each had matching smiles. Her mum was looking straight forward, but her dad had his head turned towards his daughter, his smile not for the camera, but for her.

Lewis picked up the small frame and held it out for Kelsey.

"Do you want to take this?"

"No," she said, turning back to the DVDs after a quick glance. "Can you put it back?"

"Sorry," Lewis said, returning it to the table immediately.

"It's OK. Come on."

Kelsey led Lewis into the kitchen, small but tidier than his own kitchen had ever been. "Wow. Your mum is so tidy."

"It's only because the kitchen isn't being used," Kelsey said, a flash of annoyance in her voice. "She's not cooked once since Dad . . ."

She trailed off, before opening a cupboard and pulling out a huge mug with pictures of kittens all over it and taking it back to the lounge. There were times when Kelsey first came to stay when Lewis couldn't quite understand how her being with them instead of her mum was the better choice, how it was so bad for her at home that she had to leave, but he saw it now. She was different here. Here, her grief and hurt and anger covered her completely.

Before he left the kitchen, Lewis noticed it wasn't quite as immaculate as he'd first thought. There were dirty dishes, a bowl and a single wine glass in the sink, and by the door, there was a recycling bag full of empty bottles.

"Won't be long," Kelsey called, as she headed up the stairs. "You can wait in the lounge."

Lewis did as he was told and sat on the sofa as Kelsey clanked and banged around upstairs. It was only when the noises stopped and she hadn't reappeared that Lewis thought to go up himself. He saw her on the top step of the stairs, hair straighteners and a pile of clothes by her side, a book in her hand, and tears streaming down her face.

He took the stairs two at a time to get to her.

"It's OK, it's OK," he said, putting his arms around her.

Shaking her head, she held out the book for him to see. It was *Little Women,* and it was open on the title page where large, sloping handwriting filled the blank space.

To my Kelsey,

Fourteen years old! Always my little girl, but soon to be a woman. I hope you find joy in these pages and you see reflected in these women the strength and kindness I see in you every day.

Happy birthday!

Love you,

Dad xx

"I didn't even read it," she managed now, her voice pained. "I was disappointed when he gave it me. I'd have rather had clothes or make-up. He was always trying to share the books he'd read, the films he'd watched, but I wasn't interested. I put this on my bookshelf and forgot all about it."

"It's OK. You can still read it," he said, desperate to make her feel better.

"Yeah, but he won't know I have. He won't know." She began to sob harder. Lewis held her tighter and felt her tears soak his jumper.

"I know it's not the same," he said after a while, "but I'm sure my mum has the film version of *Little Women*. It's pretty old, but we could always sack off shopping this afternoon and go back and watch it. At least that way, you'll know what he meant about seeing you in the characters."

Kelsey pulled back to look at him. "You'd do that? Give up your Saturday to sit with me and watch an old movie that's most likely completely naff?"

"Yeah, of course I would. If you think it will make you feel better?"

"I don't know if anything can make me feel better," she said, giving him a small smile. "But it's exactly what I'd like to do."

eight

Kelsey

LORRAINE BRIGHT, WIDOWER.

Not since Queen Victoria has a woman mourned so publicly and wholeheartedly as my mother. She and Dad were madly in love until the day Dad died. I was the kid who watched them slow dancing to Lionel Richie from the gap in the banister long after they thought I was asleep. I was the kid who was red-faced when we'd be out at a restaurant and they'd share lingering kisses whenever one of them got up to go to the loo. Their happiness was real, and Mum lost it at forty-two when Dad died.

But that wasn't all she lost. When Dad was alive, she was Lorraine Bright – wife, mother, daughter, friend, finance clerk, weekly karaoke singer. Since his death, she's let go of most of those things.

Not all, though. We now have our weekly coffee at Marks & Spencer. Her mothering hour. As Mum says, if we were living together, we'd talk less than we do in our hour over the whole week. I'd have my head down over my phone or be watching TV, and she'd be distracted with her errands or her coursework now she's studying for her degree in counselling at Edge Hill University. It's much better to have dedicated time to listen to one another properly without any distractions.

I know I'm lucky to have this. Lucky that we're here at all, and that we can have whole conversations now that aren't frozen midway through by the sudden appearance of grief. For a long time after Dad died, I thought our relationship was dead too. I'd accepted that Mum after Dad wasn't Mum any more. Before Dad got ill, I used to hate how involved she was in my life. We'd sit down for dinner and she'd fire off question after question. I'd shovel down my meal to get out of there before she started asking about boys. After he died, she never asked me anything at all. Before Dad got ill, I had my uniform laid out for me each night and a packed lunch waiting for me in the kitchen to collect on the way out in the morning. I would screw up the post-it notes she sometimes left on top of my sandwich and put them in my pocket before my friends could see. After he died, I'd pull out my uniform from the laundry basket in the morning and shake out the creases. I'd ask Gramps to top up my account at school, so I had enough to buy some chips at lunch.

We all reached the conclusion she couldn't look after me the way I needed her to. After trying to live with Mum again after staying with Melissa, and it becoming clear Mum wasn't in any fit state to get back into the routine of caring for a teenage daughter, it was agreed it would be better I lived with Gran and Gramps in order to stick to some semblance of my normal life, at least for my important school years. It was what I wanted, because home was no longer home, and, although I never said it to her, I was frightened of Mum's pain. I wanted to take the option that would allow me to escape it. Mum visited and we would meet up when she was doing OK. Sometimes she talked about me coming home, but we both knew this wasn't an interim solution. This was the way it was now, and Gran and Gramps's bungalow was really my home.

But then, five years after Dad passed away, she met Wendy, her grief counsellor, and was finally able to move forward into forging a new life without Dad in it. Wendy helped her see that she wasn't the same person any more. How could she be? There had been a metamorphosis, but that didn't mean she couldn't claim new things for herself on the other side, including this time each week with me.

I wished I looked forward to seeing her. I wished I counted down the days until the next time we got to catch up across a table in a cafe like other mothers and adult daughters do, but I never have. I've craved normal for years, but normal isn't only seeing your mother in Marks & Spencer.

More than any other, this particular Saturday morning catch-up I could do without. Another night had passed, waiting up with my phone in my hand, wondering what could have gone so wrong for Lewis not to call me. I'd have cancelled, but my grandparents love me seeing Mum – it helps them believe we're both doing well. And what else am I going to do but wait for Lewis to get in touch and feel the minutes piling up on top of me until they get so heavy they begin to crush me?

I arrive a few minutes earlier than normal to order our lattes and iced currant buns, and sit down before she arrives.

Everything is going so well until she turns up. Since I've been inside, it's begun to rain. Swollen summer raindrops have soaked her beige trousers, sticking them to her legs and revealing her darker knickers. When she spots me at the table, instead of joining me, she gives me a wave and points to the toilets.

Coming back, twenty minutes later, the trousers have been returned to their former glory, she has a new layer of lipstick on and she's also acquired a dark green M&S plastic bag with a new, opened pack of white knickers poking out the top.

"Sorry, Kels," she says, sitting opposite me. "I forgot my umbrella and got drenched walking from the bus stop."

"Don't worry. Here, I got you a drink."

Mum takes a sip of her latte and grimaces. "It's stone cold. I'll go and get a fresh one. Want another?"

"Go on, then."

It's another ten minutes before she gets back to the table. We are halfway through our hour already.

"You look tired, Kelsey," she tells me. "All these late nights don't agree with you."

"I've not been working late the last few nights."

"Oh."

I wait for her to begin telling me about her week, but in the pause while she chews her bun I decide I can't listen. My mind is too full of Lewis for anything else.

"I saw Melissa the other day," I say, gripping the conversation before she gets to it. She swallows before picking up her latte, taking a sip and wincing.

"Is she well?" Mum asks. She and Melissa aren't exactly friends now. They're not exactly not-friends either. There's been no falling out, but Mum has severed a lot of ties to her past with Dad in an attempt to move forward and free herself from the pain of always remembering what her life used to be like.

"I don't know. She was weird, to be honest. I saw her in the pharmacy, and she kind of ran away from me. And since seeing Melissa, Lewis has gone weird too."

Saying it like that gives me pause and makes me wonder just how connected those two occurrences are. I've barely considered whether what I told him about his mum having that medicine in his name was the reason he so abruptly stopped contact with me. I don't understand why that would be the case, but maybe I need to try to work that out.

"Well, I never," Mum says, feigning surprise. "Words out of your mouth that aren't in that boy's praise. Weird in what way?"

"He's stopped texting me," I answer, ignoring Mum's tone. "He was meant to ring, and he didn't."

"Sweetheart, have you considered that he's finally realised that this silly friendship you both insist on hanging on to does neither of you any good? I didn't think the day would come but maybe he's started doing the right thing and is letting you move on with your life, rather than dangling himself in front of you all the time, letting you believe he'll be coming back when the reality is he's moved on."

"Dangling himself in front of me? Nice image."

Mum reddens. "Yes, well. You know what I mean."

I push down the annoyance that's growing. Mum's never wanted me to be with Lewis, not since I was eighteen and first realised I was in love with him – which is bizarre given how much Mum values being in love. She's always talking about what a gift her and Dad's relationship was, but it seems she doesn't want the same for her daughter. If I give her an opening, I know she'll spend the time we have telling me that Lewis isn't the one for me, that whatever I think I have with him isn't real, and all her other feelings about our relationship that she seems to have plucked from thin air. But I don't want that. I want to talk about what's happening – maybe even get some advice – so I let it go.

"I do, but that's not it at all. He wouldn't say he'd ring and then not without there being a good reason. And then there's Melissa. Something weird is going on there."

Mum pauses and nods. "It is odd that she avoided you like that. She thinks the sun shines out of your bum, that one does."

The one good thing about our mothering hours is Mum's view of how they should run. Since their inception, she's insisted that they are based on honesty. Yes, she often does the lion's share of the talking, but we both know that, if I need to, I can tell her anything and she will treat what I say with the utmost seriousness.

Instead of dismissing me now, she continues. "Have you thought about asking her what's going on?"

"I haven't. I presumed, with Lewis being so far away, she was hardly likely to know why he hadn't called. But maybe I should check?"

"Maybe. Just don't expect too much from Melissa. The amount of time he's been away from home now, she might not know anything more than you do. Could you not ask his friends?"

I sigh. "There's no point. I saw Connor and his girlfriend at the restaurant a month or so ago, and apart from a few messages, he'd not heard a word from Lewis since he moved to New York. No one has. He was the one asking *me* for intel."

Shamefully, I was pleased about that. I could tell Connor was hurt that Lewis had ditched him and not me. Connor was a romantic when it came to Lewis – he thought their childhood friendship would stretch out indefinitely, that Lewis would be there to share all his moments. I did feel bad for him, but I also felt special that Lewis had sent me four messages that day, that I wasn't someone he'd let go of.

"Well, there you go. Friends grow apart, Kelsey," Mum says. "You can go looking for reasons all you want, but my advice is to take the hint and use this as a chance to move on. You're worth far more than Lewis Gardner. Now, have you thought any more about a new job?"

* * *

I get an hour. Mum has to get home to prepare for an essay that's due next month. When I ask if she fancies having a look around the shops, she pats her green plastic bag and reminds me she's already done her shopping for the day. She stands up sixty minutes after she arrived, lightly kisses my cheek and disappears back into the throng of M&S shoppers.

Once she's gone, I check my phone and find nothing. I read Lewis's last message for the millionth time.

LEWIS: *Speak to you at 8 x*

I return to Gramps's car, intending to head back home, but it's Melissa's house I drive towards. Mum's right – I should check to see what she knows. I could text her but given the recent bad form of her son, a quick visit feels like my best chance of getting some information.

I've not seen her house since Lewis left last year, and it remains largely unchanged. The rendering looks a little grubby and the lawn could do with mowing but essentially, it's like going back in time. I can't help but smile when I'm in front of it.

The night Melissa brought me here to stay, I was so angry with her. Angry with her for siding with Mum and agreeing it would be best for me to leave my house and spend a few nights here instead. Dad had died four months before, and now I was being pulled away from my mum too.

I knew it was what Mum wanted, but I blamed Melissa. After another argument between me and Mum – a wildly drunk one on her part – she rang her best friend to ask for help, to admit that she wasn't coping, that she couldn't spend another night pretending she was fine for my sake. I wanted to make things better – if I wasn't at home, Mum was never going to put down the wine and switch to tea instead. She wouldn't eat and she wouldn't be able to pull me close to her and say, "That's better". But Melissa agreed with her that some space from me would be a good thing and, at fifteen, I was forced to pack a rucksack and get in Melissa's car.

I didn't see it that night, but this little detached house on Beech Avenue, with its TV always on and its constant supply of Melissa's diet drinks, would become my refuge in the months that followed. It was a refuge long after that too.

But much as I love all its warmth and good memories, that's not what I'm here for now. I'm here to find out what she knows about her son.

nine

Kelsey

"HI, MELISSA. CAN I COME IN?"

"Oh, hello! What a lovely surprise." Her voice is light, but there's that same expression on her face as the other day; that strange fear I can't understand. "You've caught me at a bad time, Kels. I've got to go out in a minute." We both look down at the fluffy slippers on her feet and her loose, indoor-only tracksuit bottoms.

"I won't stay long, I promise. It's nice to see you."

"It's nice to see you too," she says, softening. "But I really don't have long."

"That's fine," I tell her, stepping past her into the hallway.

In pride of place on the wall is a school picture of Lewis, taken when he was in year eleven. He hated his mum blowing it up to poster size and displaying it so proudly, but, as I told him, it's such a great picture – big smile, those hazel eyes, that floppy hair – he really gave her no choice. Around this photo there's a cluster of smaller framed photos, and I spot my face in most of them. Planets around the sun.

I walk past them into the kitchen and sit on the breakfast bar stool while Melissa goes over to the kettle. I can't count how many times I've sat in this exact spot, talking to her as she makes us a drink. The familiarity of it aches in my chest.

"How's your mum?" she asks, her back to me.

"Fine, thanks."

"She still doing her degree?"

"Yep. So far, so good."

"That's great. Must be strange for you to see her as a student, though. I still can't quite get my head round it."

"I guess. Look, Melissa, I need to ask you something about Lewis. Do you know what's going on with him at the moment? I've not heard from him for a few days, and I'm starting to worry."

Her back straightens and she puts the milk she was about to use in my tea back on the worktop. "I'm sure there's no reason to worry at all. I imagine he'll just be having a busy spell with work."

I'd love to believe that, to dismiss my worries so easily as Melissa is able to, but 'busy' doesn't explain the wall of silence from Lewis.

"No, no, I think it's more than that. He was going to ring me the other night but he never did, and since then his phone has been off. He's normally attached to that thing. This isn't like him at all."

"I'm sure it's nothing," she repeats. "I bet you'll hear from him in a few days, and you'll feel silly for all this worrying."

"Maybe. Have you heard from him?"

"No, but like I say—"

"I know, but this phone call we were about to have – it was important. I really thought he was going to say he was coming back. Had he mentioned coming home to you?"

She turns to me then, walks towards me until there's only a foot of worktop between us. There's something about her expression that belies the calmness of her answers, that tells me maybe she does know something, and my heart speeds up as I wait for this potential piece of information that – good or bad – might explain Lewis's disappearance from my life.

"You'll have to speak to Lewis, Kelsey. Wait to speak to him, OK?"

So there *is* something. Melissa might think she's doing a good job of telling me nothing but for the first time, I know I'm not wrong. Something is going on with Lewis and I'm more – not less – determined to find out what it is.

"But that's the problem. I can't speak to him, and I'm worried. Lewis has always helped me when I've needed him, and if something's wrong, I want to be there to help him. Please tell me what it is," I plead.

"Speak to Lewis," she says, firmer this time. "Listen, I really do need to be getting on. I'm sorry. Would you mind?" she asks, pointing to the front door.

"Oh. OK," I say. "But I really think we need to talk about Lewis."

"Sorry. It really is a bad time," she says. It's clear I'm getting nothing else from her. Reluctantly, I make my way back into the hall and she opens the door for me.

"Take care, Kelsey," she says. She's back to smiling, relieved, no doubt, that I'm going. I'm almost out of the house when I catch her eyes involuntarily glance to the floor and flare with panic. I look down too.

A pharmacy bag. I can just make out the words printed on the sticky label on the top, which fastens the bag together. I read Lewis's name and an address I don't recognise.

34 Ellcott Avenue.

Melissa bends down and snatches the bag up, pressing it against her, her hand deliberately obscuring the address.

"Where's 34 Ellcott Avenue?" I ask. Her shoulders sag a little.

"It's nowhere. Just an old address from years ago we've never got round to changing with the doctors. I've got to go, Kelsey. See you soon."

The door slams in my face. There's so much more we need to talk about. Melissa is lying, no doubt about it, but my focus turns from her to the address I've just seen.

There wasn't time to see the whole postcode before Melissa grabbed the bag, but I did see the postcode started with L, which I'm hoping narrows my search of Ellcott Avenues to Liverpool. A quick Google search tells me there are only two streets of that name in the city. I type in the full postcode of the first street in Gramps's satnav and set off.

I've no idea what I'm going to find when I get there, but my gut is screaming at me that Melissa's lie is important – that there's something about the address that matters. Tom might believe in signs from the universe, but I believe in signs from my gut – I have ever since I moved in with Gran and realised how much she lets hers guide her life. Sometimes her gut will tell her to have another creme egg; sometimes it will tell her to check in on a neighbour she hasn't seen for a while, to then find they are struggling. And once her gut told her that she needed to abandon the retirement she had planned by the seaside and return home to care for her granddaughter. So, yeah, I listen to mine too. Only, the more I drive, the more my gut settles, and I begin to wonder why I'm speeding towards a house I know nothing about.

It's the nauseating lurch of disappointment I get when I reach the first Ellcott Avenue, and find 34 is actually a hairdressers, that explains it. I want answers. I want to understand why Lewis has disappeared, and I'd rather hold on to the fact that something has happened, that there's a mystery to be solved, than let in Mum's theory that he's finally had enough of me and decided to go and live his life without me in it.

I look at the second entry for Ellcott Avenue and find it's only one and a half miles away. I pull off and head straight there.

The house Lewis always wanted, the one he talked about when we were teenagers dreaming of the future while revising for our GCSEs, is what I discover when I pull up in front of the second 34 Ellcott Avenue.

The house is part of a new development of eight properties just outside Allerton. It has a solid grey composite front door with a vertical chrome handle running its length, tiny frosted windows either side and two huge opaque glass panes on the floor above. In front of the neighbouring houses are a whole host of cars Lewis would love to drive, from BMWs to Teslas to Range Rovers. No

Ferraris, but who knows what's hidden away in the double garages to the side of each property. Thankfully, there's no gate to the house, so I'm able to park and walk right up to it. I knock on the door and wait.

I don't understand it, but somehow I *know* that this is his house. I'd never be able to afford a place like this, but Lewis could. Since becoming interested in coding at university and getting a graduate job as a coder for a huge international firm in London – the same firm that poached him back from his new job up here with me and whisked him off to New York – he's had more money than he's known what to do with.

No one comes to the door, and I ring the bell again. It's a video doorbell, the camera pointing at me currently beaming an image on to the owner's phone somewhere. I try to look directly into it, to smile, but I have no idea who might be looking at me.

Theories are flying around my mind. I'm sure this *has* to be Lewis's house, but Lewis is thousands of miles away in an apartment in New York. Could he have bought the house as an investment, a property to live in when he came back? Maybe he's renting it out temporarily? If that's the case, that would be a sign that I'm right – he is planning on coming back soon. But why would he keep me in the dark?

There's no sign of life behind the door. I ring one more time before giving up.

As I reach the bottom of the drive, the car door of a Range Rover parked in the next driveway opens. A woman about my age steps out. She's wearing sportswear, but in the way the

Kardashians wear sportswear – nothing like the thin leggings and baggy T-shirt ensemble I put together when I get the rare urge to go for a run round the block. Her blonde hair is thick and wavy, and she has the full lips and clear skin of a woman who has the luxury of having hundreds of pounds a month to spend on herself.

Pushing down my immediate feelings of inferiority, I put up my hand and wave.

She cautiously smiles back as she goes to her boot and pulls out a huge bright-yellow Selfridges bag. I'd love to know what she has inside it.

"Hi there," I say, stepping onto her drive. "I was wondering if you could help me?"

"Sure," she says, giving me a big, perfect smile.

"I was hoping to speak to the person who lives next door about a friend of mine, but they aren't answering." I consider the best way to go on. "Have you seen them about recently?"

"No, I'm afraid not," she says, picking up the bag and shutting the boot.

"That's a shame. I don't suppose you know their name, do you?"

She gives me a suspicious look, which is fair enough given the amount of sniffing around I'm doing. "No, I don't."

"No problem," I say, realising I've probably pushed it too far. "It was probably a wasted trip anyway. I'll leave you in peace. Sorry to disturb." I give her an apologetic smile and start to walk away.

"No, it's fine," she says, softening. "It's just I've not been here that long. I've met a few of the neighbours, but no one from next door. Mostly, everyone keeps themselves to themselves round here. I've seen a few delivery vans coming and going, but that's about it."

"That's OK, thanks for the help." I try to sound grateful, and not as deflated as I feel.

"I hope you manage to get in touch with them," she says, before walking up the path to her colossal door, opening up and disappearing inside.

Once she's gone, I look around the street. There's no sign of life. There's nothing else to do but leave – make my way back home and get ready for my shift.

Before I reach the car, I turn back and ring the doorbell to number 34 one last time, but there's no answer.

ten

Lewis

SIXTEEN YEARS OLD

HE FOUND CONNOR AND JAKE NEXT TO THE BEER. KELSEY gave him a little wave goodbye and went further into the party to find her friends. Lewis took a seat on a sofa in the lounge and helped himself to a Budweiser.

"You two looked very . . . what's the word?" Connor said, smirking at Jake. "*Close*, just now."

"No, we did not," Lewis protested, wishing his friends hadn't had such a good view of the front door. It wasn't his fault he'd stumbled on the wonky path; not his fault Kelsey had grabbed his arm and said, "Easy there, Bambi"; not his fault he'd gone on to stumble again, and they were laughing and touching when they walked into Connor's house.

"Well, you looked it to me," Connor said. "Kissed her yet?"

"Piss off."

Connor held his hands up. "Easy. Just saying what I see."

"Well don't, all right?" Lewis was spending so much time

telling himself he saw Kelsey as just a friend, and that was how they worked, that he was annoyed at his friends for so clearly seeing something else.

"Fine, but if you're going to keep acting like mates, you really need to sort out your face whenever you're around her."

They all took a swig of their beer and the conversation moved on to how big Connor's house party had become, how half of their year was here, and how dead Connor would be if his parents found out. But Lewis didn't forget what his friends had said about Kelsey – because he knew they were right.

When Kelsey had opened the door to him earlier that evening wearing a short dress and a denim jacket, with her hair curled, he'd had to will his face not to react to how stunning he found her. He told her he'd wait outside, where the light was more forgiving and less likely to reveal his blazing red cheeks.

Kelsey had been living with her grandparents for a few weeks now and was settling in well, but when she left the house that night, the first thing she said was, "Get me out of here."

Walking to Connor's house in the dark, she told him about her mum coming round to visit her drunk that afternoon, leading to a huge family argument, and Lewis was able to temporarily forget how attractive he found her and listen to what she was saying. They'd grown accustomed to sharing parts of their lives with each other that they wouldn't with anyone else. Kelsey spoke about how much she missed her dad, how hard it was to see her mum struggling to find her place in the world without him. Lewis told her about school, how stressed he was by the pressure his teachers put on him as a high-achieving top-set student. Listening was what Lewis did best, and he fell into his familiar role as they wound their way through the maze of streets to Connor's house.

Not that it was all serious between them. Kelsey could make him snort with laughter by doing impressions of teachers in their school, and they would talk for hours about the films they loved and the places they wanted to visit when they were older. More than anything, more than how beautiful he thought she was a hundred times a day, more than how he dreamt of kissing her, Lewis thought her the best friend he'd ever had. That was what he was focusing on – because Kelsey had given him no signs she wanted anything else.

Half an hour after he arrived, the beer had all gone, and Lewis went in search of more. In the kitchen, he looked out into the large garden, decorated with fairy lights along the fence panels, and saw Kelsey sitting at a wooden table with three other girls, blankets round their shoulders. They all started laughing at once, and Lewis smiled. He wouldn't go out and disturb her. He'd find her later.

He was still looking out when a conversation struck up behind him. He turned to find Sam, one of the most popular lads from his year, huddled with a few others from the rugby team he captained. Lewis was surprised they would come to Connor's party, given that they'd never spoken to Connor or any of his friends. They were looking in the fridge, helping themselves to what was there.

"All right," Sam murmured to Lewis when he saw him. They'd once been good friends in primary school, before secondary school hit and they'd quickly discovered their natural places in the pecking order were not with each other. As always when they were thrown together, Lewis puzzled over how to be in Sam's company. They weren't friends any more – in fact, there were many parts to Sam's secondary school identity he didn't like – but he always felt duty bound to make some effort. He didn't need to in this case, as before he could open his mouth, Sam looked past him and his eyes lit up when he saw the girls.

"Kelsey's here," he said to his friend. "She's looking fit tonight."

"Kelsey? You mean the sad one whose dad died? I'd leave well alone, mate."

"Nah, sad girls are the best. Always up for a bit of comfort. So grateful," Sam said, and they both started laughing.

Lewis didn't say anything. Instead, he walked right towards Sam and shoved him as hard as he could in the chest.

"What the fuck?" Sam said, more surprised than angry at first, but he got there quickly and moved towards Lewis, ready to start a fight.

"Woah, woah," Connor said, entering the kitchen at just the right moment and rushing to come between them. "If you've come here for trouble, you can get the hell out," he said to Sam and his friends.

"It wasn't us who started it! It was him. He's tapped in the head."

Connor turned to Lewis and looked ready to say more, but Lewis's thunderous expression stopped him in his tracks.

"Wouldn't stay at this shit party anyway," Sam said, and walked out. His friends hesitated, taking one last look outside at where Kelsey and her friends were laughing and drinking, oblivious to what had happened inside, before following him out.

"I'd ask what that was all about but I'm pretty sure I can guess. Tell you what, mate, you might be saying there's nothing between you and Kelsey, but you're acting like you're already in love with her."

* * *

Later that night, after he'd walked Kelsey home, after pretending he'd had as good a night as she had, Lewis crawled into bed, his brain fuzzy with too much booze. He put the pillow over his head and tried to shut the night out. But try as he might, he couldn't get rid of it.

It wasn't Sam that bothered him. It was Connor's words he couldn't stop playing on repeat: "You're acting like you're already in love with her."

It might have been friendship for Kelsey, but not for him. Every time she told him how great a friend he was, how she couldn't have got through the last few months without him, he became more convinced it would never be anything else to her. Finally, her life was looking more settled – she was starting to smile more, she was moving forwards with him at her side. He had no idea what to do with these feelings, but he knew the last thing she needed from him right now was for him to rock this fragile new state of hers by telling her the truth.

eleven

Kelsey

LEWIS: KELSEY, I'M SO, SO SORRY.

Lewis's message is waiting for me on my phone when I open my eyes on Sunday afternoon after getting in at four in the morning from Cuba Club. I'd been dragged there by Tom, Joy and Dessie after our shift ended with the instruction to have fun and forget about men. Tom was on such a mission to forget about Luca after he found out their new relationship was one of many that Luca had going on, that every time I threatened to leave, he'd march me to the bar and buy us shots of tequila, ordering me to join him in shouting, "Worth Not Girth!" before we necked them.

Despite the hangover, as soon as I see the first line of Lewis's message, I sit upright, rubbing my eyes a few times to bring back my focus before clicking on it to read the rest.

LEWIS: Kelsey, I'm so, so sorry.

I should have messaged you much earlier than this. I know it's no excuse at all, but the thing is . . . I've kind of fallen for someone. Her name is Simone and we met in a spin class (I know, bleurgh!). We've been spending every minute together. You know what it's like when you meet someone you really like.

I know that makes me a shitty friend, and I'm so sorry. Back on my best behaviour from now on, if you'll let me. Hope all is well with you.

Also, don't worry about Mum. Before I left, I got a repeat prescription for this foot cream which she now uses herself. (Again, bleurgh!)

At first, the relief of hearing from him is so immense I'm laughing with it. *Thank God!* But then I read over his message a few times, and relief quickly turns to anger. And that anger, mixed with the tequila still in my system, makes me feel ill.

Lewis would have known how worried I was about him. To have sent that message, he must have seen all the panicked messages I sent him first and this – *this* – is what he comes back with. No mention whatsoever about the planned phone call or the message he'd sent me where he'd said we needed to talk.

And who the fuck is Simone?

I throw my phone down on my bed and get up, desperate for something to calm my churning stomach.

Gran and Gramps are in the kitchen, sitting side-by-side reading the papers.

"Oh dear," Gran says when I walk in. "You look pale, love."

"Morning."

"Here, sit down and let me fetch you something," Gramps says, jumping off his stool. "You're not coming down with something, are you?"

"I'm fine," I tell them, sitting on Gramps's stool. "Although I wouldn't say no to a banana milkshake if there's one on offer."

"Coming up," Gramps says.

Gran pushes my unbrushed hair off my face. "Good night, was it?" she asks.

"I suppose. It just got late. Tom's fault. I hope I didn't wake you."

"Wake your Gramps? If he can sleep through the burglar alarm, he can sleep through you coming back a bit drunk. We're fine. I don't expect you'll be doing much today then, will you?"

I'm so tired, I could easily sleep the day away. But if I go back in my room, my phone will be there waiting for me, tempting me to reply to Lewis. I know I'm not ready to. Not when I'm so angry at him. So hurt by the blatant glossing over of where we were up to before he disappeared. Right now, I can't bring myself to be happy Kelsey, understanding Kelsey, puts-up-with-whatever-is-thrown-at-her Kelsey.

"I don't know yet," I tell Gran. "What are you doing?"

"I'm just finishing reading the paper and I'm off to see your dad."

Ordinarily, our visits to Dad are a solitary activity. We're all regular visitors – Gran and Gramps's affection for their son-in-law never having waned – but we like to go alone. Gran often takes her gardening equipment and tidies up Dad's grave and the church garden. Gramps tends to go on a Saturday so he can update Dad on the latest football scores, and I prefer to sit by the gravestone and talk to him about whatever is on my mind.

"Mind if I come?" I ask now.

Gran's face lights up. "Not at all. I'm meeting the church ladies at half two to attempt to sort out the weeds sprouting up the pathway. If they get any worse it will be like wading through a jungle to get to the church door! You can help us, if you'd like?"

"I might be a bit too delicate for that, but I'll come along."

She looks me over before saying, "Good idea. You visit your dad, get some fresh air to help you come round after last night while we do battle – and we can all go for a cuppa once we're done."

* * *

At the church, a group of four women with gardening gloves on and trowels in hand are waiting for Gran. Leaving them to decide how to wage war against the weeds raging out of control, I walk past the faded, grey headstones nearest the building with names on them that have long since been erased by weather and time. The graveyard slopes down, and I follow the flattened grass path until I reach the row of smaller black marble headstones at the end, near the low wall that separates the sprawling graveyard of St James's from the primary school next door. The names etched on to these headstones are as clear and deep as when they were first created.

I stop when I reach the one at the end of the row.

Martin Bright
1962–2013
Loving husband of Lorraine,
Beloved father of Kelsey
For ever missed

"Hi, Dad," I say, sitting next to it.

A bouquet of dead flowers is resting against the base. Gran or Mum must have left them when they last visited. I pick them up and throw them over the wall, into the playground. Tomorrow morning, it'll be a nice treat for the pupils who find them – they can use them as a macabre bouquet in a pretend wedding or as a weapon in a game of tag.

Usually, I'd spend my visits with Dad filling him in on what's been happening, from Tom's latest boyfriend to Gran and Gramps's monthly trips out to the seaside in Gramps's battered old Nissan that end with them coming back either sunburnt and giggly or freezing cold and miserable. I'd tell him about Lewis and what he's been doing in New York. But not today.

Now I'm here, I don't feel like talking. I thought all my upset and anger at Lewis would come spilling out, and that it might be cathartic to let it do so, but a fresh wave of grief hits me that sweeps my intentions away. Instead, I lean my head on Dad's headstone and look out over the other graves, wondering who is missing those people, if it hurts them as much as it hurts me. If it's normal to still feel the pain of someone not being here ten years later, as though it's just happened.

"I miss you," I whisper to him.

It's only on the way home, when Gran nudges me on the bus and asks me what's wrong with my face today, that I feel ready to tell someone about Lewis's message.

"Well, that's wonderful, isn't it?" Gran says, when I've shown her the message on my phone. "I knew there was something up with you this last week. Well, now you don't need to worry, do you?"

"No, I suppose not," I say. "But don't you think it's all a bit, I don't know . . . a bit convenient? Not the Simone bit." Her name feels uncomfortable in my mouth. "More the explanation about his mum? I just can't believe that the way she was acting, especially that last time, was really to do with foot cream."

"I don't know what state Melissa's feet are in, love. If they're anything like mine, she might need all the help she can get." She's trying to make light of it, to lessen my worry, but I spot the concerned look on her face, the crease between her brows her smile can't disguise.

"I don't know. Meeting someone new isn't a reason not to send me a single message in a week. He'd have known that would hurt me, and that's not like Lewis. When he first moved to New York and wasn't in touch, I was upset but I could understand his reasons: the rush of it all happening, a new country to settle into, the new job. He promised he wouldn't do that to me again, but he has."

"If you're upset, Kelsey, you should tell him," Gran says. "Just because you love someone, it doesn't mean you have to please them all the time and pretend that everything is fine when it's not."

"I know that," I say, a little too defensively.

"Do you? I sometimes wonder if you're a little scared of being honest with Lewis."

"What? Why on earth would I be scared of Lewis?"

"Because you don't want to lose him." Maybe it's because of where we've just been, but when she stops talking, I can almost hear her add 'like your dad'. "But you don't need to worry," she tells me. "That boy loves the bones of you, no doubt about it. When he's pissed you off, you can tell him."

"Gran!" I can't help but laugh at the unfamiliar sound of her language, but Gran doesn't laugh along with me.

"Sorry, but no point beating around the bush with these things."

"No. You're right. I am pissed off with him."

"Good! So you'll speak to him about this?"

I consider it – going home, pouring myself a glass of wine and sitting down to write a reply that is completely honest. I nod at Gran and she nods right back, before giving my knee a squeeze.

twelve

Kelsey

GRAMPS HAS THE CAR ALL DAY, SO IT'S A TAXI THAT DROPS me off at Ellcott Avenue into a new, unexpected heatwave. One heatwave brings with it a bit of a thrill – a chance to wear clothes you'd ordinarily save for beaches and to drink more rosé wine than you'd ever ordinarily contemplate midweek – but two is a pain in the arse. I have to peel myself off the leather seat to get out of the car before stepping onto the new tarmac road which shimmers in the heat. Apart from two pigeons perched on a garage roof under a tree that affords them some shade, the road is deserted. There are no children playing, no one out tending to the neat gardens at the front of each property. From the identical stripes on each lawn, they probably get a gardener in once a week to look after them all.

As I walk towards number 34, unsticking the thick black fabric of my dress from my back, I look at its small windows and huge front door with a new appreciation. It must be so pleasantly cool in the dark rooms at the front where the sun isn't allowed in.

I reach the door and ring the bell, fully expecting to wait. I should have come better prepared. A hat, a bottle of water, sun cream. Hopefully, whoever is on the other side will take pity on me when they see me melting out here and let me in.

Yesterday, I did what Gran suggested. I went home, poured a glass of wine, opened up my messages with Lewis . . . but as my fingers hovered above the screen, I didn't know what letters to tap.

It should have been simple: *You promised you wouldn't do this again. How could you leave it so long without getting in touch when you knew how worried I'd be? Simone doesn't sound good for you . . .*

But the problem was, I didn't believe him. The more I read his message, the more I became convinced it wasn't honest. Maybe the message he sent wasn't exactly him lying to me – there could very well be a Simone and a great love blossoming across the Atlantic. But there was also a house round the corner from where I live that he hadn't mentioned, and a phone call that he was going to have with me that he seemed to have forgotten all about.

And so I put down my phone, downed the wine and made a decision. I'd go back to the house and try one more time to make sense of how it fit in to all this.

If someone answers the door today and can explain to me why a prescription in Lewis's name would be linked to this address, and if that explanation makes sense, *maybe* then I can stop thinking about it so much. If I discover Lewis has bought this house and rented it out – it's possible he did this, without my knowledge – maybe then I'll be ready to talk. The house wouldn't matter then. I could go home and write the perfect message. I could tell him how hurt I've been by his disappearing act and ask him when he decided we were going to be two people who kept things from each other. The idea I had of our future was one of us being together, madly in love, finally sharing our life. It's not meant to look like this.

I ring the bell. It really is mercilessly hot today – a solid wall of heat is pushing against my body. Already I can feel the skin on my neck burning. I will someone to open the door, to invite me to step into the cool, but no one arrives. I press my ear against the door, but there's no sign of anyone inside.

I wait a few more minutes, but it's not a day for lingering. I reluctantly admit defeat and turn my back on the house to walk away.

At the bottom of the avenue, just as I'm about to turn onto the main road, a black Range Rover turns in and stops by me. The window winds down, and the next-door neighbour of 34 leans out. Her skin is matte, make-up perfectly applied, and her hair looks as thick and in place as the last time I saw her. A blast of cool air hits me as I step towards her, and I hear the purr of her air conditioning.

"Hello again," she says, smiling pleasantly. "Any luck?"

"Hi. No, afraid not. I've rang the bell a few times, but no answer. I'd have tried for longer but I'm going to cook if I stay outside too long."

She looks me over, from my swollen feet to my flat hair. "I know. I'm the same in this heat," she says, which is kind, if not at all true.

"Don't suppose you've seen anyone around?" I ask.

"Afraid not. I have to admit, I've been a lot more curious about my neighbour since you were last here, but I've seen nothing apart from a few Amazon Prime vans, and they've been dropping their parcels around the side of the house rather than at the front door."

I'm about to thank her anyway and walk away when she says: "What a shame you've had a wasted trip again. I'd ask you into mine for a quick drink before you leave, but I'm running so late today."

"Oh, that's OK," I say, taken aback by her friendliness. "Another time, perhaps."

"Sure."

She turns to the steering wheel, ready to pull away. Before she does, and before I can stop myself, I take the chance to ask for her help. "I don't suppose I could give you my number, could I? Just in case you come across your neighbour. If you could pass it on, I'd be grateful."

"Sure." She reaches for her phone, which is on the seat next to her and hands it to me through the open window so I can type in my number. "You're hoping to talk to them about your friend, right?"

"Yeah. It's a long story, but I was hoping they could help with something. I'm Kelsey, by the way."

"Nice to meet you, Kelsey. I'm Lana. I'll keep an eye out," she promises.

I hand the phone back and thank her for being so helpful before watching her drive up to her house, pleased the trip hasn't been a complete waste after all.

* * *

I tell myself I'll wait another day to see if Lana gets in touch with any news about her neighbour before I respond to Lewis's apology message and the news about Simone. And all the messages that followed after it.

LEWIS: Kelsey, please reply.

LEWIS: OK, I get you're mad but at least let me know if there's space in that huge heart of yours to forgive me.

LEWIS: I really am sorry, Kelsey.

I'm just home from Ilk after a rubbish shift on a Thursday evening involving Dessie and I waiting on a table of twenty knobheads from an advertising firm round the corner who came in for a 'meeting' that culminated in me mopping up sick outside the gents' toilet, when her message arrives.

073645957593: Hi, Kelsey. It's Lana from Ellcott Avenue. I've finally seen someone leaving number 34, but I'm afraid she hurried off before I could pass on your number.

I wasn't holding out much hope that Lana would have anything to tell me, but I can't help being disappointed.

KELSEY: Hi, Lana. Thanks for your message – I appreciate it. Not to worry. X

I get up, needing a long shower to get rid of the lingering smell of vomit, but before I let the phone fall to my bed, curiosity makes me type out another message.

KELSEY: Out of interest, what did your neighbour look like?

I'm not sure Lana will reply to such a nosy question, but there's another message waiting for me when I get out of the shower twenty minutes later.

073645957593: She was small with cropped red hair and a pretty questionable taste in sportswear! Lana xx

My stomach drops at the exact same time my mouth does.

A small redhead with questionable taste in sportswear – I know exactly who that is.

Melissa.

thirteen

Kelsey

"IT'S ONLY AN HOUR," I EXPLAIN TO TOM THE NEXT MORNING, when I ring into work to postpone starting my shift.

"Kelsey, darling, you're a waitress. Pretty much all I need from you is for you to turn up, and you're telling me you can't manage that."

I'd tell friend Tom to fuck off for that, but it's manager Tom I'm dealing with now, so I opt for a different approach. "I understand. How about I make it up to you by staying late tonight to help Andrez and Mike give the kitchen a good clean?"

If there's one thing Tom lives in fear of, it's being surprised by the Food Standards Agency or a reality TV show for an inspection of the kitchen. Andrez and Mike are great cooks – cool-headed and creative – but their cleaning can be described as light, at best.

"Fine," he says. "But whatever the reason you're going to be late, I hope it's worth tackling the kitchen for."

"Me too."

I'm already in Liverpool city centre, and once I hang up the phone, it's a short walk to the Harold Cohen library at the university campus where Melissa's worked as a librarian for as long as I've known her. I wait outside the entrance, watching the students filing out, their bags stuffed with books. When I studied here, this was the place I visited least – Melissa would joke she'd never seen me around. But I wasn't busy partying or living any kind of typical student life – I was in my student digs, watching TV, feeling invisible. It was Lewis who made me see that I didn't need to stay, that I could leave uni and give myself time to figure out what I wanted to do before possibly studying again. It was the right thing, and I've always been grateful to him for that, but it doesn't stop the familiar ache whenever I see other students making it all look so effortless.

As arranged, Melissa comes through the glass doors at twelve sharp and walks over to me. When I rang her last night, told her she'd been seen coming out of the house and informed her I'd be waiting for her on the library steps when she came out for her lunch, I half expected her to hang up. I didn't expect her agreement and her resigned, "See you tomorrow, then," before she put down the phone.

"Hi, Melissa," I say now. "Thanks for meeting me."

She gives me a small smile. "Let's get a drink, shall we? There's a cafe just round the corner."

"Sure."

She walks off at speed and I follow behind, not trying to catch up. I watch her as she walks – her head down, shoulders ever so slightly stooped, her normally regularly-dyed red hair showing solid grey roots. Mum still seems young in her floaty tops, red lipstick and bouncy gait – but somehow Melissa has lost her youth.

There's a queue outside Suzie's Cafe, and Melissa joins the back of it. It's tiny inside, a glass-fronted counter and six tables squeezed in. I'd suggest we go to the Costa a few doors down but sense today it's best to let Melissa take charge.

"You're still working at the same restaurant then?" she asks, looking down at my uniform.

"Yep."

"Like it, do you?"

"I do."

"That's good," she says, before turning back to the queue.

It takes twenty minutes to order our coffees and get seated. I've only got forty minutes left before I need to be in work. Once we've set ourselves up and Melissa has stopped pouring sachets of sugar into her latte, I jump into the silence.

"I know it's his," I say. "The house. I knew it as soon as I saw it. You've got to tell me what's going on. Please, Melissa."

She surprises me by nodding. "All these secrets. I told him he should have never kept it from you, that it was a mistake, but you know how stubborn he can be."

"Sure do." We exchange a smile. "What's going on?" I ask again, my voice gentle.

Melissa takes a sip of her coffee and puts it down. She focuses on the cup, turning it in her hands. When she looks up there are tears in her eyes.

"If it was up to me, I'd tell you everything, Kelsey. I would.

I always told him you should know, but he made me promise not to say a word."

I'd been nervous about today, about what I would discover, but those nerves had been contained to the pit of my stomach, pushed down by the determination to get answers. Now they run through my body, down my arms and legs, into my heart, speeding it up. Whatever is going on with Lewis, it feels bigger than him buying a house and not telling me. That wouldn't upset Melissa, but something has.

"Tell me what? I don't get it. What's there not to tell me?"

She looks down at the cup again, her face tight, as though she's working hard to keep control of her emotions. I prise one of her hands off the cup and hold it in mine.

"Please, Melissa. It's me."

She looks around the cafe, at the groups of students, at the smiling girls behind the counter, and as she does, her face firms up with what I hope is resolve to be honest with me.

"I can't tell you everything, you understand? I've got to respect his wishes."

"OK." I nod encouragingly.

"I wouldn't have met you at all," she goes on, "but I don't know how much longer I can go on doing nothing. I'm only meeting you because you're the only person I can think of who can help him. But don't ask me for more than I can give."

I nod again.

"Lewis isn't in New York," she says, bluntly.

Despite my misgivings that something is wrong here, I can't

help but be excited. If he's home, there's nothing we won't be able to sort between us. "Oh my God. He's back already?"

"No." She shakes her head slowly. "He's not back from New York, because he never went." My face scrunches up in confusion, because those words make absolutely no sense.

"What? Of course he went. He's been living there for a year."

Now it's Melissa's turn to squeeze my hand. "No, darling, he hasn't been."

She pulls away from me and sits back as she waits for me to take this in, but I can't do it. I shake my head against what she is telling me.

"That's not true."

"I'm sorry," Melissa says. "I know this is hard, and I told Lewis it was unfair, but he decided that's what he was going to tell you. And he stuck to it."

We sit in silence for a few moments. "You mean there was no job offer?"

"No."

"No reason for him to rush off like he did?"

"No."

"And the house . . ."

She nods. "The house. He's been living there the last few months, since the sale went through."

Every truth she's saying hammers at my heart – the heart I've had to guard so feverishly since he left after we kissed. The heart I've only managed to keep intact because I've spent the last year telling myself one day he'll come home to me and, when he does, we can finally be together as we were always meant to be. But if this is true, everything I've told myself has been a lie. Those daily mantras that have got me out of bed in the morning – *this won't be for ever, true love doesn't fade with distance, he'll come back* – were built on lies I didn't even know about. Because he never even went away.

"I don't get it," I finally say. "Why would say he was in New York?"

"I'm sorry. That's the bit I can't tell you. For that, you'll have to speak to Lewis."

"After he's lied to me?" I ask. My voice comes out loud and high-pitched, causing the girls on the next table to look our way. "What makes you think I'm ever going to speak to him again?"

I want to be furious at him. How easy it should be to hate him for this monumental, conniving, gigantic *year-old* lie – to swear I'll never speak to him again, and to mean it. As I sit, welded to my seat with shock, I picture myself getting up and walking out of this cafe, telling Melissa to tell her son to go to hell, my head held high. I try to summon that energy, but I can't. Because I know from Melissa's distraught face that there's too much of this I'm missing to be able to settle on something as simple as anger.

She lets a silence open up between us. I fill it by trying to reassess everything I think I know.

"The medicine bag," I say, when my mind snags on how I came across the address. "That really was for him? Not foot cream like he told me."

Melissa nods. "He's still not got round to setting up his

89

prescriptions to be delivered, so I've been collecting them for him the last few months."

"It was a pretty big bag," I recall. "What was in it?"

She shakes her head. "Sorry, Kelsey, I—"

"You can't tell me," I finish for her. "Why don't we make this easier then, because I've not got long left. I can't begin to imagine what would have possessed the Lewis I thought I knew to do this – to choose to lie and lie and lie for this long. So, if there's anything else you *can* say before I go, will you please say it now?"

In return, she simply asks, "Do you remember the last time you saw Lewis?"

"Of course I do. It was two weeks before he messaged me saying he was in New York," I answer instantly. "He'd come round to see me before a night out in Chester he couldn't get out of with some work mates. It was the night we had our first kiss," I add, quietly.

She closes her eyes and lets out a line of long, ragged breaths. "When you speak to him, you need to ask him about that night."

"Why?" I say, uselessly.

"Just ask him. When you do, I really hope he'll be able to tell you what happened." Then Melissa stands up, brushing my shoulder with her hand as she passes, and pushing past the queue to get back outside.

fourteen

Kelsey

AS I WALK UP THE PATH TO LEWIS'S FRONT DOOR, THE first drops of rain begin to fall from a sky that has threatened a downpour all morning.

It doesn't matter. I reach into my canvas bag and pull out my umbrella. In there, I also have sun cream in case the weather swivels again, as well as a cardigan, a bottle of water and a bag of Fruitella. I've come prepared. I ring the bell to let him know I'm here, but then sit down on the step, knowing he won't answer. I should have brought a camping chair, too.

I've had two full days to prepare. Two days to consider what Melissa told me, to try to work it out, to understand it. But I'm no further forward than I was when the words came out of her mouth.

He's not back from New York, because he never went.

I would have marched round here as soon as Melissa left the cafe if it weren't for work. By the time my shift had finally ended, I was so heavy with exhaustion, the only thing I wanted to do was go home and curl up in bed. I slept for ten hours, my body protecting me like it's done before by holding back the hurt until I was better able to face it.

Yesterday morning, after I'd let Gran take my temperature and promised her I wasn't ill, just tired, I went to the best place I could think of to try and find some space in which to begin to work all this out, to try and find a reason to explain why Lewis would put a stop to our new-found relationship just after we'd kissed.

I got in the car and drove to Speke Hall, the National Trust place I spent so many Sundays with Dad in my childhood. In the few years before he died, I would moan whenever he suggested another trip there. Teenagers and National Trust sites are not a natural combination, and the place held no appeal for me. But since he's been gone, I've been drawn to this place, with its warm memories of even the bitterest of cold days. Walks in the woods where he wouldn't ask me about school or friends or my goals in life, but what I liked, what music I was into that week or what I'd watched recently. Timed runs around the maze we knew so well but always managed to take a wrong turn in. Hot chocolates and ice creams before returning to the car, where he would always say the same thing before turning on the engine. "See, not so bad to spend time with your old man, is it?" I would always answer no. Not so bad at all.

Walking its familiar paths, I did laps around the estate as I waited for the explanation for Lewis's lies to click into place. But the more I looked back over the time before he left and the stories he concocted to take himself out of my life, the more my confusion grew. Nothing made sense – I could think of nothing to explain why Lewis would behave like this. I got back in my car, angry and hurt and disappointed that the soothing magic of this place only covered me when my dad was next to me.

This morning, I knew that there was no option but to go there – to push open the letterbox and to try and get him to help me understand.

"Come on, Lewis," I say now, after sitting down on his front doorstep. "You know I'm here, and I know you're there. I'm guessing from the lack of messages you've sent since I saw your mum that she's filled you in about what she told me. Don't you think you owe it to me to let me know what's going on?"

I'm met with silence. I look through the letterbox into the cavernous hallway, but there's no sign of him. In fact, there's not much of sign of life at all. The place has the appearance of a show home, beautiful but eerily flawless. There are no shoes kicked off by the door, no letters on the side table, not a coffee cup or coat in sight. Each of the wooden doors leading off the hall is shut, keeping the rooms beyond hidden away. I breathe in deeply, trying to get a smell of something I might recognise, but even the air is empty of cooked food or laundry or scented candles. When we lived together as teenagers, I constantly took the piss about how overly organised Lewis was, his obsession for everything being put in the right place which he'd inherited from Melissa. But even for him, this is extreme.

"This is a good thing," I tell him, my voice louder this time. "Now I know you're here, you won't need to spend so much time googling about the Lower East Side to convince me you actually live there."

I mean it as a joke, but I hear the sharpness in how it comes out. As much as I don't understand this, the weight of his deception hasn't completely buried my faith in Lewis. My loyal heart is still shouting over the noise in my head, telling me that he wouldn't disappear without good reason. Melissa was upset, not annoyed with him. If he was being a dick, trying to get rid of me by pretending to move away, she'd have never gone along with the lie. She wouldn't have done that to me, and she wouldn't have allowed Lewis to do so either. The Melissa I know would have made him come to my front door and explain himself if she felt he was being underhand. But she's supported him in this lie. Not fully, perhaps, but enough. There's got to be a good reason for that.

And then there's the medicine bag. The size of it has been keeping me awake at night. When I thought he was in New York, I'd dismissed it as not being his. But now I know he's in Liverpool, that bag is significant.

When Dad became ill, he didn't tell me for months. He hid himself from me so I wouldn't see it. He wanted to protect me for as long as he could, to keep me in the life I knew before it was blown apart. First, he was busy with work, then he was tired, then he was just so grumpy with me that I wouldn't go to him, wouldn't want to ask him to take me to the shops or to watch a film. It was a kindness – cancer, or the thought of losing him, didn't cross my mind during those months – but it didn't feel like it at the time.

Now, I can't help but worry that Lewis is doing the same. He could be ill. He could be trying to protect me. But if that's the case, he needs to know that it won't work. I'd rather know. I'd rather face this with him than miss a second more with him than I need to.

Whatever's happening, first I need Lewis to come to this door to tell me.

"I'm sorry," I say. "That was harsh. I know there's got to be a good reason you lied to me. I hope you'll tell me what it is."

The rain's coming down heavier now, and I'm not sure how much longer this Home Bargains brolly is going to stand up to it.

"I like your house," I say. "Very Bond villain. I bet you've got a dark room filled with computer screens in there, haven't you? All set for world domination. Have you got a cat, too?"

Nothing.

I sigh. "Look, Lewis. I've been going back over the days before you left and trying to understand what happened. Your mum said I should ask you about the night you were going out with your work mates. If it's something I did or said that night, something that made you think you couldn't tell me the truth, I'm sorry. If I messed up—"

I stop, sure I heard movement behind the door. I look through the letterbox again. Everything's the same, but that doesn't stop my heart crashing against my chest wall. There's a faint shuffle, close, and I realise where he is. Where he must have been this whole time – sat on the other side of the door, his back pressed against it, his knees pulled up under his chin, so I wouldn't be able to see him.

"Lewis?"

His voice when I hear it is so near to me, yet miles away from the solid, confident voice I know.

"Please, go away."

fifteen

Kelsey

THE PAIN IN HIS VOICE CEMENTS IT.

"I can't," I tell him. "I'm staying here until I know you're OK."

"Kelsey, please," he begs. "I'm not ready to do this."

"Do what?" I push, hating to hear him like this but knowing at the same time we've come to the moment of truth and I need to keep going.

He doesn't answer, and I begin to think that's it – that's all I'm getting – until he speaks again, his voice more controlled this time.

"Look, can we at least talk over Whatsapp?"

"What? I'm right here. Why can't you just tell me what's going on?"

"Please, Kelsey. I'll explain, I promise, but it would be a hell of a lot easier if you'd let me do it in my own way, rather than turning up and demanding answers."

A peal of incredulous laughter comes out of my mouth – at how *he* could possibly be angry at *me* in this situation, how he could act like I'm the one in the wrong when I'm outside the house he never told me about, and if it wasn't for his mum, he'd likely still be texting me today pretending he was in New York.

"Oh, I'm sorry. I'm the one in the wrong, am I?" I snap back.

"No. Obviously, I'm to blame. All I'm asking is for you to help me out, to make this a tiny bit easier."

"Fine. Fine. Have you any idea when you might be getting in touch, or shall I not get my hopes up to hear from you anytime soon?" My voice is still full-on anger, but I'm already settling my bag on my shoulder, ready to move away.

"Give me an hour," he says.

"OK," I agree. "But you better mean it. You know I'll only keep coming back, hounding you, until I get an explanation."

I mean it. Lewis never backed off from me when I would push everyone away after Dad died. He kept showing up for me, and it helped me to know I wasn't alone. In this big house, with seemingly everyone apart from Melissa being kept out of it, Lewis seems more alone than I ever was. I owe it to him to keep pushing.

For the first time, there's a hint of the old Lewis in the warmth of his voice as he replies, and it fills me with hope that we might be able to get through this. "Oh, I know that very well."

"Good. I'll go then, but I want to hear from you in an hour."

"You will."

I let the letterbox fall shut and get up. Huge droplets of rain fall from his guttering as I do so, landing on my neck before I have a chance to rearrange the umbrella.

There would be plenty of time to get back home before the hour's up, but, as I walk away from him, I know it's not where I'm going to go. I'm not ready to return to the bungalow yet, to set eyes on Gran and Gramps's disappointed faces as I tell them he wouldn't let me in. There's a chain pub a few minutes' walk away from his house that I've never been in but always looks inviting, with its sage green paintwork and copper lanterns in the window. I settle on walking across, ordering a hot chocolate and waiting the hour out on my own.

It can't have been more than ten minutes since I left his house but once I've got my drink and have settled on a sofa next to the window, I get my phone out and place it on the table next to my mug.

The hot chocolate is long gone and a nice, underworked barman who came over to try and make chit-chat is fetching me a large glass of red wine when my phone finally pings, forty-four minutes later.

LEWIS: Hi.

KELSEY: Hi. Ready now?

He begins to type, and I hold the phone in my hand, keeping a close eye on the top of the screen that tells me *Lewis is typing.* I watch and watch, and still no message arrives. Rather than a few words to put me out of my misery, he seems to be constructing an essay of an explanation.

Finally, it comes through.

LEWIS: OK. Here goes. First off, I'm sorry about lying to you. I never meant to hurt you, but now I can see that not being honest has done that. Being in touch with you, hearing about what you get up to and talking shit with you, has been the one thing that's kept me going this last year, but the messages we shared were built on lies. If I could go back, I'd make different decisions about how I've behaved. But I wouldn't change everything, Kels. I need to know I can tell you this without you trying to change the way my life is now. Promise me you won't try?

Without any consideration, I reply.

KELSEY: Promise.

LEWIS: Thanks. I know Mum told you to ask me about the last night we saw each other, when I came round to yours before going to meet people from work for that night out in Chester. I felt terrible leaving you after we'd kissed, but it was work – I didn't know everyone that well and was still trying to fit in, and I felt I had no choice. So stupid. You know I didn't want to go, right?

I didn't know that at all. I had no idea what was going through Lewis's mind after we kissed, because he just left. But I don't write that.

KELSEY: I know.

LEWIS: The plan was to stick to the bars, but a few pints in, one of the lads decided he wanted to go on the pull and we ended up in a club. It was rammed. As soon as I got in, I wanted to go. I wanted to check in with you and make sure you were OK, but Matty wanted a wingman. Matty was my supervisor, so I didn't feel I could say no. At one point we were on the dancefloor and a girl fell into me. Seeing how wasted she was, I led her off and took her to the bar for a glass of water.

I stop reading and take a large gulp of the wine. A night out? A girl? This isn't at all what I thought I would get, and I have to steel myself to go on.

Turns out her boyfriend had seen us, and we exchanged a few words before I walked off. Not long after, I decided I'd leave and try ringing you to see if you were still awake. I came out of the club on my own, and he and his mates were waiting for me outside. They jumped me and beat me up so badly I was knocked out and ended up with three broken ribs. Then the girl's boyfriend smashed up a bottle and used the glass to destroy the right side of my face while I was lying on the ground.

The violence of those words on my screen makes me miss a breath. It's the sharp pain in my chest that reminds me to breathe, but when I do, I'm hit by a wave of sickness and have to put my phone down and grip on to the table with my head down until it settles.

Lewis, attacked? Glassed? The viciousness of it is incomprehensible. The words I've just read don't belong in Lewis's world. His world isn't violent or aggressive, but kind and compassionate. I hate that someone has pushed into it and filled it with this.

I need to reply. To say something, anything. But this is so far from what I'd imagined he'd say that I just keep rereading what he's told me.

There are so many questions running through my mind. How bad was it? What do you mean by 'destroyed'? How much pain were you in? Who did this to you? Why didn't you tell me? Why couldn't you have stayed with me that night? But these aren't the kinds of questions I want to ask him by message. In the end, there's only one thing I can think to write.

KELSEY: Oh my God, Lewis. I'm so sorry.

There are a few minutes when he doesn't text back and my

fingers hesitate over the buttons, unsure whether I should say more, if that sorry went anywhere near close enough to telling him how devastated I am for him. I exhale when I see that he's typing again.

LEWIS: *Thank you. I'm sorry I've had to tell you over text, but I hate talking about it. I spend most of my time pretending it never happened. Saying it out loud with you on the other side of the door felt too hard.*

That's when I start to cry. Huge tears drop onto my T-shirt and spread to form patterns on the thin, navy material. The barman is looking over and I smile at him, nodding to signal that I'm OK, that I don't want him to come over. But the tears won't stop as the enormity of the situation washes over me.

Lewis was attacked, and not only did he have to deal with the physical pain of that, but the fear and trauma of it must have completely altered his life. Back in college we'd go on nights out, and I'd see fights break out between the lads we were with. Not long ago, Tom had to break up a fight that erupted at Ilk. But those were all scraps, the result of too much booze. This was something else entirely – something that made my friend who used to tell me everything not able to say the truth out loud to me for a whole year.

KELSEY: *You don't need to say sorry. I just wish I'd known sooner. I could have . . .*

I stop writing. What could I have done? I could have sat by his side, but I couldn't have changed the events. Right now, I can't even understand the events.

KELSEY: *You don't need to say sorry. I just wish you'd told me.*

LEWIS: I know. I am sorry I couldn't. It was selfish of me not to.

KELSEY: Lewis, you are the actual least selfish person in the world. You're the Jason to my Kylie, remember?

Despite the pain, I smile at the memory of Lewis turning up to the bungalow to pick me up for Elle's seventeenth birthday fancy-dress party wearing an open white shirt and a blonde wig, just so I wouldn't feel so self-conscious walking into the cricket club as Kylie Minogue in her gold hot pants.

LEWIS: I very much do remember. But this was selfish, and I am sorry. When I woke up at the hospital, I was in so much shock and so much pain, I couldn't think about anything. My eye had been damaged, and I had to have an operation to reduce the fluid around it. I had my face stitched back together in four places, and I was in agony all over. It was only once I came home that the shock wore off and I was left to deal with what had happened. Or not deal with it. Hide from it, I guess.

KELSEY: I get that. I reckon most people would have wanted to do the same.

LEWIS: That's overly generous of you, and questionable. But thank you. I did try a few times to carry on as normal – to do the small things I used to do without thinking, like going out for coffee or to the supermarket – but it soon became obvious the only way I was going to cope was to shut myself away. All I wanted was to make it disappear. Only, I couldn't make it disappear when I was outside. Every time I left the house, I felt terrified. I'd gone through my whole life never once considering how vulnerable I was whenever I left home, how exposed I was to so many dangers, to so many things out of my control. It's what everyone does, I suppose, but after what happened, the thought of that was crippling. The solution was simple. Don't go outside.

A chill runs down my back at that, at where his brain had taken him in order to protect him from the hurt of what happened. *Don't go outside.*

LEWIS: I know the best thing would have been to just remove myself from your life, not to pretend to be in New York. But when it came down to it, I couldn't let go of you.

New York. The lies. At some point, I know we'll need to talk about that. But not now. All of the things that mattered so much to me a week, a day, even an hour ago, have shrunk in the light of what happened . . . and what is still happening as a result of that attack. Right now, all that matters is Lewis.

KELSEY: I'm glad you didn't let go. I just wish I could have been there for you.

LEWIS: But you were there for me. More than anyone. When I came home from the hospital, I told Mum to keep everyone away. Even you. When you rang her phone, I begged her not to answer. That time you came round, I told her to pretend we were out. I couldn't talk about it, I didn't even want to think about it, and I just wasn't ready for you to become part of what happened, when I hated that it had happened so much.

But I didn't intend to tell the lie until Mum got my smashed phone repaired for me and I looked at it for the first time, a few weeks after the attack. There were all these messages from you. You were so concerned about me, and pissed off with me for disappearing on you. But despite not hearing from me, you'd still send me stupid GIFS and links to articles you thought I'd like. It hurt like hell, the state my face was in, but you made me smile for the first time since the attack. Everything else was unrecognisable, but not you. I came up with New York that day to hold you off for a bit. To delay the change between us that was coming. It was wrong, but when we were texting, I felt a bit like my old self, like what had happened to me wasn't there – even if only for a few minutes each day. I knew if you found out the truth, that would disappear. I told myself you were used to me being away for work so it wasn't that big a lie, and when I was ready to tell you, you'd understand. I'm so sorry I let it carry on as long as I did. I wanted to tell you so many times, but the more days that passed, the bigger the lie felt. I know this is selfish, I do, but as I came to terms with my face, my scars and the fact going outside was no longer an option, the messages between us became a lifeline, and I couldn't bear the thought of losing them.

I remember sending those messages when he first disappeared. Second-guessing how he was feeling, so terrified that I'd lost him that for every honest message I sent, I'd sent another to try and make it seem like I wasn't hurt or confused, that we were still the same. Giving him the out if he wanted to go back to being friends after kissing me, showing him I was cool with that.

I look up from the screen, the upset and anger and shock whirling inside me at odds to the pleasant, warm atmosphere of the pub. I want to leave, to be alone, but we're not finished yet. We're only up to today.

KELSEY: But what now? Now I do know. What happens next?

He doesn't reply straightaway. For a while nothing appears on my screen, my question hanging there.

LEWIS: I can't let you in. I'm sorry, Kelsey. If I do that, you'll try and be normal, try and stay the same as always. But you won't be able to. You'll see my scars, and you'll pity me. I'll hate it. I don't think I can handle you becoming another person trying to get me to come out of the house, to get on with my life. And I definitely can't cope with us not being us any more. I'm sorry.

KELSEY: Stop apologising! And we can stay us. I can't even begin to imagine what you've been through, but it doesn't mean we have to change. If you need us to be the same, that's what we'll be.

LEWIS: Really?

I don't know whether I'm right or not. I can't say how I'm going to react to this. I know I won't *want* to pity him, and I won't *want* to make him do anything he doesn't want to do. I want for us to stay us, but this is such new ground, it feels premature to talk about certainties. Instead, I give him something that we both need. Honesty.

KELSEY: Really, I don't know. I can't promise anything, but at least let's try. If you don't want me to come in, I won't come in. You won't need to see me. But how about we try sitting on either side of that big front door of yours and see how we get on?

sixteen

Lewis

SIXTEEN YEARS OLD

HIS MUM HELPED HIM WITH THE FLOWERS.

Lewis hadn't even considered buying them. Connor, and the majority of people in year eleven who had decided to use the prom as a chance to get a date, had asked the person that they fancied to go with them weeks ago. Those invites had taken place at school, via notes passed in class or in between lessons, usually through other people – "My mate says will your mate go to the prom with them?" He was sure that neither Connor nor any of the other lads from his year would have thought to buy flowers for the occasion, but last night, once Melissa had brought the prom up over dinner and he'd told her he wanted to ask Kelsey to go with him, she'd reached over the table to squeeze Lewis's hand and asked him what the plan was.

"Oh, come on. This is Kelsey. You've got to make it special for her," she'd said, in response to his shrug.

"And I want it to be special," he said, only realising how much this was true as the words left his mouth. "But given that she probably has no idea I'm going to ask her, I don't want her to feel pressured into saying yes. Maybe I should avoid anything too romantic – keep it casual, like it's no big deal."

Melissa laughed at that. "Unless Kelsey's taken to keeping her eyes shut whenever she's with you, I don't think it's going to be quite the surprise you think it is, love."

"Maybe not," Lewis admitted. Even he knew these last few months, as school drew to a close and the air was filled with the smell of the future and talk of next steps, he'd been struggling to pretend that Kelsey didn't fill his mind the whole time. The new haircut she'd got with the long fringe that worked like an arrow to draw him to her beautiful eyes hadn't helped. The last few weeks, they'd spent more time together in school than ever before – he'd sought her out at lunch, happy to sit with her friends instead of his. He'd walked her home and sat in her grandparents' kitchen pretty much every night for the last fortnight, and their text chats were becoming so long he was beginning to worry about the lack of revision he'd been getting in.

Kelsey's grandparents arriving had made Kelsey's life stable. She told Lewis she didn't feel like she was spinning any more, going through her life in a blur. Now she was able to be still, Lewis was sure she was starting to look at him more closely, and what she saw wasn't entirely a friend. Their cover of friendship was wearing thinner by the day, and, for the first time since she came into his life, he felt like it might OK, that he could stop pretending not to have fallen for her.

"In that case, get her some flowers. Make it nice," Melissa said.

He went to get them the next day. Melissa had insisted on being there when he made his choice, because his selection, she explained, would say far more than he thought it would. She took him into a little florist's shop near their house that he must have walked past a hundred times and never properly noticed. Inside, with the overwhelming smell of lilies threatening to bring out his hay fever, he let his mum and the florist do most of the talking, his own excitement building as he imagined handing them over to Kelsey – this well-thought-out bouquet that would help him show her how much she meant to him.

Buoyed by the prospect, he soon took charge. The flowers should be purple, Kelsey's favourite colour. Definitely no roses – Kelsey had hated them ever since her mum had chosen them for her father's funeral. They shouldn't be too big or showy; pretty rather than stylish.

Twenty minutes later, they left the florist with his mum holding on to a small bouquet of stocks, blue irises and eucalyptus tied together with straw. Even to Lewis's untrained eye, he had to admit they were far better than the supermarket bunches he would most likely have chosen if left to his own devices.

"Go on, then," Melissa said at the end of the road. Turning right would lead him home, turning left would lead him to Kelsey's house.

"Now?" he asked, suddenly not ready.

"Yes, now. You've got a delivery to make."

He took the flowers from her and set off, self-conscious to have them in his possession. If Connor or anyone from school were to drive past now, they'd have ammunition to take the piss out of him for weeks. When he got to her front door, he remembered his mum's words about making this special, pulled the flowers up to his chest, put on his best smile and knocked.

"Oh, it's you," Kelsey's gramps said, opening the door. "Hiya, lad," he added as an afterthought, moving to the side to let him in, his eyes not meeting Lewis's but looking behind him at the empty path.

"Were you expecting someone else?" Lewis asked, as he stepped inside.

"I was hoping it would be Lorraine, coming back to say sorry."

"Oh." Lewis lowered his arm, the bouquet resting upside down against his leg. "What's happened?"

"Lorraine's cancelled on Kelsey for next week. She was meant to be staying back home for a few nights, but Lorraine's just been round to say she's not up to it." He shook his head sadly.

Lewis knew how much Kelsey was looking forward to going home for a while, how much she hoped it was a sign of better things to come between her and her mum.

"What's all this, anyway?" her gramps asked, pointing to the flowers by his side.

"I-I was going to ask Kelsey if she wanted to, erm, come to the prom with me."

"Right. That's nice," he said, smiling at Lewis, but not managing to disguise the evening's upset in his voice.

"I hope she thinks so." He tried to keep his tone light in an attempt to cancel out the misgivings that had arrived since he'd stepped inside.

He started to walk on, towards Kelsey's room, but felt a firm hand on his shoulder. He stopped.

"Listen, none of my business, but . . . do you think that's a good idea?"

Lewis paused. He wanted to say yes, of course it's a good idea. He wanted to say he loved her, so it was simple. You love someone and you tell them, and you hope they'll feel the same. That's how it was meant to work.

"I've no doubt she'd say yes," Gramps continued, a small smile on his face. "I'm just not sure that's the best thing right now. You've been such good friends this last year. It would be a shame if you changed things and it didn't work out, and you ended up losing each other. Especially when she's already lost so much."

"I'd never stop being her friend," Lewis said.

"I know you wouldn't. But what about Kelsey? I'm not sure she would be able to handle any more hurt."

He knew what her gramps was saying was right.

He took a long breath before speaking. "OK. I won't ask her."

As soon as he said it, he was amazed that it had taken him until then, until he was standing in her hallway with flowers in hand, to work it out.

Walking into the function room at the Hilton with Kelsey on his arm for the prom, slow dancing under the disco lights, venturing off somewhere dark and private as the night drew to an end, were all the things his heart wanted. Only it wasn't *his* heart he needed to be thinking of. Lewis needed to protect Kelsey and her shattered heart that he'd started to hope he was helping to piece back together but knew was still so fragile. She needed him to stay as her friend, and he couldn't risk anything that could jeopardise that.

"Good lad," Gramps said, giving Lewis's shoulder a quick squeeze. "It's for the best. Now, why don't you go and see if you can cheer her up."

Lewis remembered the flowers in his hand. It was as though they'd suddenly doubled in weight and he needed to put them down after holding on to them for so long.

"Give them here," Gramps said, noticing him looking down. "I'm off to church in a bit. I'll take them there."

Lewis handed over the flowers and kept walking until he was outside Kelsey's bedroom door.

He knocked gently.

"It's me," he said. "Can I come in?"

"OK."

She was on the bed, her face pink and blotchy from crying. She got up as soon as he came in.

"I'm so glad you're here," she said, as she went to hug him.

He put his arms around her and held her while she sobbed on to his T-shirt.

seventeen

Kelsey

"FOR THE LAST TIME, *YOU* SAID THAT GARLIC BREAD WAS on the house to make up for the wait and I am not paying for it."

I've been locked in this argument for the last ten minutes. I smile at the customer again, swallowing the urge to tell him he's making himself look a complete dick in front of the date he's been trying to impress since he came in here by arguing about an extra four pounds fifty on top of a three hundred pound bill.

"I'm sorry for the confusion, sir, but what I actually asked was whether you wanted some garlic bread while you waited."

Honestly, I don't have a clue if that's what I said or not. I've spent the shift counting down the hours until I can leave again, and I've hardly the space in my brain to hold on to garlic-bread-related discussions. But I can't afford for Tom to notice there's a problem. "Thin ice, Kelsey. Thin ice," he'd said to me this morning when I appeared a minute before my shift started without having yet changed into my uniform.

"No, you did not!" the customer shouts. I glance at his date and her widened eyes. If I was her, the alarm bells going off in my mind would be deafening.

At his raised voice, Joy appears by my side.

"Is there a problem I can help you with, sir?" she asks, her voice syrupy.

"I bloody well hope you can. As I've been trying to explain, the garlic bread was on the house and I'm not paying for it."

"I see," Joy says, scrunching up her face. "The thing is, it's company policy not to offer free food, and I know Kelsey here is a stickler for following policy, so I'm afraid there must have been a mix-up. We won't be able to take the item off the bill, but I can offer you a complimentary shot of limoncello each to make up for the confusion. How does that sound?" she asks, beaming at him, while making it clear he's the one completely in the wrong.

"If you make them doubles, that's fine," he grumbles.

"No problem, sir. Kelsey will get that for you right now."

We walk away from the table together, only starting to laugh when we get behind the bar and our backs are to the diners.

"What a prick," Joy says. "Make sure it's a good double you pour him. And give the woman some of the decent stuff. She deserves it after putting up with him all afternoon."

I reach for the two bottles of limoncello we stock, one a nice bottle we order in from our suppliers, the other a toilet-cleaner -reminiscent bottle Tom picked up from Costco for a fiver.

Once I've delivered the drinks and finally taken payment, I head back to where Joy is waiting for me at the bar.

"How you holding up?" she asks.

"Great. Top of my game," I say, wafting my hand over my shirt

I stained half an hour earlier by spilling a half-eaten aubergine parmigiana all down my front on the way back to the kitchen.

"You know, I still can't believe what happened to Lewis. It's awful. And all those lies he told . . ."

"I know," I say. "But I'm not focusing on the lies. It still hurts to think about it; to think I believed he was in New bloody York for an entire year. But those lies helped him. And I'm glad I was helping him, even if I didn't know I was doing it at the time."

"I get that. But you know you can't completely ignore the lying, don't you?"

I nod my head. "I'm not. We'll deal with that. But right now, more than anything else, I just feel so sad for him. So sad that it happened and that the only way he could deal with it was to shut himself away." I begin to cry again, and Joy puts her arms round me for the third time this shift.

"Why don't you tell Tom about Lewis? I'm sure he'll let you go early if you do."

"No. I'm better off here than worrying at home. I will tell Tom, but I'd rather get tonight out of the way first."

"Sure. But no more handing out free food," she says, before walking back to one of her tables to take away their empty plates.

It wasn't my intention to tell Joy about Lewis, but when she caught me crying in the toilets half an hour into our shift, it all came out. Everything Lewis had told me – the attack, his decision to keep it from me, the lies about New York – and everything lurking behind all that I didn't yet know.

Last night, when I got home, I googled Lewis's name. I typed it into the search bar and slowly, with trembling fingers, added the words 'glass attack' and 'Chester'. I hesitated before pressing enter, certain that as soon as I did, all the details of the attack would be laid out before me. Only, once I found the courage to do it, nothing came up. No news coverage, no images, no reference to Lewis's attack at all, just the usual search results I'm used to – his LinkedIn profile, a local news report about a charity football match he organised when he was at university, an old biography from the company he used to work for – and underneath each link in small font the line, 'does not include: glass and attack'.

As I told this to Joy, and she asked whether I was going to ask him to tell me more about it tonight, it hit me how nervous I was about going to his house again. I don't know what I'm going to say to him, and I haven't a clue what Lewis is going to say to me. I'm going round with the promise that we'll still stay us. Us is talking about the first things that come into our heads, sharing everything. If I ask too much, will he decide that's it, he can't do it any more? But if I don't ask anything, how can we really be us?

I've never had to think through what I say to Lewis before, never worried about how he'd take my words. With Gran and Gramps, it's necessary to give them a positive spin on every life development so they don't stay up all night worrying about me. In my mothering hours, I'm used to providing an edited version of whatever news I want to tell Mum, so I've a chance to fit it into the conversation. Me and Lewis have always been each other's no-filter person – but now, I find myself planning out our conversation, thinking of lines I could use to make tonight work.

My shift ends at six. Dessie comes in for the evening shift, with the grimy make-up from her dress rehearsal of Sweeny Todd still on her face. Joy and I ask her about it, and we laugh as she tells us about the director deciding to change a bunch of lines last minute to bring it up-to-date, so they've ended up with some weird mash up of Victorian musical thriller and an episode of *Succession*. When I get my chance, though, I gratefully leave them to it. After getting changed into jeans, a floaty top and trainers in the toilets, I wave goodbye and walk away from the docks to the main road to get my bus.

Each time the bus lurches to a stop to let passengers off, my stomach lurches too. The closer I get to him, the more I want to pull out my phone and type an excuse that will get me out of this.

Calm down, I tell myself once I'm off the bus and walking towards his house.

I force myself to march up to his front door.

* * *

His voice comes out of the electronic doorbell instantly. "Coming."

I hover on Lewis's doorstep, standing rather than taking a seat in case he changes his mind and decides to swing open the door. Best for his first view of me in a year not to be the top of my head.

The door stays shut, though, and the next sound is of him opening the letterbox.

"You there?" he asks.

I sit down on his step and peer into the rectangular opening hoping to catch sight of him, but the only view I get is the immaculate hallway.

"Yeah. I'm here."

"Hi."

"Hi."

"How are you?"

"Good. I'm good. You?"

"Good."

A silence opens up that strikes panic into my heart. Everything that's made us friends is absent in this moment. All we're left with is this crushing formality and the truth neither of us know how to navigate.

"Have you come from work?" he asks at exactly the same time I ask, "Why is your hallway so clean?"

We both laugh, and I feel a brief moment of relief. "Who should go first?" Lewis asks.

"You."

"OK. My hallway is so clean because I don't spend any time in my hallway. I can guarantee it's a different story in the kitchen."

"I bet it's not," I say. "You were always so annoyingly tidy. But really, it's like luxury hotel level immaculate."

"Thank you very much."

"I'm not sure I meant it as a compliment."

"No, I didn't think so. OK, your turn. How was work?"

"Oh, it was fine. Knobhead customer, but I got my revenge."

"Very *Gladiator*. I approve. What did you do?"

"Let's just say don't cross a member of staff at Ilk and go on to accept a shot of Limoncello."

"Noted," he says, and I can hear the smile in his voice. There's another pause, but this one feels different.

"See, this isn't so bad, is it?" he asks, reading my thoughts before going on to add, "Opening doors is very overrated, if you ask me."

It's his attempt at a joke, but there's so much sadness in it, it instantly propels us towards the real reason I'm here.

"I'm so sorry, Kelsey. I should never have lied to you. You've no idea how much I regret it."

"I know," I say, truthfully. I've no doubt his regret is real. "But I've got to say, I'm not sure I understand why you did. Not completely. You being attacked is so awful, and I can't begin to imagine how afraid you must have been, not just when it was happening but afterwards too. But shutting yourself away like this, it's such a huge decision to have made, and not telling me about what was happening to you—"

"I don't think it ever was a decision," he says, cutting me off. "It wasn't like I weighed it up, drawing up the pros and cons like I was deciding whether to take a job or where to go on holiday."

"Sorry. Of course not."

"No, it's OK. That sounded flippant, and I didn't mean it to. All I meant was that it wasn't like that. I knew early on there was going to be no bouncing back from this, but I hadn't formulated a plan or anything. Those first weeks after, I was so tired, Kels. So unbelievably exhausted from it all, and in so much pain, I don't think I could have come up with a plan if I wanted to."

I shut my eyes tight, trying to scrunch out the image my brain has just provided of Lewis battered and bruised, lying in a bed in agony.

"After being discharged," he continues, "I had to go back for outpatient appointments to monitor my eye the glass had penetrated. Despite the operation, I was starting to develop blurred vision. The second time I had to go, I was so scared to leave the house. Mum kept telling me I'd be fine, and I'd see there was nothing to be afraid of, but she was wrong. I ended up having a panic attack. I hadn't had one since I was in sixth form, and it was awful. My brain must have blanked out how awful because I remember thinking, it's a good job I'm in the hospital because I'm having a heart attack. I came out of it eventually, and the doctor who helped me told me it was common after a trauma like mine. That assault like that leaves not only physical injuries but psychological ones too. I went home and hoped it wouldn't happen again. But it did, when I was walking to Costa with Mum on a busy Saturday afternoon, after she'd convinced me to get out of the house for some fresh air."

"Lewis, I—"

"No, it's OK. I came back after that and I knew I wasn't going to go out again, not unless I absolutely had to. It wasn't a decision, rather something I just knew. I know that once I'd accepted it, I should have been honest with you about it. Or I should have removed myself from your life."

My stomach drops at him saying this to me again, like he did in his message.

"Why would you ever feel you needed to do that? I'm your best friend. What have I ever done to make you believe that was your best option?"

"Nothing," he says, firmly. "Only we weren't only best friends when this happened, were we? Things had been weird between us. We'd kissed the night I got attacked. I don't know, it just felt too much. I thought if I told you and you rushed over to see me, we'd have to deal with that at some point, and I couldn't face it. What I really needed was you as my friend."

"If that's what you needed, that's what I would have been."

"I know," he says gently, and I hear the sadness in his voice. "You'd have tried so hard. But back then, you were ready for us to fall in love, to become more, and I knew there couldn't be more. I knew I couldn't give you the relationship you wanted with me. I couldn't begin to think about letting you down on top of everything else. I wasn't in a place where I could deal with anything other than getting through each day, so I accepted your friendship and pushed the rest away."

I knew there couldn't be more. A whole year of wondering, of dreaming of what might happen between us, of hoping he would come back to me and we would finally become a couple, when he'd decided all along it was never going to happen.

"Couldn't you have at least told me that part of it? That we could never be together? You must have known I was waiting to find that out," I tell him, my own truth coming to the surface. He might have been able to push the prospect of us being together away, but, despite the jokey, light messages I sent, he would've known I couldn't do the same.

"You're right. I should have done. Truth is, I clung to you like a life raft those first few months, and I didn't think anywhere near enough about what it all meant for you."

"And six months later? Ten months later?"

"I know, Kels. I shouldn't have kept the lie going as long as I did."

"And Chloe, the other women you peppered your messages with?" I say, my own burst of anger escaping. "God, Lewis. Did you really need to do that?"

"I know. There's no excuse. As the weeks went on and I started to think more about what I was doing, I started to worry about you. I started to see that you were pretending too – that really, you were waiting for me. And that's completely understandable," he adds.

"Thanks for that," I say sarcastically.

"No, it is. We have all this history and we finally kissed for the first time. Of course you'd want to know if there's a future for us. It was exactly what I was thinking about too, before it happened. Then I woke up to find my future, my world, had completely changed. I feel so stupid now, making up girls that I was seeing. It was obviously going to hurt you, but you have to believe that was never my intention. I wanted you to move on. To be happy. I was too selfish, too much of a coward to tell the truth, but I felt like I had to do something to show you that you shouldn't wait for me – that there was nothing to wait for. For a while, I thought I'd done enough. You started dating. You got the job at Ilk. You had new friends. I was happy for you."

"Can't you see how manipulative that is?" My voice is laced with more upset than I expect. I remember the first attack of crushing disappointment and the depression that followed each time Lewis told me there was another girl. Seeing those days now for what they really were doesn't make it much easier. It almost makes it worse.

"Yeah, well there's a lot I didn't know I had in me," he answers bitterly. "If it helps at all, before you found out about me being here, I was about to put a stop to it."

"The phone call," I say, it suddenly slotting into place. "That's what it was about?"

"Yeah. I was going to tell you we needed a break from each other. I'd been worried about you again. You kept telling me you were fine, that you were busy and had all these plans, that life was great. But, I don't know, nothing really seemed to happen. The odd date, the odd night out, but nothing more. You and I were having all these wonderful, hilarious text chats every day and I began to worry that maybe you were giving so much of yourself to me, you weren't opening yourself up for anything else. So I decided to finally stop."

"To stop but still not tell the truth."

"No," he admits, his voice small.

I don't want to cry here on his doorstep, not when the plan was to come here and make him believe we could carry on as normal. But a year's worth of waiting for him, of loving him, only for it to end like this is too much to contain. I try to hide it from him by moving to the side of the door and covering my mouth with my hand, but the sound of my heartache escapes.

"Are you crying?"

I don't answer, not trusting my voice.

"Please don't cry, Kels. This is why I didn't want to tell you. I can't bear you being upset."

"Tough," I say, sniffing. "I am upset. I get it about other people, but this was me. This was us. You could have been honest with me about what you needed. I would have understood. After Dad died, you were there for me, and you always put me first. You always gave me what I needed without question, so I don't understand why you thought I wouldn't have done the same for you."

"You're right. I'm so sorry."

"And now?"

"Now?"

"Now I know everything. Do you still want to tell me that we should go our separate ways?" He doesn't answer immediately, and I wait nervously for his reply.

"No. I thought I did – only now you're here, I hate the thought of this being the end. But the choice is yours. I should have given you that choice a long time ago. You know how my life is now and, if you can handle that, I'd like you to be in it."

He's saying exactly what I hoped he'd say. But now the choice is mine, laid out in front of me, it's like being handed a piece of jewellery that in the display cabinet looks sparkly and perfect, but in my hands is heavy and doesn't shine as brightly as I hoped.

I don't want to let Lewis go, but at the same time, I can't pretend that our future isn't going to be bound by the tangle of lies behind us. And I don't know if I'm quite as ready to accept that as I thought.

eighteen

Kelsey

I'M IN THE KITCHEN, FLICKING THROUGH A COPY OF *Good Food* and typing the ingredients for a no-bake Biscoff cheesecake into my phone to make later for Tom as a thank you for putting up with my terrible waitressing this week, when Gran shouts to me from the garden.

"Kelsey, you have a visitor."

There's an excited trill to her voice, and my mind immediately jumps to Lewis. The excitement only lasts the second it takes for my brain to recall that, no, it cannot be Lewis, because Lewis isn't able to leave his house. Still, intrigued by my rare visitor – a visitor who has gone through the iron gate at the side of the house into the back garden where Gran's been tending to her pot plants instead of ringing the front doorbell – I slip my feet into my flip-flops and head outside.

It's strange to see the woman who only last week was going out of her way to avoid me now on her knees next to Gran, admiring her chrysanthemums.

"Hello," I say, and both women turn to me, big smiles on their faces. Melissa looks more like the Melissa in my memory than the one I encountered last week. Her smile is particularly generous this morning, brightening her face.

"There you are," she says, getting up and wiping imaginary dirt from her cropped jeans. "I was hoping you might be free for a quick chat."

"Sure."

I should invite her in for a cup of tea, one of Gramps's rock cakes, but I'm so taken aback she's now the one seeking me out, my manners fail me. Gran steps in.

"Sit down over there, Melissa, and I'll put the kettle on. Honestly, Kelsey," she says, tutting while she passes me.

"Sorry," I say, joining Melissa at the wrought iron table on the patio. It's a warm day, and Gramps has already been out here this morning to put up the parasol and get out the floral seat cushions. We sit side by side, looking out at the garden with its full borders and colourful pots dotted around.

"It's looking lovely, isn't it?" Melissa says.

"Yeah. This garden's my grandparents' pride and joy. You wouldn't believe the hours they spend on it."

"You haven't told them, have you?" she asks. There's no need for her to elaborate further.

"No," I admit. "I've tried, but every time I remember the lies I'll need to explain, I stop myself. Do you have any idea how embarrassing it is to have been lied to for an entire year?"

"I'm sorry, Kelsey. I wish I could have told you what happened. I would have done if he hadn't sworn me to secrecy. He knows he shouldn't have lied to you, but if you'd seen him after it had happened . . . you'd understand better."

I'm about to snap back that he made sure I couldn't see him, but I quash the anger that's been growing inside me the more I've thought about his deception. Because, really, I don't want to be angry. I want to understand. "Tell me, then."

"I don't know if I can come close to explaining how awful it was," she begins. "He was a mess, Kelsey. He was unconscious and bleeding heavily when his workmates found him and called the ambulance. By the time I got to him, he'd come round, but he was in agony. I remember standing in the empty cubicle in A&E, his blood on the floor, thinking to myself, *please let him live*."

I reach out my hand and place it on hers, the horror of what she must have been through hitting me for the first time.

"But it wasn't just the injuries, Kelsey," she continues. "After it happened, he changed in a way I never could have imagined. It was like my son was disappearing before my eyes. That he held on to your friendship, despite the way he went about keeping it, was the most hopeful sign I had that his life wouldn't be completely ruined. He got rid of everyone and everything else that had been good."

"I can't imagine what he's been through. How it must have felt for him to do that."

"No," Melissa agrees. "I don't think any of us can."

Gran opens the back door, carrying our drinks, and Melissa wipes under her eyes before changing the subject. As she asks me about work, whether I've inherited any gardening skills of my own – which I haven't – and how Gran and Gramps are keeping, I immediately sense her relief in stepping back from the pain of having to think of Lewis like that. After Gran joins us and has poured the tea, the three of us continue a stilted conversation of the same kind.

"I think I'll take my tea inside and let you two catch up. Too hot for me to be sitting about outside," Gran says, getting up after the small talk has been used up.

Once she's shut the back door behind her, Melissa puts down her tea and turns back to me.

"Look, Kelsey. I'm sorry I couldn't tell you everything. Believe me, I wanted to. Now Lewis has told you, I wanted to come round to apologise and to say I'm glad you know. It's huge that he's told you."

"It's not like he called me up and volunteered the information," I point out.

"No. But now you know everything, and that's the main thing."

I think about that – about how the amount of things I don't know by far outweighs the things I do.

"Not everything. I know about what happened after, but not a lot about the attack itself – who did it, and what happened to them after."

Melissa shifts in her chair. "No, he doesn't like to talk about those things. What did he tell you?"

"He told me about being at the club, and that his attacker thought he was coming on to his girlfriend, that the attack was revenge. But he didn't tell me his name."

"Does his name matter?" she asks. "Does it help to know, to think of who did this as a person and not a monster? I certainly don't want to speak his name, and I know Lewis feels the same. It would be a kindness not to ask him."

I think about how much I've wanted to know who was responsible, but I can understand what she's saying. I don't want to make Lewis have to talk about who it was when it must be so traumatic for him to think about. "OK, I get that. But at least tell me what happened to him after he did it. Did he get arrested? I've looked online to find news reports, but there's nothing."

"No, there won't be. The police told us at the time that assaults, even ones as awful as this, are all-too-common. They're everyday occurrences, so they don't get picked up by the news."

I cross my arms around my body, chilled by her words. "Did he get arrested?" I ask again.

"Yes. There was CCTV outside the club and it took less than ten hours for the police to find and arrest him. He confessed to it straight away. Later, at the trial, he tried to change his story. By then, he'd had plenty of time to sober up and work out how serious this was for him, but it was too late. He was found guilty."

"Good." I'm able to breathe out a little, relieved about that at least.

"I suppose so. His defence argued it was a moment of madness, a drunken mistake, but CCTV also caught him in the club smashing a bottle and putting a piece in his pocket before leaving. It was enough for the prosecution to prove it was premeditated and to push for GBH with intent. He got six years."

There's barely a breeze today. It's hard to sit among Gran and Gramps's flowers, to look up at a bubble-gum blue sky, and to think of such a violent act and the horrors that followed. I don't know how Melissa has coped with having all this in her head this last year.

"He told me he won't leave the house," I say.

"No. He's not been out of his front door since the day he moved into that house. The scars on his face will improve over time, but inside . . . who knows? That's where the real cruelty lies. It took only a few minutes for the attack to take place, but he's been left agoraphobic because of it. It's another fact he's had to incorporate into his life, like having blurred vision and having to take medicine multiple times a day to keep the nerve pain in his cheek at bay. He sees it as the way it is. He's been offered all sorts of help this last year and, apart from the physical side of things, he's always turned it down. He's accepted it and that's that."

I nod, taking all of this in.

"It was the panic attacks that did it. Do you remember how bad the first ones he had were? Back in school, when he was sitting his exams?"

"Of course," I say, pulling up the memory of Lewis struggling at the end of sixth form, pushing himself to his limit revising for his A-levels until his body rebelled and he'd had two panic attacks. His last few weeks of sixth form had been peppered with days off school and nights out missed.

"He told me about them back then, but I never saw one happen. I had no idea it could be so bad. He had one when we were out, shortly after he was attacked. I'd insisted we go out and have a coffee, but it was too much for him. He was gasping for breath, Kels." She looks away, as she goes somewhere painful in her mind.

I gulp down the pain in my throat. "That's awful."

"Yeah. His freedom to live a life without fear. The attack took that from him."

My throat is hurting from the pressure of not breaking down, but I'm not ready to yet. There's something else I still want to know. "Do you think he'll try again? To go outside."

"I don't know. The way he explains it is if you tripped over a dodgy pavement and fell, you would avoid walking over it the next time. You wouldn't keep doing the same thing, in case it happened again. He's a long way from leaving that house, you know."

"Yeah, I'm starting to see that."

She gives me a smile. "But then again, I didn't think he'd ever tell you the truth, and look where we are. Now you do know, what I'd like to find out is what you're planning to do."

"I'd like to help him," I tell her.

"That's good," she says. "But it's what kind of help you plan on giving him that I'm interested in. I know you were in love with him when it happened, Kels," she says, her voice gentle.

I've never told her that. The times we did meet in the last year, I played the game of being Lewis's friend and nothing more, and I can see now she was playing along with me. By the way she's looking at me, a strange mix of understanding and pity in her eyes, there's no point denying it.

"He's made it clear that's not what he needs from me right now."

"I'm sorry, love, but it isn't."

I nod, before taking my hand back and looking away from her to the comforting pastel colours of Gran's flowers.

"I know, and I'm trying to get back to thinking of him as just a friend," I say. "But I can't help wondering what might have happened if he hadn't gone out that night, if he'd stayed with me. We were so close to being happy together, and it was taken away from us. It all feels so unfair."

"It is. Maybe you would have become an item. You might be happily together now. But if there's one thing I've learnt not to do this last year, it's to give space to alternative realities, to those *what ifs*. The only scenario worth focusing on is the one we've actually got, and that's Lewis alone in that house. If you're going to be in his life again, you need to understand that what Lewis needs from you right now is your friendship, nothing else. Do you think you can give him that?"

* * *

I send him the message as soon as Melissa has gone. I pass Gran in the kitchen and she doesn't ask about our conversation. We've long since reached an understanding, stemming from my teenage days, that I'll come to her with my problems rather than her looking for them. She gives me a wide space in which to operate, and I'm grateful not to have to repeat any of what Melissa told me.

There's never really been a question of what I'm going to do next. It was hurt feelings that made me back off, but hurt feelings are never going to win out over the constant thrumming in my heart. *He's here, he's here, he's here.*

Melissa's right. There's no point thinking about what might have happened. No point being fixated on the night he was attacked and who did it. All we have is what we have now, and I'm ready to accept that. I *have* to accept it to keep him in my life.

KELSEY: Thought I might nip over tonight. Fancy a drink?

nineteen

Lewis

EIGHTEEN YEARS OLD

"YOU'RE GOING TO IRON THE LOGO OFF THAT T-SHIRT."

Lewis had been standing ironing his clothes in front of the TV for the last hour. On the couch he had the pile he still needed to do, and on the armchair was a smaller pile of neatly folded clothes. He looked down at the Adidas T-shirt that didn't need much ironing to begin with and took it off the board.

"Here, let me take over," Melissa offered, but Lewis turned her down. It was helping, the ironing. His job that day was to get his clothes ready. That's what he wanted to concentrate on, not what came next. Melissa pushed the clothes on the couch to one side and sat down.

"Have you started on your room yet? I mean, you don't need to take everything, but you'll want your PlayStation, the TV, a few home comforts. Shall I do that?"

Ordinarily, he'd have said no. With his mum taking care of the rest of the house, it had always been agreed Lewis's room was his responsibility. But if it meant her not sitting watching him as she'd taken to doing over the last week, he'd happily let her take over the job.

"Sure, thanks."

"OK, then. I'll get started. We'll get the car loaded together once you've finished all that, so we can get away early in the morning."

"OK. Thanks."

Melissa stood up and touched his arm as she passed him on the way out. "It's the adventure of a lifetime, sweetheart. Don't be so worried."

"I know, Mum," he lied. He didn't know that at all. What if he hated it? What if the pressure of doing well, of meeting all the deadlines, was too much for him?

Sitting his A-levels had resulted in insomnia and two terrifying panic attacks when he'd felt like the air couldn't get into his lungs, that his body had forgotten how to breathe. That he would die. His maths teacher had found him in the corridor that first time, explained to him what was happening, and got him to focus on breathing in for two seconds and out for three until it passed.

What if university brought on more of that?

Everyone around him saw university as a chance to have fun, to drink more, to meet girls, to be free. But all Lewis could think about was the degree he'd have to get through. Filling in his UCAS form in the college IT room and putting Computer Science at King's College as his first choice, he'd never really imagined he'd be going. He needed three As, he needed money to live in the most expensive city in the country, he needed to make his peace with leaving Kelsey. It wasn't real. It was his second choice of University of Liverpool that he planned for. He'd continue to live with Melissa, he'd see Kelsey all the time, he'd get a job around his studies so he could pay his way a bit. He was happy with that.

But then he got the results. He got an offer. The student loan. The room in halls. He'd arranged it all in a daze, waiting for the excitement to kick in but never experiencing anything other than nausea when he thought for too long about going.

If Kelsey or his mum had given him the smallest sign they wanted him to stay, he'd have given up his place in a heartbeat. But he received nothing but pride from them both. Sometimes it felt like that pride was pushing him out the door.

After Melissa had brought down two bin bags filled with the contents of Lewis's room, and Lewis had placed his ironed clothes in the suitcase his mum had bought him the year before when they went to Mallorca, they headed to the pub, where they were meeting Kelsey for a send-off meal.

Lewis didn't want to tell Kelsey not to bring Sam, but he hoped she'd come alone. Since Sam asked her to the prom the day after Lewis chose not to, they'd been a couple. He hated that Sam, of all people, had asked her instead of him. He couldn't forget his comments at Connor's party – calling her a sad girl, laughing with his friends about how desperate that made her. When Kelsey came over to his house, gushing about how Sam had come up to her after English, handed her a crappy cellophane-wrapped rose and asked her out, he tried to warn her off him, but she just told him not to worry. He repeated what Sam had said at the party, and she'd replied that she knew exactly what Sam was like. She wasn't a fool. That was two years ago now.

On the surface, Sam was the perfect boyfriend. He hadn't put a foot wrong and, whenever Kelsey was around, he treated Lewis as though they'd remained best mates from primary school. Lewis didn't pretend at all with Sam, much as Kelsey wished he would. No matter how much time passed, no matter how much he acted like he was caring and considerate, Lewis knew it was just that: an act. There had been a number of times Lewis had seen Sam out at parties or in their local when Kesley wasn't there, and he couldn't reconcile the cocky, bullish person Sam was with his mates to this version of himself around Kelsey.

Thankfully, when they walked into the pub, Kelsey was waiting alone for them at the table. He smiled when he saw only empty space around her. The table was covered in gold confetti, and in the middle of it there was a 'Good Luck' helium balloon. She had a huge grin on her face that he tried to focus on instead of the tight fine-wool dress she was wearing.

"You didn't need to do this," he said, giving her a hug.

"I think you know I really did."

Lewis laughed. "You're going to uni too, remember?"

"I know, but I'm staying at home. You're the one leaving us for the big smoke. Who knows when we'll see you again?"

Funny how his plans had become hers – how she was the one going to university in Liverpool, staying at home. He wished he could undo it all, that his day hadn't been spent packing, that there was no farewell meal.

"Exactly. We can't let you go without a send-off," Melissa said from behind him. She and Kelsey hugged, and Melissa went off to buy a bottle of fizz.

Over fish and chips and Prosecco, they talked not about the future, but the past. Lewis was the instigator. Whenever there was a pause in conversation, he'd fumble around for another story, a 'Remember when . . .' Melissa and Kelsey knew he was nervous, that he was arming himself with memories before he left, and they happily obliged.

"We best get back," Melissa said, once she'd paid the bill. "Meet you in the car,"

"Come here," Kelsey said, standing up and coming over to him.

Normally she hugged him loosely and quickly, the same way he saw her hug her other friends, but that night she clung to him. He clung back, wanting to communicate everything he couldn't say to her by the pressure of his arms around her body. How he loved her, how he wanted to stay, to go to university with her and, most of all, how he wanted her to love him back.

"Go," she said, breaking off. "Before I start crying."

"Yeah."

"I'm going to miss you so much."

"Me too."

twenty

Kelsey

I CLIMB INTO THE FRONT SEAT OF GRAMPS'S CAR AND settle the canvas bag I've filled with three mini cans of wine, a sharing size pack of crisps and an umbrella between my legs. I'm wearing a short black dress with tiny roses on it that looked perfectly cute and not too try-hard when I put it on but is pulling tightly against my thighs now I'm sitting, inches of the hem disappearing as it bunches up.

Gramps takes an age to check his mirrors, his steering wheel height, the angle at which his chair is reclined, as he does every time he gets in the car, despite being the last person to drive it.

"Ready?" he asks.

"Yep."

"Great. What's the address?"

"It's fine, I know the way. I'll tell you."

"Let's put it in the satnav to be on the safe side. You know what you're like with your lefts and rights."

"Fine," I concede. "It's 34 Ellcott Avenue."

"Thank you," he trills, never happier than when he's typing

a new destination into his satnav.

He indicates before he pulls off the drive, and slowly starts to reverse. I smile as I watch him, his forehead crinkled in concentration, his eyes darting from satnav to rearview mirror to windscreen to me in a constant loop. I could have walked – it wouldn't have taken too much longer – but Gramps insisted, and I did have my bag of goodies to contend with, so I agreed.

After Melissa left and Gramps got back from the shop, I sat him and Gran down and told them about Lewis. I received the expected mixture of upset for Lewis and anger about him not telling me, but there was also a look I caught between them right after I'd finished speaking. It's hard to make sense of it, but it looked like disappointment.

"One point two miles away. Isn't it amazing he lives so close? That's going to be handy," I say now, in an attempt to prompt Gramps to reveal more about what he really thinks. If he has any misgivings, I'd rather be getting out of the car having assuaged them.

"I suppose," he says. "Although, if he's not planning on letting you see him, the fact he lives close by doesn't really matter. He might as well actually be in New York."

It's a fair point but it still stings to have it spelt out, especially when I've been trying so hard to get on board with this new situation and to find the positives in it.

"That's not true. Now I know where he is, I can be there for him. Not just on the phone, but properly be there. I can help him."

"Can you? From what you said, help is exactly what he doesn't want. You can hardly go turning up at his doorstep every night begging to be let in." After a pause, in which I don't reply, he takes his eyes off the road to look at me. "We don't want this to set you back, love. That's all. You were doing well, making friends, going out and, even though we didn't like it at the start, the waitressing has been good for you. I don't want you to throw all those good things away by focusing entirely on Lewis again, putting your life on hold like you did when he first left – or didn't, as it turns out."

"I'm not throwing anything away, but this is Lewis, Gramps. Of course I'm going to help him. If that means turning up at his doorstep every night, that's exactly what I'll do."

"We know you will," he says. "That's the problem."

It's rare that there's tension between Gramps and me. Gramps has always been so careful with me, so determined to see me happy since Dad passed away, he's normally unassailably pleasant. I turn to look out the window, wanting out of the conversation now I've drawn him into it, and Gramps focuses on the remaining journey with even more concentration than normal.

As we get closer, I wonder what Dad would have thought about this whole situation – and what he would have made of Lewis. To Dad, Lewis was only ever the son of Mum's best friend. A child who he saw every now and again. It was only after he died that Lewis became such a big part of my world. I've always been certain Dad would have loved Lewis if he got to know him, but I'm not quite as sure what he'd make of what's happening with us now. Would he have been more understanding than Gramps? Would he have had more faith in me that I knew what I was doing, going back into his life? Or would he have hated it even more than my grandparents did, his love for me rendering it impossible to see past the lies and the ensuing hurt his little girl had endured? But he died without me ever having talked about boys with him. I'd never nervously introduced him to a boyfriend, never waited upon his verdict. The painful truth is I have no idea how Dad would have reacted to all this.

"How the other half live," Gramps says, as he pulls into Ellcott Avenue. He doesn't mean it as a good thing. On our road, most houses have their own splash of personality – from the borders filled with flowers that separate the front gardens and the pavement, to the ornaments in the windows, to the football flags that go up and down throughout the year, to the multi-coloured Christmas tat the Rolands cover their house and garage with from early November to mid-January every year. On Ellcott Avenue, every house is beautiful but exactly the same as the one next to it – all without any sign of life.

"It's that one over there. The one without the car," I say, pointing out the only difference Lewis's house has. I noticed it the first time I came here but didn't understand its significance. Lewis doesn't have a car because he doesn't need one.

"Give me a ring when you're done," Gramps says, once he's stopped the car. "Don't sit out too long, will you?"

"I won't." I lean in to give him a kiss on his cheek. "Stop worrying, OK?"

"OK," he says, but he can't bring himself to smile at me or to say 'ta-ra', like he normally would.

Once he's let me out, reversed into the drive and pulled away, I push the car journey out my mind and walk up to Lewis's door. I'm here, he's waiting for me, and that's all that matters.

The letterbox is open before I've even rung the bell.

"What's this creation?" I ask, taking in the two sticks that are holding open the letterbox, saving us the trouble of keeping it pushed up.

"Seeing as this is becoming a regular fixture, I thought I'd make it easier for us to talk."

"Good thinking."

"Why, thank you."

I peer through the gap he's created. The hallway is dark, and wherever he's sitting, he's made sure to position himself out of view.

When he doesn't say anything else and there's the tiniest silence, I suddenly feel nervous again. "Erm, hi."

"Hi, yourself."

"So have you got your drink ready?"

"Yep."

He holds his bottle of beer in front of the open letterbox and I catch a glimpse of his slender fingers, the first part of him I've set eyes on in over a year. "You?" he says.

"Give me a minute." I rustle around in my bag and pull out my first can of wine. I hold it in front of the letterbox, although he's already disappeared from view.

"Delicious," he says, the familiar teasing note in his voice.

"It is."

"Well, cheers then."

"Cheers."

We take a few sips – mine, I suspect, being much larger than his in a bid to get rid of my nerves.

"I'm glad you forced me to do this," he says.

"Yeah?" I ask.

"Yeah. Despite the resistance I put up to this plan of yours, I have to admit, it's good to speak to you again. In person. There's a slight chance I might have underestimated the *in-person* part of our friendship."

"A chance?"

"OK, more than a chance."

"Well, I'm glad you've come to that realisation," I say, a laugh in my voice. I take another sip of my drink and when I speak again, I'm serious. "Can I ask you something?"

"Sure."

"How have you kept this a secret? I still can't believe I didn't know you were here. What have you told everyone else? They don't all think you're in New York, too?"

"I guess I don't have that many people who make up my 'everyone else'. Some of my family know what has happened. My auntie, a few cousins. They text me every now and again, and they make sure Mum is OK. I'm glad she's got them to talk to, because I know she hates seeing my life like this. People at work know too, but I was new-ish when it happened, wasn't quite at the friends stage with any of them. No one has batted an eyelid that I switched to working from home once I went back to work. Then there's Connor." He pauses before continuing. "Once I said to you about being in New York, it kind of made sense to have that as my story, so I told him and a few of the other lads from college the same. We're so long out of the habit of regularly meeting up, nothing has really changed. We still have our WhatsApp group, and Connor still sends me the odd pissed message about how he wishes we were around for each other more, but that's about it. Same with uni friends. They're mostly down south, and there are no regular meet ups with them either. It's actually been surprisingly easy to disappear from people's lives. With the exception of you, of course."

"Of course." I try to be light, but it's hard when there's so much sadness in what he's just told me.

Another silence opens up, and this time it's Lewis who rushes to fill it.

"If this is too weird for you—"

"No. If this is what you need, it's fine. It's just . . ." I hesitate. "It's just, I guess I don't fully understand why you can't let me in. I get that you don't want to go outside, but I don't see why that means I'm sat here."

"I can't pretend I fully understand either," he says, taking me by surprise. "One thing I've discovered this last year is that logic doesn't always come into my decision-making. Logically, there's no reason why you couldn't come in. I know it's going outside that's the problem but, and I'm sorry if this sounds harsh, I also know that it will be too much for me to let you in.

You probably see my life and think it's a mess, but it's taken

146

months of work and planning to get this point. I have a nice home, a good job, a life I can live. You coming into that wasn't part of the plan. When you spend so long meticulously planning every aspect of your life like I've had to, the idea of losing control of a little bit of that life is terrifying."

When I don't say anything, too busy contemplating what he's said rather than responding, he laughs. "Blunt honesty, eh? Can't beat it."

"No, I'm glad you're telling me this. It's important to me you do. I want to know how you feel."

"But?"

"No buts. I suppose I was just thinking how lonely you must be."

"I'm OK. Being alone isn't all that bad. I work from home like half the population, I make dinner, I watch too much TV. I've got Mum here most evenings. It's not that big a deal."

It's a huge deal, I want to tell him, *we're sitting on opposite sides of a door.* But I can tell he needs to believe what he's just told me. My experience with psychologists stretches to occasionally watching them on true life documentaries, but even I know they'd tell me that bulldozing my way in, trying to pull him back to the life he had before this happened, is only going to push him away. Instead, I go for lightness, trying to bring back the flavour of the evening I'd been hoping for.

"Have you watched anything good on TV recently?"

He laughs and begins to tell me about a new series on Prime I've never heard of. I sip my wine and listen. In a way, it's kind of like old times – I'd forgotten the passion he has for the things he enjoys, be it a TV show or a good day at work or a meal he's eaten, and the familiarity of the animation in his voice makes me smile. But I can't see his face, can't watch his expressive face and his flailing hands as he tells me 'how fucking good the twist was'. I don't know what his face looks like now, if it can hold those same expressions – and I can't savour his whole body speaking to me like I used to.

I hadn't understood before now how it was possible to be with a person and miss them at the same time.

We keep going, a ping-pong game of small talk, but it's much harder than I thought it would be. I can hear how hard he's trying, and I wince at the sound of my forced laughs. We cover every subject we can possibly conjure up, from football to how my mum is getting on with her studies. We're talking about each other's lives, but it doesn't feel right – it feels polite and removed and unnatural. It's the way I speak to Gramps's friends when they come to collect him to go to his weekly bowling night, and he's never ready, and it's left to me to entertain them while he charges around locating his lucky shirt and change for the slot machines. All the time I'm listening to Lewis, or I'm giggling, I can't ignore the voice inside my head saying 'This isn't us'.

Earlier, I'd worried three cans of wine wouldn't be enough, but an hour after I arrive, Lewis's voice begins to grow tired, and I sense he's waiting for me to go. I'm ready to go too.

We've run out of things to say.

twenty-one

Kelsey

THE NEXT DAY IS RESOLUTELY GREY AND COLD, LIKE England has had enough of summer and wants to get back to what it knows best. I'm glad. I'm done with summer too, and I relish the chance to disappear inside my thick cardigan.

"Come on, let's get this lot unpacked and you can tell me what went wrong with Lewis last night," Gran says when we get back from doing the weekly shop at the supermarket and are standing in the kitchen.

"Nothing went wrong," I tell her, as I pull out the chocolate biscuits I chose from the bag.

"Nothing? Then why have you been so quiet all morning, and why did you throw all that junk food in the trolley?"

I sigh. "It just didn't exactly go as I'd hoped, that's all."

"In what way?"

"I was excited about last night. I thought it was the start of us getting back to being us, only it wasn't. I tried, but it wasn't the same."

"Well, of course it's not going to be the same," she says, rubbing my arm. "Too much has happened for that. The main thing is, you're there for him. I hope Lewis sees that."

"I don't know, Gran," I say, tearing open the biscuits. "We tried to be like we were, but the more we talked, the more obvious it became that things aren't the same any more. It was painful."

"Do you want my advice?"

I hesitate. Gran's pride lies in her ability to dispense world-class advice to me, Mum and her many friends. It's as terrible as much as it is perfect.

"Try again," she says, not waiting for a response. "Only this time, don't make it about going back, but moving forwards. Maybe your relationship is going to look different, but that's not necessarily a bad thing. The most important thing now is that you're both honest with each other. Don't pretend for him, Kels. If something isn't working, you make sure you tell him."

"You're right." I can't deny Gran's on the money about us having to be honest, but it's complex. "Of course. But I've got to be careful here. I'm only just back in his life, and he's not sure at all about me being in it. I don't want to push him away."

"Listen, love. If you're not honest with one another, eventually you are going to push each other away. The way I see it, if you want to stay in his life – if you want to really help him – you've not got another choice."

She gives me nod, as if to say, 'I have spoken, now all is right with the world', and gets to work on the unpacking. After everything has been put away, I go to my room and pick up my phone. I wasn't going to text him today – I wanted him to be the one to get in touch with me. But Gran is right. I need to be honest with him, and there's no need to wait for that.

KELSEY: I'm sorry if last night felt awkward.

He replies immediately.

LEWIS: Me too.

KELSEY: Not sure we were quite ready for all that small talk.

LEWIS: I know. I just wanted last night to be you and me chatting away like normal.

KELSEY: I'm not sure it could have been normal. It feels like too much has happened, doesn't it?

LEWIS: Yeah.

Honesty. Here goes.

KELSEY: This has been a lot for me to handle. Although I'm determined to be your friend, at times I'm going to struggle with where we are now. We kissed, and that mattered to me. Even when you went out of my life, I still thought it mattered. I'll be your friend, but you have to accept that my feelings for you were more than being friends and that's something I'll be dealing with.

LEWIS: I get that. I do. I know this isn't easy for you. I'm just glad you're here.

KELSEY: Me too. A wise woman (Gran) has reminded me today that I'm not perfect, but I am trying. If that's enough and you want to try again, I'd like to.

LEWIS: Me too x

* * *

"These are amazing," Lewis says. "You can tell your Gramps from me he just gets better and better with age. There's a roaring trade in postable baked good these days. He should definitely consider going into business."

"I know, right?"

We both take a minute to chew the gooey white chocolate and raspberry blondies Gramps made specially for me this morning to take round to Lewis's house.

"Are you still drinking that ridiculously strong Peruvian coffee you always used to try and ply me with?" he asks.

"Sure am. And are you still drinking cups full of milk with the tiniest smidge of caffeine and calling yourself a coffee lover?"

I take a loud sip of the flask of milky coffee I made up this morning. "Sure am."

Things feel easier this morning. The fact the sun is out again, that I walked here and am wearing my trainers, a T-shirt and a pair of leggings instead of a dress, and I followed Gran's advice, has brought an ease to sitting on his step, drinking morning coffee with him that wasn't there last time. This morning gives me hope I can do this. I can fall all the way out of love with him, and we can get back to being friends.

"I'm so glad," I begin, at the same time he says, "This is nice, I—"

"Sorry," I say. "You go first."

'No, no, it's OK. I was just saying this is nice. It kind of reminds me of when I was living with Mum and working from home doing that ridiculous junior coding job, where I'd have to work eighteen-hour days or face being sacked. You'd constantly be popping round, telling me I needed to take a break before pulling out whatever shite magazine you'd bought from the shop that day and reading me the highlights while I drank much-needed coffee."

I smile at the memory. "It reminds me of that too. But no magazines today, I'm afraid. Which means you won't be able to tell me I'm derailing your entire career by detaining you to share how Brenda from Devon ended up having an affair with her stepson's best friend."

"No, that's true. Maybe you can bring some next time."

I'm tempted to remind him of some of my favourite stories over the years just to hear him laugh – 'I married my ghost-lover but now he never visits' being my all-time favourite – but there's so much I want to know about him now, I decide to keep us in the present.

"How is your job going?" I ask, enjoying the space this conversation has in it to talk about normal, everyday things.

"It's all right," he says. "How about yours? Can you see yourself staying at Ilk for a long time?"

If Mum asked me that, it would be with a heavy dollop of implication on top that I should definitely not be thinking of staying for long. But there's no judgement in Lewis's voice. He has never rushed me along my career path. His certainty that I'd find what I wanted to do, and that whatever I chose would be good enough, has given me the same belief.

"Maybe not for ever, but yeah, I enjoy it – and I've got friends there. Since Mum's gone back to uni, she's been on at me constantly to do the same, telling me it's never too late. But I've no idea what I'd study. Until I find out what I'm passionate about, what's the point?"

"Exactly. And you will find out. I've no doubt about it."

"I hope so. Thanks."

"For what?"

"For always saying the right thing."

He laughs. "I'm not sure you can give me credit for that any more."

"No, maybe not."

A silence opens up for the first time since I arrived.

"The other night was harder than I thought it would be," he says.

"Yeah. It was."

"When you turned up, I panicked a bit. I told myself I was ready to see you, but all the time you were there, it felt like too much."

"You should have said."

"I know," he admits. "Not an easy thing to tell your best mate though, is it? That it's too much to sit on the other side of the door to them."

I hear the annoyance in his voice, not at me but at himself.

"It wasn't exactly an ordinary situation. You've been through so much, and I was trying too hard—"

"You were fine," he says.

"Thanks, but you're allowed to tell me when you're feeling uncomfortable."

"Deal."

I put my coffee cup on the doorstep, uncross my legs and

straighten up. "In that case, can I ask you something? And you have to say if you don't want to answer."

"OK," he says, uncertainty clear in his voice.

"What is your face like? I keep trying to picture you, and I can't."

He takes a moment to consider the question. I'm about to take it back, tell him he doesn't need to answer, when he starts to speak.

"I'm not sure I want you to picture me. Mum says I look the same, but she's lying. I've got four thick scars on the right side of my face and an eye that's almost permanently bloodshot. I hate it."

I press my hand against the door, wishing I could put my arms around him to offer him some comfort. "I'm so sorry, Lewis."

"That's OK. You can ask me stuff. I'm all right with that. It's the getting-me-to-come-out-of-the-house bit I don't like."

"I can take that on board."

He coughs, and when he speaks again his voice is light and playful. "Right then, I'm going to get started on another blondie, and you can tell me all the latest gossip from work."

I take another sip of my coffee, and I'm smiling before I begin. I know we can make this work.

twenty-two

Lewis

EIGHTEEN YEARS OLD

SHE CALLED HIM WHEN HE WAS STANDING AT THE BAR IN
The Vault, waiting to order two pints, one for himself and one for
Douggie, his next-door neighbour in halls. He'd been standing
there for twenty minutes, wondering what the key to success was
for getting served in this pub, because whatever it was the other
students possessed – who sauntered up and came away minutes
later, their arms full of drinks – he didn't have it. Any other name
on his screen and he'd have let his phone ring out, but it was hers.
He stood back, letting two girls take his prime position in front of
the till, and answered the call.

"Hi, Kels. Everything OK? I'm just out," he shouted above the
music.

"Don't worry. I'll call you back," she said, too brightly. He could
picture the disappointment on her face – her eyelids dropping,
her mouth tightening as she tried to sound OK. He immediately
changed his mind.

"No, it's fine. I can talk now. Give me thirty seconds to go outside."

"Great," she said, and he knew she was smiling.

He walked past his table, mouthing 'sorry' to Douggie, who held his arms up, looking horrified that Lewis was coming back this way without beer. Once he made it to the corridor outside the main entrance where the music was no more than a continual thudding, he asked, "What's up?"

"Nothing much. Where are you?"

"A bar. There's this pound-a-pint night on a Wednesday I've started coming along to with a few lads from halls."

"Oh God. How long does it normally take for them to run out of everything apart from Guinness?"

Lewis thought wistfully of the pints of lager he'd seen being served as he stood at the bar. He was doubtful he'd be able to re-join the queue in time to catch the last of it now.

"On a good week, about an hour."

She laughed, and he waited for her to start explaining what it was she'd called about. Since he'd started at King's College, Lewis had grown used to Melissa's twice daily check-in phone calls, but it was rare for Kelsey to call. They would text all the time but phone calls were infrequent, like she didn't want to disturb him. If she did ring, the calls were short and for a specific reason – like asking him if he could remember the name of the science teacher they had in year ten because Kelsey was sure she'd seen her falling out of a pub on Smithdown Road, or to make an arrangement for the weekends he came home.

"Everything all right?" he asked when she didn't speak.

"Yeah. I'm fine. Well, Sam and I broke up, but I'm fine."

"Oh God. I'm sorry, Kelsey," he said. He'd never liked Sam, but he knew how much Kelsey did. He knew how much she'd be hurting now.

"Do you want to talk about it?"

"Not really. I needed to end it. We were well past our expiry date. Gramps and I agree that the best thing to do now is to try to forget about him."

"Good plan. How are you going to do that?"

"That's kind of why I'm ringing. I don't suppose you're coming home this weekend? If you are, I thought we could go out together, the two of us."

"I'm sorry, I'm not. I've got plans," he admitted, guiltily. "But, hey, I'm sure you've got loads of other people to go out with."

"I suppose," she said, without any real conviction. "I just always have the most fun with you."

"Me too. I'm sorry, maybe I could—"

"No, don't worry about me. I'll be fine. Anyway, you're out! I'll let you get back to it."

* * *

For his first month of university, Lewis had to force himself out every morning to attend lectures, to join sports clubs, to knock on the doors of the lads on his floor in halls, to join their nights out when his strongest impulse was to hide away in his room. He'd missed Kelsey and home desperately, had packed up his belongings three times, planning to leave, and had called Melissa in tears one early morning in October asking her to pick him up. She'd driven down the next morning and taken Lewis out for lunch. After a long conversation, he'd agreed that he would keep trying until Christmas. If it wasn't working at that point, he could come home.

He'd watched his mum go, believing that there was no way anything could change enough that would make him come back for another semester. He was fearful, as he'd felt every day since he arrived, that the panic attacks would come back. But, as time passed, he was surprised to wake each morning feeling a little better. He got used to how his day was filled with lecture theatres and seminars. Rather than being intimidated by his course mates, he began to grow interested in them and what they had to say. Returning to halls each night began to feel a little like coming home, and there waiting for him were not strangers but new friends. Knowing he didn't have to stay if he didn't want to made it strangely easier to do just that.

It didn't feel like when he first started his studies and was overwhelmed with all the different lectures and seminars and work he'd need to complete, but he'd chosen well with his course. Computer science suited him. Once he found his feet, he discovered it was interesting and challenging, and, as his tutors would often remind him, a degree that would lead to bright and exciting future prospects. He'd find himself looking forward to the work he was set. He loved the feeling of starting on a project and looking at his watch to find he'd been so engrossed that hours had passed. Douggie was in his tutor group for his Foundation of Computing module and, for the first time, he'd found someone just as happy as he was to spend hours talking about computer programmes and cyber security. He didn't have to worry about being boring or coming across as too geeky, like he had at home.

Now it was the start of December and he had a weekend filled with exciting, hard-won plans that he was proud to have – his first rugby match for the college and a trip into Soho on Saturday night with Douggie and the two lads who lived in the rooms opposite. But Kelsey hadn't asked him to come home before. He knew she missed him, that him going away had been difficult for her. He wanted her to know that he was still there, still the same Lewis, that she could always rely on him.

"It's OK," he told her. "I'll come home."

"You will? Thank you, thank you, thank you. But I thought you were busy?"

"Not with anything important. I can cancel."

"Are you sure?" she asked. Her voice was so full of relief it was impossible to be honest with her; to tell her how hard he'd had to work to find his place, how he wasn't sure at all that coming back and seeing her again when he'd just got over her was the best thing for him.

"Of course. I can't wait to see you."

twenty-three

Kelsey

"HOW CAN YOU BE OK WITH THIS?"

"I don't know, but I am. Really," I say, turning round to where Joy is sitting in the back seat of Dessie's Fiat 500 to answer her.

The trip started off as intended: a fun afternoon out, singing along to songs on the radio, Joy leaning forward to take selfies of us to put on her Instagram account with the hashtag #girlsdayout. That was until we reached the Birkenhead tunnel and the radio cut out, leaving a silence which Dessie had filled by asking me what the latest was with Lewis. Now Joy is scowling at me, and even Dessie is alternating between weaving in and out of lanes at horrifying speed and staring at me incredulously.

"But you're never going to be able to be just friends," Joy says. "I can't believe you told him you could be."

I've always been upfront with Joy and Dessie about my feelings for Lewis – I never saw a reason not to be – but I regret sharing quite so much, pining quite so openly in front of them now.

"If it was anyone else, maybe not. But it's Lewis. He was my friend for a hell of a long time before he was anything else to me, and if that's what he needs for me to be able to stick around in his life and help him, that's what I will do."

"Yeah, you might say that now," Dessie says, taking her eyes off the road to look at me for an alarmingly long time, "but there's no way you can keep this up. Sooner or later, the fact you're wildly in love with him is going to become a problem."

"It won't be. I don't plan on staying in love with him. I plan on getting back to the way things were between us when we actually were just friends."

"You're not going to try to convince him to fall back in love with you along the way?" Joy asks.

"No, of course not. He can't come out of his house, remember? His life has been destroyed by what happened."

"I'm glad you're there for him," Dessie says, the softness in her voice surprising me. "What happened to Lewis was terrible and I can't begin to understand what it must be like to feel it's not safe to step outside your house. But he's been honest now. He's told you he can't be with you. So what happens next with you?"

"What do you mean?"

"Well, you've spent a year waiting for him to come back, and now you know there's no future. Does that mean you'll finally move on? Finally start dating men for more than two seconds?"

"I don't know. It's not something I've being thinking about."

"But it's important," Joy says. "This is your life too, Kelsey, and you can't keep putting it on hold. If you're really going to be friends and you're really going to accept that, you need to make your peace with properly moving on."

"Maybe," I concede.

"No, definitely," Dessie tells me, before blasting her horn at a Mercedes that wouldn't let her cut into the fast last and shouting, "Wanker!"

"Please let me get out of this tunnel alive, please let me get out of this tunnel alive," Joy chants, holding her hands together in prayer.

"Shut up," Dessie tells her. "I'm a great driver. It's not my fault I'm the only one on the road."

"You are right," Joy says. "Not about your driving, obviously, but about Lewis. You're really going to have to start moving on from him now, Kelsey."

"You could join my amateur dramatics group, if you want," Dessie offers. "Once we've finished Sweeny Todd, we'll be accepting new members."

Joy shakes her head at me and I smother a laugh, recalling all the times Dessie's regaled us with stories of how awful it is.

It takes another fifteen minutes to reach Irby and the destination for today's trip out. Pulling into the car park of The Anchor Inn, a gorgeous country pub with newly painted Georgian windows and a pretty garden filled with flowers of purple and red, we spot Tom outside the front door, pacing up and down the path, his neck craned trying to spot us.

"Is he high?" Dessie asks. "Look how jittery he is."

"He's more likely nervous. You know how much he wants this to go well."

Yesterday, at the start of the Saturday night shift, the three of us were summoned to the staff room and invited to Sunday lunch in order to meet Tom's new boyfriend, Henry. It was sweet, really, the way he revelled in starting almost every sentence 'Henry and I', and kissed each of our cheeks when we said we'd love to come.

For my part, it's nice to have a plan for the day. Savouring a Sunday roast in a nice pub with a glass or two of red wine is one of my all-time favourite hobbies, and it's one I don't do nearly enough. Gran and Gramps don't believe in eating out unless it's a special occasion, Mum doesn't have time to savour anything, and Joy, Dessie and Tom usually hate to plan anything on a Sunday other than recovering from the night before.

Lewis used to love a Sunday roast too. This morning, I wrote him a message letting him know about my plans, but I hesitated before sending, worried the mention of a nice thing he can no longer do would pain him. I deleted the message and rewrote one to say I was meeting Tom's new boyfriend at some pub in the Wirral, missing out the lovely bits that might hurt him.

Dessie parks the car, and we all get out to be greeted by Tom. He has come very much dressed for the occasion, wearing a maroon woolly jumper and Timberlands, a far cry from his uniform of skin-tight black jeans and equally tight T-shirt. I'd taken care to dress the part too this morning, but looking down at my denim mini skirt, wedges and floral top, I feel I might have missed the mark.

"There you are. Talk about leaving it last minute."

"We're right on time," Dessie protests. "You should have told us it was fancy dress."

164

"Hilarious." With a quick look back at the pub door to check no one is there, he adds, "Don't forget, you promised best behaviour."

Dessie salutes and marches straight past him towards the bar area, which has been beautifully decorated with navy walls, a wooden floor and bright floral armchairs arranged around oak tables. We don't need to ask where Henry is. Seconds after stepping in with Tom, we're each taken into the arms of a man who is identical in appearance to Tom, aside from being at least a decade older.

"So great to meet you," he says, right into my ear, leaving a wetness I have to work very hard not to rub away immediately once I pull out of his hug.

"Hi, Henry. Good to meet you too," I say, from a much more respectable distance. "Tom has told us lots of great things about you." That bit isn't true. Tom has only warned us how to behave around Henry.

"Drinks!" he says and takes Tom's hand, pulling him to the bar. Tom turns around and beams at us.

"Jesus," Dessie says. "I'm not even hugged that closely when I'm having sex."

"He seems nice," Joy says, her voice lacking conviction.

"Tom clearly seems to think so," I say.

Henry takes it upon himself to buy us ladies a bottle of Prosecco and to make a meal of pouring it out and handing each of us a glass, telling Joy to wait when she starts to take a sip.

"A little toast. To new friends," Henry says, and clinks each of our glasses with a delicious looking glass of Malbec.

"To new friends," we parrot.

"Now, I want to hear all your best stories about Tom," he says, putting his arm around Tom, who is inexplicably drinking a brown-black pint of something with a huge head on top. "I said to him on our second date, there's no better way of getting to know someone than to meet his friends! You can tell all the stories you want about yourself, but it's your friends who will give you the real gems. So, no holding back now, do you hear me?"

Tom laughs and looks down into his pint.

"How many dates have you two been on?" I find myself asking.

"This will be number five, won't it, Tom?"

Not that I'm an expert in fifth dates, but if I liked someone enough to get to one, there'd be no way I'd want anyone else on it. Henry and Tom should be in here tucked away at a table for two near the log fire, not taking their seats at a table for five by the window, where Henry chooses to sit in between me and Joy, rather than next to Tom.

Once we're all seated, and I've shrugged at Dessie in response to the seating plan, a waitress arrives and gives us paper menus with today's date on the top and a list of five different roast dinner options.

"Wow."

"I know," Henry agrees with me. "It's a fabulous little place. Best Yorkshire puddings on the Wirral. I said to Tom when I suggested booking it this would be a brilliant place for him to work. What do you think of it, Tom?"

"Yeah, it's great," Tom says, deliberately beaming.

"Much better than where you are now. Think of the better hours, the better clientele."

"Are you thinking of leaving us, Tom?" Dessie asks, surprised.

"No, course not. It's just—"

"Much better prospects here, though," says Henry, cutting him off. "A stint here would look much better than at a chain restaurant. It could lead you to much better places."

"Yeah, I suppose . . ."

"Tom!" Dessie is genuinely affronted now, and Joy hasn't looked up from her menu since it was handed to her. "You love your job."

"I know," Tom says, not meeting her eyes. "But I do need to think about these things. I can't be a manager at Ilk for ever."

"Why not?" Dessie asks.

"Because he's a talent, Dessie," Henry says, answering for Tom. "We can't have him wilting away because he likes having a laugh with you lot, can we?"

"I think I'll have the turkey," Tom practically shouts in an attempt to shut this conversation down.

Poor Tom seems to be shrinking in his chair, his face now almost hidden behind his disgusting looking pint. Joy and I exchange a worried look and Dessie fumes behind her menu.

Once the waitress has come back and taken our menus, Henry reminds us he's waiting for our best Tom stories. I try to come up with something, if only to help Tom out, and tell Henry about the time at work a pigeon got into the restaurant and Tom, who is terrified of birds, had to chase it out with a mop, much to the amusement of the diners. A glance at Tom after I've finished tells me I've missed the mark completely.

Joy tells the story of how kind Tom had been to her when she started waitressing and was hopeless. Instead of sacking her – as she really did deserve – he stayed with her after her shift and pretended to be a whole variety of different customers, from the complaining knobhead to the leary drunk to the entitled girls who won't even look at you, so she could practise her table-side manner. Her story is much better received than mine, and Tom visibly relaxes after she's told it.

When it came to Dessie's turn, however, she refused to take part, excusing herself to go to the toilet.

* * *

"Can you believe that?" Dessie asks, once we're back in the car. She pulls her hair back off her face into a ponytail. "Who the hell was that person?"

"I know, but Tom seems to like him," I say. "Maybe he was nervous and over-egged his part."

"I didn't mean that arsehole, I meant Tom. Who the hell was *he*?"

"I didn't like it," Joy agrees. "Not one bit. Do you really think he'll leave Ilk?"

I put my hand on her arm from my place in the back seat. "No, course not. He's just in that first bit of a relationship when you want the other person to think you possess all the qualities they presume you do. Tom loves his job."

"It's not just that, though, is it?" Dessie says. "The beer, the outfit . . . he wasn't being himself at all. Not one bit of that person was the Tom we all know and love. It was sad."

"But people do that," I say to Dessie. "He'll soon come out of it."

"Will he? Look at you. You're still doing it with Lewis, and you've known him since you were kids."

I balk at the harshness of her words, at how she can see both Tom's relationship and mine in the same unforgiving light.

"That's not the same," Joy says, coming to my defence.

"Sure about that? Telling Lewis what he wants to hear, pretending to be fine with something she's not? It's exactly the same. It was the same when you thought he was in New York too. You didn't tell him how you really felt once. I don't like it for you, Kels, and I don't like it for Tom either."

"That's not true," I protest. "I am fine with how things are now, and I'm completely myself when I'm with Lewis."

"Really?"

"Sometimes, you need to make allowances for another person. A relationship – any relationship – is about being flexible. It doesn't mean you're not being yourself."

"Sweetheart, there's being flexible and there's bending over backwards. You and Tom are doing the latter. In fact, I'd say you're both so bendy, you could form a double act and go on *Britain's Got Talent*."

I don't bother to respond to that, too stung by her words to want to keep going and hear anything else she might say about Lewis and me. We spend the rest of the trip in silence, the traffic perfectly light. Dessie drops me off at the bungalow and gets out of her seat so she can pull it forward and let me out. I intend to say a quick goodbye but as I pass her, she catches my arm.

"Sorry if that was too harsh. I'm just worried about Tom. Didn't mean to take it out on you."

I tell her it's fine, that Tom will be fine, and go inside.

When I say goodnight to Gran and Gramps at the unusually early hour of nine, Gran asks what's wrong. I give them a short version of the day's events, about how Tom was behaving, but leave out the part I've worked out is bothering me most – the bit about Dessie not believing I'm being honest with Lewis.

"There's nothing so blind as love," Gran says, nodding her head towards Gramps, who bellows with laughter.

"She means she was blind with love for me," he says.

"It's true. You'll never believe this, Kels, but when me and your Gramps met, I was infatuated. Infatuated!" She stops to laugh at the thought. "Took me until I was married and living with him to realise what he was actually like."

"Eh, it was the same for me," Gramps says. "If I had any idea how long your Gran would sit in the bath every night and how much she'd spend on face cream over the years, things might have been very different."

"You cheeky swine," Gran says, but they're both smiling at each other, blind love still very much in evidence all these years later.

"OK. I'm going to bed before this kicks off," I say, smiling too.

I love hearing them teasing each other. I used to imagine me and Lewis like this when we were older. Sat together on matching armchairs, the TV on, laughing at our memories, our home filled with love. Maybe even our own granddaughter, who we'd cheer up after she's had a rubbish day by showing her our happiness.

Despite what Dessie thinks, I am being honest with Lewis. I am OK, now. It's the future that's the problem. It's taking Lewis out of every dream I have of myself as I get older. He's remained the person who gets grey and teases me about the amount of time I spend trying to hold on to my looks as the years pass. His is the face in the photographs that line my walls. Now when I think about that person, there's only a blank space. That's the hard bit. That's the bit I need to work on.

twenty-four

Kelsey

"DELIVERY!" I SAY WHEN LEWIS COMES TO THE DOOR and lifts the letterbox. I post through a copy of *Breaktime!* and a pack of Jelly Tots.

"Sorry, you've got the wrong address. The woman with a penchant for disturbing true stories and kids' sweets lives a few streets away."

"My mistake. I'll take them back then."

"You can have the magazine, but I'm holding on to the sweets."

"Fair deal."

Lewis posts back the magazine and I spend the next half an hour reading the juiciest articles out loud in my best impression of a news reporter. *This just in . . . bride-to-be shocks groom by revealing she's married to three other men. And they're invited to the wedding!*

"I really shouldn't let you derail my day like this," Lewis says, after I've finished reading and we've laughed over the finer details of the story. "I was preparing for a very important Zoom I'm having this afternoon with two company directors. Now all I'm going to be thinking about is how Clare from Leeds decided to have her first dance to 'Sexual Healing' not once, but four times!"

"You're welcome. Don't want you working too hard."

"No danger of that with you around."

I smile before taking the last sip of coffee from my new flask.

"Speaking of work, I best get going. See you tonight?"

"Tonight? Christ, how many magazines did you buy?"

"No more magazines. I just thought we could chat."

"Kelsey, we've spent the last hour chatting, and you've been round the last three nights, too. Are you really sure you're OK to be coming round this much?"

"Course. I like coming round."

"But it's raining, and you'll only get wet. How about you take the night off?"

I consider it. Tonight is the opening night of *Sweeny Todd*, and Joy's plan is that we'll meet at Ilk a couple of hours before, so we can pilfer free drinks off Tom and get tipsy enough to get through two hours of am-dram theatre. Joy keeps rolling her eyes whenever Dessie is around but I know she's been looking forward to tonight, and I have too. Things have been going so well with Lewis though that I don't want to take a night off. I feel bad for Dessie and Joy, I do, but my heart doesn't want to be in a makeshift theatre tonight – it wants to be here.

Instead of agreeing, I loudly pat the blue plastic box I bought from Tesco and have set up next to his front door. "Don't worry, I've got all my essentials. I'll be fine."

The box was actually Lewis's idea. After a week of trekking camp chairs up his street and forgetting umbrellas and lamenting the lack of a jumper when it got cold, he suggested I keep some of those things by the door, so I'll know I've got them if I need them.

It was a great sign.

For the last two weeks, I've been sure this has been working, that my visits have been doing him good. On the bad days when he's in pain or feeling low about missing something – like the smell of walking into a bakery or the buzz of travelling to London for a meeting and getting swept up in the masses at Euston – I'm there to cheer him up, remind him of all the things he can still do, like feel the sun on his face when he opens the bifold doors in his kitchen or read the classics he made a list of in college that he swore to work his way through before uni but never did. On the one really bad day when he came to the front door and told me he couldn't do this, couldn't make conversation with me when he was in pain and feeling that his life was so far away from what he thought it would be that he didn't recognise himself any more, I didn't say anything. I just sat on the other side of the door with him, so he knew he wasn't alone.

I never tell him to go out, never say that those things he loved are still there waiting for him. One thing I've learnt over the two weeks since I found out the truth is that Lewis really isn't ready to leave his house. Nowhere near ready. He might feel low and frustrated, but those feelings pale against the fear of going outside.

Not that he shares much of that fear with me. It is Melissa who does. We've met three times for coffee now. Between meeting Mum once a week, the regular morning coffees at Lewis's before work and now meeting Melissa too, I've more than tripled my caffeine intake of late. Me coming back into Lewis's life is a huge change, and Melissa can't hide the hope that I'll be able to help him. But I know she's worried. As much as she thinks this is working, she keeps reminding me how fragile Lewis is now, how I should be careful how I tread.

The box was my clearest sign yet he thinks it is working too.

"You know, I'm sure I put some chewing gum in here last time. I can still taste that horrendous coffee you made me buy. Even Gramps said it was an abomination, and he doesn't even drink nice coffee to compare it to."

I rummage around the box to find the gum, unloading half the contents on to the path to help me get to the bottom.

"How much stuff have you got in that box?" Lewis asks, a laugh in his voice.

"Enough that I'm prepared for any eventuality."

"Good. But, Kels," he says, before pausing slightly, "I don't want you feeling you have to spend all your free time with me. You've barely spoken about your friends from work since you started coming round."

Since the Sunday roast, we've not met up outside work. Tom has retreated into Henry's world, with no further mention of us getting together. All Dessie's free time has been swallowed up by last-minute rehearsals, and Joy has finally agreed to go out with someone from her seminar group who has had a crush on her all year. But it's been good to not have the late nights out, not to have to make plans and trek across the city on my days off. I've had more energy to get up early and spend mornings like this with Lewis.

"We're all busy right now," I say, omitting tonight's plans. "There'll be plenty more nights out with them. I'll see you tonight and when we've all got more time, I'll see the work lot. OK?"

"OK," he says.

* * *

Tom is standing at the reception desk and feigns absolute shock when I walk into work fifteen minutes early the next morning.

"This is three times in a row. I had no idea Lewis was going to be such a good influence on you."

"Yep. He always has been."

"Well, I like it."

I walk past him but stop and turn back. "What's that smell?"

"Oh, do you like it?"

"Um, yeah, it's very . . ." I search for the right word to describe the worst aftershave I've ever smelt. "Earthy."

"It's not what I'd normally go for, but it was a gift from Henry. He says it's more mature than Calvin Klein."

"Nothing wrong with Calvin," I tell him, and walk downstairs to the ladies.

"Have you smelt him?" Joy asks, the second I walk in.

"Sure have."

"So now Henry is telling him how he should smell. I'm telling you, Kels, that man is a control freak."

"Or he bought Tom a gift and Tom genuinely likes it?" I offer.

"No way. He's trying to make Tom as unattractive to other men as he can. It's worrying. Do you think we should say something?

176

Stage some sort of intervention?"

"Not over aftershave. Let's keep an eye on him, OK? Anything else that worries us, we'll talk to him."

"Yeah," Joy says. "OK. Let's do that. Now, do you want to tell me why you lied about being ill last night or should I not bother asking?"

She's giving me such a sceptical look, there's no point pretending I was unwell like I told her. Guilt twists in my stomach. Last night, I was thinking about Lewis, about putting his friendship above everything else – but I know I've hurt another friendship in doing so. "I'm really sorry, Joy. Was Dessie annoyed at me?"

"No, she was upset. She really wanted you there. I did too. I wanted us to drink wine together and laugh our heads off. It was meant to be a fun night. Without you, I actually had to watch the play."

"Was it bad?"

"Oh, Kels. Dessie was a star, but the play itself was woeful. Part of the set collapsed midway through, and Sweeny Todd himself had such bad stage fright, he forgot all his lines and ended up having to perform the entire play reading from the script."

I want to laugh, but Joy's face isn't warm. I forfeited my chance for laughing, and it hits me how much I've missed out, how much I let her down by not being with her last night.

"I'm sorry," I tell her again. I hope she can hear how much I mean it.

"You need to say that to Dessie," Joy says, before heading back upstairs.

I should follow her up to the restaurant, but I send a message to Dessie first, apologising to her. It's only a four-hour shift today for the lunchtime rush, but I know it's going to be a long one, not being able to check my phone to see if I'm forgiven.

It's quiet inside, so I head to the outdoor seating area where three tables are already occupied. Two women sit next to each other rather than across from each other as the table has been set, holding hands; there's a couple dressed in business gear, both on their phones and, waving at me, along with Tom, my grandparents.

"Hello, you two," I say, joining them. "You didn't tell me you were planning on coming down today."

"We thought it would be a nice surprise," Gran says, reaching out to hold my hand.

"I best get back to it," Tom says, his swift departure making me wonder which health concern Gramps has shared with him today. He smiles sweetly at them before flashing me a warning glance above their heads, reminding me I'm on the clock.

"I won't be able to chat for too long," I say loudly, making sure Tom hears as he walks back into the restaurant. Once the glass door has shut behind him and he's out of sight, I take the seat next to Gran and kiss her cheek. "This is nice. It'll make my shift go much quicker having you to wait on."

"Oh, we're not staying, love," Gramps says. "A quick coffee, and we'll be off. Far too much to do today." He winks at Gran.

"Why, what's going on?"

"You tell her," Gran says.

"No, you. Go on," Gramps insists.

"OK." She smiles widely at me. "We've decided to book a little holiday for us all next week. We only came down to make sure Tom could give you the time off. He says it's fine, so we're going to go back home and ring the holiday park. A week in Wales. What do you think?"

I think it's a disaster. I've been back in Lewis's life for such a short time. I want to be here, not in a caravan park outside of Abseroch.

"That's lovely," I tell them. "But I'm on the rota until the end of the month. You go without me. You'll have a lovely time."

"Don't be silly! Tom has just told us you can go. In fact, he was delighted to hear you'll be taking some of your holidays for a change."

I make a note to myself to speak sternly to Tom about sharing my holiday information. Surely that's the kind of thing that should be confidential so you can use lack of holidays as an excuse to get out of going on holidays you really don't want to go on.

"That's nice of him, but me missing a week when I'm on rota will mean the others will have to cover for me. It's not fair on them. How about you go this time and I'll try and organise some time off later in the year?"

"Kelsey," Gramps says, his voice suddenly low and sharp. "You're coming."

When I turn to him, his white eyebrows are an inch higher than their usual resting place. This clearly matters to him. I can't help but wonder if there's more to this than them simply fancying a week away, and when his eyes flick to Gran, my stomach drops.

"Come on, love," coaxes Gran. "They'll cope. And there's more. Your mum is coming too! Won't that be lovely?"

Oh, God.

twenty-five

Lewis

TWENTY-ONE YEARS OLD

"THIS IS NICE," LEWIS SAID, LOOKING INTO THE APARTMENT from the doorway. He was deathly tired after the delayed flight from Liverpool to Tenerife and the two-hour wait at the airport for the private transfer Kelsey had booked that never arrived, but he didn't put his heavy rucksack down or move to crash out on the bed like he'd told Kelsey on the bus he was planning to do. Not when his body was rooted to the spot in horror.

"It looked so much better online," she said.

"What website did you book it on? Crime Scenes to Rent?"

He turned to her, smiling, but she was looking past him, her eyes starting to fill with tears.

"Hey, it's fine. It's not like we'll be spending any time in here."

"It's not fine! It looks like a prison cell."

"A bit," Lewis agreed. The room was bare, apart from two narrow beds against the wall and a high slat of a window letting in little light. The roughly plastered walls had been painted white at some point but had since been heavily stained. "Though I'm definitely getting murder-scene vibes too," he said, pointing to two severe slashes of a red substance behind the beds.

"Don't. You could have been interrailing around Europe right now, and instead you're going to be stuck in the worst room in the whole of Tenerife."

It was true. If Douggie hadn't got glandular fever two weeks before they finished for the summer, they'd have spent three weeks celebrating the end of university by travelling from museum to museum, riverside cafe to riverside cafe. He was devastated when those plans fell through and had let Kelsey book the last-minute holiday to cheer him up. The start of it couldn't have been worse but even so, he found himself laughing.

"I'm sure it will grow on us. Let's dump our stuff and come back in a bit after a few drinks. I'll just go to the—" He opened the bathroom door and quickly shut it again. "Never mind. I'll find a toilet in a bar."

He put his arm around Kelsey and escorted her out. They went in search of the sea. While the Apollo Apartments had nothing to offer in the way of luxury or basic sanitation, the one very redeeming feature was their location. They were in walking distance of an upmarket family resort and they found a quiet, beautiful beach lined with elegant restaurants and bars a ten-minute walk away from their front door.

"Sangria?" Lewis asked, as they sat on blue and white cushioned chairs at a bleached wooden table on the beach.

"Definitely."

With a glass in his hand, sand between his toes and his face pointed up to the sun, Lewis felt his holiday begin, but even with his eyes closed, he could feel Kelsey tense and unhappy beside him.

"Please stop worrying about the room. We can always try and find something else, and if we can't, we'll have a funny story to tell people when we get back home."

"There won't be anything else we can afford. We're stuck here for ten days." Her mouth set into a hard line. Lewis put down his glass and reached for her hand.

"It doesn't matter. We're going to have a great holiday. This isn't too bad, is it?"

"It does matter!" she argued. "I wanted it to be perfect."

He didn't understand why until much later in the holiday. After the first few days of letting their bad luck hang over her like a rain cloud, Kelsey had started to forget about the room. They only slept and changed there, and the rest of the time was so pleasant it was hard to let it dampen the holiday. One night, in the little restaurant at the marina they'd declared their favourite, they sat drinking wine at the end of the meal, both a little tipsy, just getting over the point of being painfully full, and Kelsey said, "Can you believe it's taken us this long to go away together?"

"I know. I always knew you'd be great on holiday. We should pledge a holiday per year with each other from now on."

"It's a deal," she said. They clinked their glasses together, and Kelsey leant in closer.

"Everyone must think we're here as a couple."

Lewis, who had thought the same all holiday, nodded. "Definitely."

"Have you ever thought of us like that?" she asked. "Wondered what it would be like if we weren't just friends?" She was trying to keep her voice light, but he heard the nerves in it.

Only ever since I was thirteen, Lewis thought. Instead, he answered, "A few times."

"How many times?"

"A few," he repeated. "But we never quite lined up like that, did we? I might have thought about it in school, but you got with Sam and stayed together for years, and then I moved to London, and Phoebe came along. It never seemed like it was meant to happen for us, did it?"

"No. There was always something in our way," she agreed. "I guess it's only recently we've been in a place where we might be closer to maybe becoming more. Where we both might want that." He could see that she was careful with her words, didn't want to push too much. And suddenly he saw the reason behind the holiday – her need for it to be perfect and not to become a source of jokes for his uni mates when he got back home.

Oh no, he thought. *No, no, no, no.*

If there had been even so much as a hint that Kelsey had liked him before he left for university, he'd have been overjoyed. But their lives had changed. They'd *had* to change. They'd been so tightly woven together before university, to have any success moving on from her, he'd had to work hard to unwind himself from her – and then restitch them back together as best friends, nothing more.

He'd put everything into making a new life for himself, and he hadn't wanted to believe that Kelsey might have developed feelings for him since he'd been gone because going back to that place in his heart again made him feel vulnerable. It made him scared that he wouldn't be able to put himself back together again if anything went wrong.

And it was all working. He'd met Phoebe in the final year of his degree when they'd been placed in the same seminar group. It hadn't lasted, but they'd been together for eight months and he'd experienced being in love for a second time – having a girlfriend, a real relationship. Right now, he was too heartsore from their break-up to contemplate being with anyone else. He wanted to focus on his career. He'd aced his degree. Everyone kept telling him his future was going to be so exciting, so full of possibilities.

He knew he was going to be swallowed by work for the next few years, especially now he'd accepted the internship at a top coding company.

How could she have thought this was the right time?

"Look, Kels, I—"

"Forget I said anything," Kelsey said back, before looking away from him, her features pulled tight.

"You know you mean the world to me, it's not that. It's—" but before he could finish, her expression changed. She smiled, made sure it reached all the way to her eyes, and sat back in her chair.

"Relax, Lewis. It was just a drunk question. Nothing more than that," she said. "Let's get the bill."

When it had been paid and she'd downed their free shot,

Kelsey pushed her chair back and stood up. "I'm tired," she told him. "You carry on if you want, but I think I'm going to go back to the apartment."

He watched her walk away with a heavy feeling in his heart. She was upset with him, and that was the last thing he ever wanted.

twenty-six

Kelsey

"THIS IS RIDICULOUS," I TELL GRAMPS, GETTING INTO THE back seat of his car at five in the morning.

"You won't be saying that when we've missed the traffic and are sitting having our lunch at the caravan, looking out to sea. Now, hurry up and get belted up. Your mum will be waiting."

I do as I'm told. Once Gran has gone back to check all the locks on the windows for the third time and made Gramps turn back at the end of the road to make certain the iron hasn't been left on, we start the journey to Abersoch, via Waverley Crescent.

It's been nearly two years since I last went back to my family house. All week the uneasiness about leaving Liverpool and Lewis just as things are going so well has been growing in my stomach, and a new discomfort on the ride over to collect Mum mixes with it, leaving me nauseous.

If Mum isn't already outside with her suitcase when we arrive, I'll wait in the car for her. With the bags around me, it will look like it's too much effort to displace everything to go into the house. Mum won't be expecting a warm welcome given that my inclusion on this trip was a result of her shouting down the phone at me last night to 'get a grip and make bloody well sure you're in the car when Gramps and Gran set off in the morning'.

I'd tried to convince Tom to ring Gramps to tell him he couldn't spare me, which was met with a strange amount of laughter and a firm no. Once Dessie and I had text back and forth enough for me to feel sure she meant it when she said she forgave me for missing her play, I'd asked her and Joy if they could help me get out of the trip by pretending to Tom they couldn't take my shifts, but neither of them would agree, telling me, like everyone else, that a trip would be good for me. I'd thought about feigning illness again to get me out of it. In my desperation, I'd even rung Mum last night to suggest to her that she should be focusing on her coursework and that I'd be happy to sort out postponing the trip.

But, even if any of my plans had worked, it wouldn't have mattered in the end. Getting off the phone to Mum, I could hear Gramps watching the football in the lounge. I intended to have one final chat with him to see if I could convince him to at least let me go for a few days and be back for the weekend. On the way to him, I passed Gran and Gramps's bedroom and paused in the doorway.

Gran was sitting on the bed next to the open suitcase, a folded cardigan in her hands, lost in thought.

"You OK, Gran?" I asked, startling her, making her jump off the bed and continue packing with such focus it was as though she'd been caught doing something she shouldn't have been.

"Fine, love, fine. Have you started packing yet? I can help you, if you like."

Her voice was a shade too bright. I remembered the worry on Gramps's face yesterday, the involuntary glance at Gran when I was ordered to come on the holiday. Whatever this spur-of-the-moment holiday is about – and my grandparents are very much not spur-of-the-moment people – it matters to them. My grandparents ask so little from me, but this they did ask.

I made up my mind not to argue any more, but to return to my room and begin to pack.

"Can't wait for tomorrow," I said on my way past.

Now, as we approach the semi-circle of worn detached houses that make up Waverley Crescent, a desperate urge to get away from this street, to breathe in the caravan-site air and look out at the Irish Sea, comes over me.

After my first stay with Melissa at fifteen, this house changed for me. For Mum, living here is a connection to Dad that she will never sever. She'll stay in this house for ever, because it comforts her being in their home, with its happy history and marks of Dad in the dodgy plumbing and the wallpaper he taught himself to put up. For me, it hasn't been home since Dad died. It's like he turned out the lights and switched the heating off on his way out. Without him in it, it ceased to be my bright, warm, happy place.

This is a house that's meant to smell of Dad's pancakes on a Sunday morning, a smell that often veered towards burnt. It's meant to have a hallway covered in mud from when he came back from his rugby matches at the weekend, and a sports bag by the door that wouldn't get moved until Tuesday at the earliest, despite Mum's nagging. It's meant to be filled by a five-foot-eleven man with the kindest eyes.

All my good memories of being here with Dad became too mixed up with Mum's grief, with all of the days I felt helpless and alone. Each time I came and went – first to Melissa's, before moving in with Gran and Gramps – I took more of myself out of the house, until nothing of my happy childhood remained there at all.

Gramps lets himself in, and Gran and I are left waiting in the car for a full fifteen minutes before he re-emerges with Mum in tow.

"All set, Mum?" she asks Gran as she climbs in the back with me, adding a large rucksack to the pile of bags already between us – Gramps is struggling to put her suitcase in the boot.

"I am, but nowhere near as set as you are, love. You look like you've packed for a month."

"Well, September in Wales can be quite temperamental and I've got an essay due, so I've had to bring my books."

"I hope you won't be working too much," I say to her.

"Only as much as I need to. Not all of us are lucky enough to have commitments we can entirely switch off from," she says, turning to face me and following up with, "Christ, Kelsey. You look knackered. I hope you come back off this trip looking better than you do now."

And with that, we're off.

* * *

I text Lewis two hours later when we're sitting in traffic on the M56, Gramps apoplectic at the number of lorries on the road this early in the morning. It's probably too early for Lewis to read it yet. Looking back, I should have always been suspicious of those messages when Lewis told me he was up at the crack of dawn over in NYC, when the Lewis I'd always known never got out of bed a minute before he had to. A red flag if ever there was one.

KELSEY: In traffic after a hideously early start. Thought you said this trip was a good idea!

When I told him about the plan last night, calling round to his house on my way back from work, Lewis seemed delighted by it.

"You deserve a break, Kelsey. Enjoy it. Spend time with your mum, let your grandparents make the most of you all being together. It will be good for you," he'd told me.

I didn't believe that at first. It was being with Lewis that was good for me. But I did wonder as I left him if, actually, this trip might be good for the both of us. I'm running very low on amusing anecdotes to share with him when I'm sitting on the doorstep. In the old days, we'd have spent our time watching films together, talking to other people when we were out. Our new situation relies on a lot of conversation. It'll be good to restock my supplies.

I put my phone back in my bag after messaging and reach my hand through the gap between the seat and headrest on the front passenger seat so I can touch Gran's shoulder.

"Not too much longer now," I tell her, knowing how much she hates being on the motorway.

"I hope not. Should we not pull over for a while, George?" she asks Gramps. "Let it clear up."

"Good idea. There are services coming up. I'd love a coffee," Mum says.

"Absolutely not," Gramps protests. "Mark my words, this will clear up in a mile or two and we'll be there before we know it."

Fifty minutes later, we've moved two miles and are sandwiched between two tall lorries that block out the sky. Gramps's car is stuffy and keeps steaming up, and it's starting to feel like it's going to suck the life out of us.

"Can you please get us off this motorway?" Mum asks. As soon as we'd hit the motorway, she'd pulled out a textbook to read, but it now sits abandoned by her feet.

I spot Gran's reflection in the mirror as a lorry undertakes Gramps, making it feel like we're going backwards. I put my hand on her shoulder again, and this time she clings on to it.

"Fine!" Gramps says. "If you want to waste the day, I'll stop. Don't blame me when we're on our way back home and it feels like we've only had half a holiday."

Another twenty minutes later, Gramps parks in front of the service station and Mum flings open the door, jumping out and stretching her legs before bending down to rub them, like she's come off a long-haul flight from Australia. Gran lets herself out and walks towards Gramps. She holds out her hand for him, the smile on her face softening him up again.

"Right. Let's have twenty minutes," he says. "Loo break, and I suppose we should get some supplies."

"Ooh, McDonalds," Gran says, her eyes lighting up when she notices the sign. "It's been an age since I had a burger."

They all pile out, but I stay where I am.

I take out my phone and find a message from Lewis.

LEWIS: The trip is a great idea! Hope it doesn't take too long to get there. Once you arrive it will be just what you need. MARK MY WORDS!

I smile at the message and start to reply but change my mind and call him instead.

"Hello, you," he says, picking up on the second ring. "You there yet?"

"God, no. We're at a service station. Gran's gone to get a McDonalds."

He laughs. "Wow. That must be one of the most shocking statements I've ever heard."

"I know. She's beside herself with excitement."

"That's nice."

"Yeah. I hope it perks her up. She's been quiet this journey. I can tell this holiday means a lot to her, but she seems a bit off today. Quiet," I say. "I can't help but feel something's going on with her."

I look out of the window to the service station where I can see Gramps, Gran and Mum now in front of one of the self-service kiosks in McDonalds. Mum is gesticulating wildly to the three members of staff who are gathered around them as Gramps tries to shove a tenner into one of their hands, the woman shaking her head and refusing to take it. Gran is still jabbing the screen.

"I've got to go. Bit of a McDonalds emergency. I'll text you later."

"Make sure you do. I'm not going to be able to do any work until I hear from you with an update."

I hang up and get out of the car. Once I've paid for the McDonalds and ordered everyone back to the car while I collect it, and once Gran has declared the Egg McMuffin an abomination and thrown it away, we're ready to set off again, in much better spirits than when we arrived. Gran is laughing at the state of them all, poking fun at Gramps and his moaning about the cost of everything, and Mum can't stop cracking up whenever she remembers Gran's face when she took her first bite.

I don't text Lewis back straight away but do compose the reply I'm going to send to him in my head, as we continue the crawl towards Wales. I muse over the finer details I'm going to include, like Gran accidentally ordering an extra three Cheesy Bacon Flatbreads on top of her order and Mum quoting the Dalai Lama to the manager when they wouldn't refund them and it all got a bit heated. If we hadn't come away, I wouldn't have this story to tell him – and he'll bloody well love this story.

"What are you smiling at?" Mum asks.

"Nothing. I'm just glad we're going away. It's exactly what we all need."

twenty-seven

Kelsey

BAY'S HEAD CARAVAN PARK IS BEAUTIFUL IF YOU ARE allocated the static caravans at the end of the site, the ones which overlook the Irish sea. We, however, are not allocated a caravan at the end of the site but end up with a view of a row of other slightly worn static caravans and the cars parked up next to them. No sea or sun in sight.

When we arrived yesterday afternoon, Gramps was too tired from the six hours of driving to do anything but put the TV on and snooze in front of it. Mum and I walked into Abersoch for fish and chips, but Mum didn't want to extend our trip by taking a walk down to the beach or having a drink inside one of the many pubs. Instead, we headed straight back to the caravan, ate the soggy chips and settled down with heavy stomachs, an empty night ahead of us, which Mum put a stop to at half eight by declaring she was going to bed. Gramps, Gran and I stayed up a little longer, but by ten we were all tucked up in bed.

I'm woken up this morning at half six by the sound of rain tapping on the window. When I come round and remember where

I am, I choose to focus on its steady beat instead of the sound of Mum's snoring. Ten minutes after waking, I'm ready to abandon the warmth and worn-in softness of the single bed and start the day.

Cold and tired, I fill the white plastic kettle and wait for it to boil, placing my hands over the steam as it heats up. We need a plan today. Something to get us outside and keep us busy for enough hours that returning to the caravan feels like a reward rather than a punishment. A long walk and lunch outside should do it, or shopping. Last time I checked, I had seven hundred and forty-eight pounds in my account. I could spend some of it on Gran – she always likes coming home from a holiday owning more than when she set off. I could take her into town, buy her a scarf or some other pretty thing that takes her fancy.

I was watching her last night, watching how she rarely had her eyes on the TV, how whenever the rest of us laughed at something on the soaps or a daft comment Gramps had made, she was always a beat behind. Something is worrying her, and even though my feelings towards this holiday are less than favourable so far, I want her to enjoy it. Actually, I want her to tell me what the hell is going on – but I get the feeling that's the last thing Gramps and Gran intend on doing this holiday.

Once I've finished my coffee, I creep back into the bedroom to get my shower things. Mum is awake, sitting up in bed, *The Happiness Hypothesis* resting on her legs.

"Oh, I thought you were still asleep."

"No, you woke me with all that noise out there."

"Sorry. Thin walls."

"Not to worry," she says, smiling. "I wanted to be up early. I've had an idea about this essay, and I need to do some more reading."

"Great," I say, rifling through my bag for my nice raspberry coloured jumper and fresh jeans. "I was thinking of taking Gran shopping later. Do you fancy it?"

"Oh no, darling. I don't think I'll have the time. I'm going to take myself off to a cafe, or the beach if it's nice enough, and I'm going to try and get ahead with all this." She points to the thin book. "I'll be back for dinner. Let's have something nice, eh? Something that's not fish and chips."

"Yeah, OK," I say.

"But you take Gran out. She'd like that."

Once I'm ready, I sit in the lounge and wait for Gramps and Gran to get up, so I can share the plan. Only there's no sign of them. Mum passes through on her way out, her bag packed and perfume on. She kisses my cheek and says she'll call me later to see what we're up to. A few minutes after she's gone, I spot her phone still charging in the kitchen.

I'm tempted to ring Lewis, to make him laugh by describing what I can see out of the caravan window – 'And to your left, you will see a collection of rusty outdoor furniture positioned beautifully against a shed covered in Wales's finest bird poo.' Instead, I decide to hold off, to focus on my plan and call him later when I've more of the day to share with him.

Gramps emerges at ten, his dressing gown on. "Morning, love. Your Gran is knackered," he says. "I'm bringing her a tea. Want one?"

Suddenly, I can't wait any more. I need to be out in the fresh air, outside of these caravan walls. If I'm going to get through this week, I can't spend it sitting around.

"No, thanks. I'm going to go for a walk."

"Good idea. I'll try and rouse your Gran by lunch. You enjoy the morning."

* * *

Thanks to a biting wind and the endlessly grey sky, there's not a great deal about the morning to enjoy. Once out of the caravan, I turn in the direction of the wind, hoping it will guide me to the sea. The beach, when I find it twenty minutes later, is quiet. There's no sign of Mum, and I imagine she would have given up trying to find it in favour of somewhere warmer. There are a few families braving the wind, optimistically digging holes with bright spades and enjoying the benefits of damp sand for their sandcastles. Away from them, before the beach narrows, a group of men are playing a game of rugby, or some approximation of it that involves a ball and lots of shouting.

At the edge of the sand, I take off my trainers and socks, moving towards the water's edge to dip my toes in.

The bite of the water and the wind slapping my face makes me feel more awake than I've been since we set off from Liverpool. This is a holiday: the horizon, the water, the break from who you normally are. I wish I could wade in deeper, to keep walking and dip down when I'm deep enough until the only part of me not submerged is my head. I contemplate doing it. I imagine the cold on my stomach as the water hits it, the shock of the Irish Sea as it reaches my nipples.

It's the family next to me that stop me. You can't very well watch a fully clothed woman walk into the sea without doing something about it, can you? There would be a scene, and they're getting on so well with their sandcastles. It would be a shame to blight their morning.

I'm just wondering how to describe this to Lewis, wondering whether the reminder of how the sea feels on his own toes, of how beautiful it is to stand at the edge of a beach with nothing ahead but the blue water, might help him or hurt him when there's a change in the air behind me. I turn round to it – and immediately after, the rugby ball hits me in the face.

"Watch out!"

I begin to topple backwards, my body on course to meet the water after all, when someone grabs my arm and pulls me back up.

My eyes are closed against the pain in my nose and the left side of my face. When I open them, I'm faced with the dad from the family next to me.

"Bloody hell. Are you all right?"

"Erm, yeah. I think so," I tell him, putting a hand to my nose and feeling blood.

"Selfish idiots playing like that when there are folk around them. He could have hit one of the kids," he says, as one of the selfish idiots – a tall and very guilty looking one in a red T-shirt and black shorts – rushes towards me.

"I'm so sorry," he says, scrutinising me all over to assess the damage. He smells of sweat and something sweeter and artificial that's not altogether unpleasant. "I'm an idiot. And a terrible thrower."

"Not if you were aiming at me," I say.

"I really wasn't." His voice has traces of a European accent I can't place, and his words come out in a rush, although I can't tell if that's just from the panic of knocking someone into the sea.

"Then, yeah. I'd say you're a pretty terrible thrower."

He grimaces but then laughs, grateful I've let him off the hook.

Some of his friends have rushed up to join him, and they gather round me in a semi-circle once I've stepped back out of the sea. There's a lot of fussing and apologising, but I keep my focus on him, as he takes off his T-shirt and presses it on my nose to stem the blood. Once he's happy I'm not going to die from blood loss, he picks up my shoes and socks.

"Come on. We should find somewhere for you to sit down. I really am so very sorry," he says, as he leads me off the beach.

"At least your T-shirt is red," I say. "I can give it back to you in minute. I don't think it will last long."

"Oh no, that's fine. You keep it. I insist. Where are you staying? Do you want me to take you home or shall we head to that cafe?"

He points at a small, naff-looking cafe at the top of the beach with net curtains in the window and a board outside advertising that every item on the menu is 99p before eleven.

Returning to Gramps and Gran bleeding and in the care of a tall, bare-chested stranger doesn't scream 'good idea' so I opt for the cafe.

"Good," he smiles. "My treat."

"I should think so."

"Come on though, we best get a move on if we want to get in before eleven."

"Generous." I begin to smile, but it hurts too much. I hope he won't try and be funny again.

He leads me inside to a dented Formica table. I watch him as he goes over to the counter and beings to talk far more than necessary to ask for a menu. To be fair, our bloody/semi-naked appearance probably demands a level of explanation. The sour-faced woman behind the counter begins to smile, and by the time she looks my way she's positively beaming.

After a trip into the back with the woman, he returns to our table with the menus and two coffees in stained white cups, now wearing a T-shirt with *Jan's* in black letters pulling across his wide chest.

"Did you pay 99p for that too?" I ask.

"No, it was a freebie. I was in violation of their dress code, so Jan sorted me out. How are you feeling? I really am sorry."

"It's hurting a little less," I lie.

"Good. So, do you live here?"

The question throws up a memory of Mum. Mum, who would live for that question on our annual trips to Mallorca when Dad was still alive. She'd dress in the most Spanish way she could, studying the Spanish women in the hotel and copying their hair, the way they carried themselves, their mannerisms, all for the payoff of that question. *Do you live here?* What better compliment than for someone to think you belonged in the place you'd spent money to escape to.

"No, I'm here with my family for a week. You?"

"A boys' trip. We come here every year."

"That's nice."

"It was until I ruined your holiday."

"You really haven't."

He looks up from his coffee and studies my face. He has piercing blue eyes, eyes that anyone would struggle to be under the scrutiny of. I have to look away.

"I'm here until Friday," he continues. "How about you?"

"Sunday."

"Lucky you. Now we've met, maybe I could see you again." He's rushing his words again. "Just so I can check up on you, make sure I haven't caused too much damage," he adds.

"There's no need. Really."

"No, of course not." But after a pause, he adds, "I don't know how your holiday is going, but I could do with a break from all the ladishness for a bit."

I think about the caravan I've just left, of Gran and Gramps sitting watching TV on their own when this holiday was meant to be about family time. Nice as this man is, there are other people I need to be spending time with now, not him. "Sorry, I don't think so."

"Boyfriend?" he asks.

"No," I say, surprised that's what he thought. "It's not that. It's my grandparents. I should be getting back to them. They'll be worrying."

He pushes his chair back and stands up, his cup of coffee still almost full. "Of course. I should get back to the boys. We've hired boats for this afternoon."

"Sounds fun."

"That's the plan," he says, in a way that makes it sound like it will be anything but.

I stand up too, the movement reminding me how much my nose and face is still throbbing. I'll need to rifle through Gran and Gramps's medicine bag when I get back for some of their super-strength painkillers.

"Well, nice to meet you," he says. Then, he adds, "I'm Jakub, by the way."

"Kelsey."

"Kelsey." He repeats my name, like he's logging it in his brain. "Sorry again, Kelsey."

He walks towards the door but stops in front of Jan to remove his T-shirt and hand it back to her.

"Keep it on, you daft sod. I don't want it back," I hear Jan object, her face reddening a shade deeper than it already was.

"Oh." It would be too much of a show to put it back on again, so he bunches the material up in his hand, turns to give me a little wave and walks out with it by his side.

Jan and I watch him make his way down the steps towards the beach. Then we watch him pause at the end and put the T-shirt back on. Once he's disappeared from view, Jan turns to me.

"You lucky thing," she says.

I touch the sticky blood that's pooled under my left nostril. "Sorry?"

"What I wouldn't do to be thirty years younger and to have someone like that looking at me the way he was looking at you."

"Oh," I say. "I think you'll find that was guilt."

Jan's thin eyebrows raise high on her forehead as she gives me such a sceptical look that it's clear whatever she saw wasn't guilt at all.

twenty-eight

Kelsey

ONCE I'VE RETURNED TO THE CARAVAN, CALMED GRAN down and promised I don't need to be rushed to A&E, once I've had the painkillers and a bowl of tomato soup, once I've cleaned my face and covered it with concealer, once I've persuaded Gramps that a trip to the town centre is exactly what I need, I go and lie down while I wait for Gran to get ready.

I don't want to fall asleep, as Gran and Gramps wouldn't wake me if I did and the day would be lost. So I get out my phone instead and see there's a missed call from Lewis.

"Hi," he says, when he answers the phone. "I was wondering when you'd call me back, but figured you'd be too busy having fun."

"Not exactly. It's pissing down, and I'm now the owner of a black eye and a bust nose."

"What? What on earth is going on down there?"

I smile at the worry in his voice. "Long story, but it involved a beach and a rugby ball in my face."

"Oh my God. Are you OK?"

"I'm fine."

My face is still sore and rather than dwell on the finer details of what happened, I move on to ask him about his day instead. A little while later, Gran pokes her head round the door to check if I'm ready. I hang up, promising to call him later to let him know how I am.

It's starting to brighten up when we eventually set off, and most people have had the same idea as us to come into the town centre. Gramps can't find anywhere to park. After a few rounds he gives up, pulling over on double yellow lines and ordering Gran and me out of the car for a quick nip into the shops while he goes for a drive. Our long afternoon out of the caravan wilts away to a twenty-minute dash, with Gran fretting about Gramps driving on the clogged up, narrow roads.

I divert Gran by pointing out all the pretty things FatFace has to offer and persuade her to let me buy her a pale blue scarf with a print of seagulls and boats. But I can tell she doesn't love it. She doesn't love anything in FatFace today. Not once has she run her hands over the dresses or T-shirts and commented on the good quality. She hasn't picked up a purse and admired it before putting it back down. She hasn't been tempted by the sale rack. She's not interested in anything other than getting back to Gramps.

Before we leave the shop, I take her arm and pull her to a quiet corner near the children's clothes.

"What is going on?" It's so apparent she's not herself, I can't help but ask. "And don't tell me it's nothing, because you normally love shopping, yet today you can't wait to get out of here."

It's not the best place for this conversation, granted, and she is clearly uncomfortable as she looks round to see if anyone has heard, but I can't spend the holiday pretending to have a good time when something is so clearly bothering her.

"I'm fine. Come on, let's go."

"No, Gran. Not until you tell me what's wrong. Whatever it is, I'd much rather know than have you try and hide it from me. Is this anything to do with Lewis? I know it's been a lot for all of us, and I know you and Gramps have been worried about me, but—"

"It's not that, love."

"Then can you please tell me what it is."

She exhales, the strength of keeping the secret leaving her as she does. She looks so small in that moment I wonder if I've got it wrong, if maybe I am better not knowing after all.

"I don't know what's wrong yet, so there's no need to worry, OK? No need at all. I've had a little biopsy, that's all, for a lump I found under my arm. I won't know what it is for a couple of weeks, so until then I'm trying very hard not to think about it."

My whole body stiffens, my chest pulling unbearably tight. This is the start of a picture I know all too well. A picture that may begin with the faint outlines of uncertainty and biopsies and waiting-to-find-out-more, before, all too soon, thick black marks of months left and pain and nothing-more-we-can-do fills the canvas.

"Oh, Gran. I'm sorry," I say, pulling her into a hug, in part so she can't see how gutturally devastated I am when she wants the opposite from me. "You should have told me."

"I didn't want to mention it until I knew for sure if there was anything you needed to know. And you mustn't tell your mum, you hear me? I don't want to have to bring up the c-word until I absolutely have to."

"I won't." I can't argue with Gran on that point. Mum doesn't have any ability to be calm when cancer is mentioned. It's her sworn enemy, and the thought Gran might have it would only panic her – and therefore panic Gran. I might feel the same, but I'm certain I can do a better job of hiding it than Mum can. "But if I've noticed something's wrong, chances are Mum will have too."

"You're right. I am trying to be positive and to put it out of my mind, but, by God, the waiting is hard. I'm not sure your Gramps was right about this holiday being a good idea."

"No," I say, firmly. "It's a great idea. Much better than sitting at home waiting for the results. We'll have a lovely time," I tell her, determined to help take her mind off the results.

"Thanks, love. Now, come on. Let's see if we can find your gramps. He'll be desperate to go back to the caravan."

She walks out of the shop, and I follow after. The pavement is narrow and busy. We manage to walk a few steps before we have to stop and move to the side to let a large group past.

"Hello, again." Jakub is there, at the back of the group, wearing a blue and white rugby top and denim shorts – a decided upgrade from his last outfit.

"Oh, hi."

"Wow, your face looks so much better already," he says, letting his friends pass us before stopping by my side.

I smile at the lie. I know my face does not look better at all.

"Thanks," I tell him.

"Is it still hurting?"

"A tad."

"Kelsey?" Gran says, her face confused.

"Oh, sorry Gran. This is Jakub. He, erm . . ." I stall over how to explain our connection, but Jakub helps me out.

"Pleased to meet you. I'm afraid I was the clown who hit your granddaughter with the ball on the beach."

"Oh." He's smiling warmly at her, and I can see Gran struggling between the urge to respond to his charm or to bollock him for hurting me.

I link her arm. "We should be getting on. Nice to see you again."

"And you, Kelsey."

"OK, bye," I say, rushing off, not sure why I'm the one out of the two of us who is feeling awkward and embarrassed.

* * *

When we return to the caravan, Mum is back too, sleeping, laid out on the thin plastic-covered couch. I wake her immediately so she'll get up and let Gran sit down.

"Hello, darling," she says, the couch squeaking under her as she moves. "I've had a very successful day. One thousand words written – can you believe it? It must be the sea air. To celebrate, I've booked us in at The Swan for tea. How does that sound?"

"I don't know," Gramps says, looking at Gran, but she cuts him off.

"That'll be lovely. Do they do fish and chips?"

"I'm sure they do."

It's nice to find myself aligned with Mum's thinking. An evening at the pub is perfect, something to look forward to. It makes the two hours of *A Place in the Sun* Gramps watches that bit more bearable. When it's time to get changed to go out, Mum and I get ready together in our little room.

"This is lovely," she says holding up my new black skater dress from Zara, the one with lacy sleeves and a flattering waistline. "Why don't you put this on?"

"I was going to wear jeans."

"No, not jeans. You should get dressed up!"

"For The Swan?"

"Yes, for The Swan. I can't remember the last time I saw you all dolled up. How about I get dressed up too? I've been looking for a chance to wear this."

Mum isn't one for unpacking. She pulls out of her case a bright blue dress I've never seen before. I've not seen Mum wear a dress for years. It's lovely.

"OK, then. Let's get dressed up."

She grins. "Goody. In that case, we should really do something about your face."

Coming out of our room half an hour later, trussed up, our hair curled and make-up caking our faces, we're both smiling. It's the most fun I've had all holiday, and all of the hours in Marks & Spencer with Mum over the years haven't been a patch on this one.

"Look at you two," Gran says, beaming. "You could be sisters."

One of us is delighted, the other mortified, but we both say thank you and tell Gran it's time to get her coat.

* * *

The Swan is dark and pleasantly old-fashioned. We take our seats in the corner and the waitress brings us cushioned leather folders holding the menu. Before she disappears, Gramps gets in our drinks order, a bitter for him and a bottle of wine for me, Mum and Gran to share. He gives a happy sigh as the waitress walks off, and I suddenly feel incredibly happy that we're here together.

There's an easy silence as we look at our menus – the usual prawn cocktail, pie and everything-with-chips kind of fare.

"I'll just nip to the loo before the waitress comes," I say.

"You went before we left," Gramps says.

"Oh, it's nothing to do with needing to go. Kelsey's been obsessed with checking out the toilets of any bar or restaurant since she was a little girl, isn't that right, Kelsey? Your Dad and I couldn't take you anywhere without you asking to go every two minutes."

It's true. To this day, I make my judgement on the quality of any establishment I enter based on the toilets. I like that Mum's remembered that. I used to love going out for meals with Mum and Dad when I was little. Dad would let me order a lemonade, and he'd always remember to bring some paper and pencils with him so we could take turns drawing silly characters while we waited for our food to arrive.

Mum rarely talks about my childhood. Sometimes I wonder if she tries to forget it, because it's too tied up with Dad and the happy memories that threatened to destroy her when we lost him. We smile at each other, both remembering Dad, and it's nice. I wish we could talk about those days more.

The toilets, when I get to them, are as expected. Dark and in need of a lick of paint but clean and with plenty of soap in the dispensers. I catch my reflection in the mirror as I finish washing my hands and am surprised at how happy I look. Gran's news has rocked me, but it's been such a long time since we were all together like this. Not together because we had to be, because of Christmas or birthdays, Mum clearly counting down the minutes until she could leave – but together through choice. Gramps was right to organise this holiday. It's the best thing we've done as a family in years.

"You again?" A voice at the bar says when I come out from the ladies.

He's sitting on a stool in a tartan shirt, holding a pint in his hands. He looks like part of the furniture. I notice Mum, Gramps and Gran looking over to see who I'm talking to. When Gran starts talking, Gramps begins to frown and I take it she's regaling them with the details of how we met.

"Jakub, hi."

I don't know if it's because the meal is going well or because he looks so lovely and his smile is so warm, but I find myself smiling up at him, pleased to see him. Like bumping into him fits into this night somehow.

"Three times in one day," he says. "That's got to be a sign, right?"

"A sign of what, exactly?" I step closer to him, distantly aware that I may be doing something resembling flirting.

"That you and I are meant to go out. The first two times, I let it lie, but three times . . . I think I'm really going to have to ask you out on a date."

I laugh. "A date?"

"Yes."

"I don't think so."

"Is it because of how we met?" He pulls his face into a grimace.

I laugh again. "No, although hitting someone in the face with a ball doesn't naturally scream *let's date*. It's like I said, I'm here with my family. I should get back to them."

Jakub turns to follow the incline of my head and, from their gawping, there's no mistaking who I'm with. He gives them an embarrassed wave and they all smile and wave back.

"OK. I'll say goodnight then, but how about this? If I see you for a fourth time, will you seriously consider not angering the gods and letting me take you for a drink?"

"I'll tell you what. If I see you for a fourth time, I'll begin to think about it."

His eyes widen in surprise, and he smiles broadly at me. He really does have the best smile.

"Deal. I really hope I bump into you again."

"Goodnight, Jakub." As I walk back to the table, I'm shocked that I find myself thinking, *me too*.

twenty-nine

Kelsey

COULD I GO ON A DATE WITH JAKUB?

It's hardly the worst offer I've ever had in my life. With those blue eyes and floppy, thick hair, he's so gorgeous it's hard to look directly at him – and he just so happens to be funny and charming too. A harmless holiday date that doesn't really count for anything. Could I do that?

I lie awake after getting back from the pub. The wine, Gran's awful news, Jakub's offer and thoughts of Lewis swirl round together in my head.

Dating Jakub and having some fun is exactly what Dessie and Joy would be telling me to do right now, and maybe they'd have a point. Lewis and I are in a good place, but we're not in a romantic place. If I dated when I thought he was in New York, there's even more reason to date now that I know the truth. And Jakub is in a whole other league to the men I've been out with this last year.

I fall asleep before I make a decision but when I wake the next morning, it's there waiting for me.

I'm not ready.

I know it in my gut. Jakub and I could have a great date. We could end up really liking each other. We could end up deciding that it should be more than a bit of fun, we could decide to try and carry things on when we got home. If I said yes to him, anything *could* happen. But I'm not looking for anything *to* happen. My mind is still too full of Lewis, the place we've found ourselves in is still too new, and mixing Jakub up in that would be too complicated.

Just to make sure I've convinced myself I'm in the right by dismissing Jakub's offer, I press my fingers against my sore, swollen nose and reacquaint myself with the story of how Jakub and I met.

Mum is already up and out of the room. When I retrieve my phone and my home screen lights up, I'm shocked to see it's gone nine. I sit up and call Lewis.

"Hi, Kels."

"Good morning. Do you know, I'm lying in a bed so old it must have had hundreds and hundreds of different bums resting against it? A whole history of bums before mine. It's quite disturbing if you think about it too much."

"Sure is," he says. I don't expect the flatness to his voice.

"What you up to?"

"Nothing much. Work and a visit from Mum later."

"That's nice."

"Yeah. Look, sorry Kelsey, I've got a report to write so I'd best get on. If you're not ringing for anything in particular, I'll speak to you later. OK?"

"Sure."

He hangs up.

I immediately wish I hadn't called him. Normally, we're perfectly happy talking rubbish. It's what we spend most of our time doing. So I don't get the shut down to it this morning.

A heavy feeling settles on my chest as I realise this might be harder for him than I appreciated. I'm ringing on holiday, when he's at home. That's got to be hard. I promise myself I won't get in touch again until the evening, and when I do, I'll check in with him and only share my day if I'm sure doing so isn't going to hurt him.

When I get dressed and go into the kitchen, I'm surprised no one else is around. I'm scrolling on Facebook when Gran passes through and tells me Mum was up and out first thing again and her and Gramps have hardly slept, so she's making herself a cup of tea and getting back in bed for a bit.

I turn on the TV, but quickly realise, two days in, I've had my fill of TV already this holiday. I really don't want to sit around all morning.

I make a coffee in my travel flask and leave the caravan.

* * *

This September morning is as it should be, bright and warm and begging for people to be out in it. While wandering down to the beach, I keep an eye out for Mum but don't see her anywhere. I dip my toes in the water again and consider whether I would be brave enough to come here in my swimming costume at any point in the holiday. Probably not.

I walk up and down the stretch of sand a few times, before heading up to Jan's to get myself a 99p orange juice to get rid of the taste of coffee. There are four picnic tables outside the cafe and only one isn't taken. It's big enough for six or more, but I perch on the end of it as I sip my drink, ready to move if the family who lined up behind me come along and want it. I close my eyes and point my head up to the sky, the sun on my face. *You can enjoy this,* I tell myself.

My enjoyment doesn't last for long. The peace is shattered by a commotion. I open my eyes to look down on a large group of men setting up a football pitch on the beach, shouting across the sand. There's at least a dozen of them and they're arsing around, pushing each other about and shouting instructions from one end to the other. And there, at the far end before the rocks sweep into the sea, pushing the end of a football net into the sand, is Jakub. A laugh escapes between my lips. *Of course* Jakub is here. This is getting ridiculous. It seems I can't leave the caravan without bumping into him.

I consider turning back into Jan's and hiding in the toilets, but he spots me almost as soon as I've spotted him. He beckons me down and I make my way towards him, where he's waiting for me at the water's edge. I have a strange awareness of my body as I walk, my spine straightening like I've been told off for slouching and am trying to correct it. My stomach muscles are pulled in, and I'm very aware of my hair. I want to tuck it behind my ears but don't because I know I look better when it frames my face.

It's not my fault I'm reacting like this, I tell myself as I get closer. It's a natural response to someone who is ridiculously attractive and who is standing without a top on, waiting for you in the glistening water with the sun shining on his six pack. It'll pass.

"So, I've seen you again," he says.

"You have."

"You know what this means, don't you?"

"I do."

"I have to ask you out on a date and, rather than turning me down flat, you have to think about it."

"I do."

"Will you go out with me then? Tonight?"

This morning, I thought my decision was final. But now we're here, now he's asked and he's standing a foot away from me, looking down at me with a nervous smile, it's harder to be rational.

"I'm sorry, no," I say eventually.

Jakub doesn't lose his smile, but I catch the flash of surprise in his eyes, the way his shoulders move back, as though my words have pushed him.

"You're lovely," I go on, wanting to soften my answer. "You are, but I'm here with my family and really not looking to get into anything."

"No problem," he says warmly. "I understand."

"OK," I say back, surprised. I'm a little miffed he's not tried even a tiny bit harder.

"How about a walk then?"

"What about your game?"

He looks back at his group of friends who seem to be getting

218

on fine passing the ball among themselves without him.

"Trust me, they'll see my absence as a favour." He points to my nose. "You've seen for yourself how good my sporting accuracy is. It looks great, by the way. You'd never know."

I laugh. I spent ten minutes this morning trying to cover the redness and bruising with concealer before giving up and washing it off when I'd only managed to emphasise what a mess it was. "Yeah, right. Thanks to you, my face is so swollen I look like Henry VIII during his gout years."

"*That's* who you remind me of!" he says. I pretend to be offended but I can't help but laugh.

"No, seriously, you look fine. I can tell behind the swelling you actually have a very pretty nose."

"Why, thank you."

"So, this walk?"

I should keep looking for Mum, but I find myself saying yes. A walk isn't a date. It's not the same thing. There's no reason we can't keep talking a little longer.

He goes back to tell his friends to keep playing without him and I take one last scan around the beach.

"Ready?" he asks when he comes back, now wearing a white T-shirt that makes it easier for me to be next to him without thinking about his pecs.

"Yeah."

We walk in the shallows of the waves, holding our shoes in our hands, neither of us speaking at first. We look out to sea, at the glistening surface and the promontory in the distance.

"How old are you?" I ask, taking the chance to put the attention on Jakub rather than me.

"Thirty."

"And you're still going on lads' holidays with a dozen mates?"

"Er, yeah. Are you suggesting there's something wrong with that?" He looks down at me and pretends to be serious, but there's a glint in his eyes that betrays him.

"No, of course not. It's nice. I was just thinking that you have a lot of friends. Most people don't have that once school and university are over."

He nods. "Maybe not. They're not all equal friends, though. My best mate Luke organised the holiday, so we're a mash up of the lads Luke and I used to live with, some of his football team and a few who I'm still not entirely sure about."

"Right. Are you all enjoying yourselves?"

"They definitely are," he says. "And, yeah, I think I am, too."

"You think you are?"

He takes a moment to answer, running his hands through his hair as he thinks.

"Truthfully, I'm not actually into big groups at all. I wasn't going to come, but Luke got married last year and we've barely spent any time together since, so I came to spend time with him. Not that I've had much chance. He's been absolutely hammered most of the time."

"Oh dear. Well, if you're here to spend time with him, don't feel like you have to be with me instead. You should go back to him."

"No point. He's still in bed nursing a hangover. Being with you

220

is definitely the better option. Speaking of you, how's your holiday working out?"

I picture Mum in her blue dress, the four of us sitting together, as well as Gran in the caravan this morning, looking tired. "It's been good for us. I think," I answer. "I love being with my family. But I've just found out my Gran is waiting for test results after a biopsy, and she needed the distraction. I don't think it's working that well."

"I'm so sorry. Are you OK?"

"I'm fine," I say. I've been so focused on keeping Gran busy I've not stopped to think about how I am, but there's a heaviness to my chest as I answer Jakub that tells me I'm not being honest. "Next question," I say, wanting to get back to him. "Where are you from?"

"London now. Poland originally."

"What do you do?"

He smiles. "I'm an accountant. You?"

"A waitress. How long have you been an accountant for?" I ask.

"Four years and," he pauses slightly, "seven months. Next?"

"Sorry?"

"Your next question. This is beginning to feel like a job interview." He raises his eyebrows at me.

He must see the spread of embarrassment crawling up my face, because he follows it up with, "It's fine. You can ask me whatever you like."

Weirdly, I'm sure I could. There's an openness to Jakub that tells me if I asked for his deepest, darkest secret he'd offer it to me without hesitation. I shouldn't want to know anything, but I find myself wondering what else I could find out about him.

Maybe it's because my brain is filled with worry for Gran, but the rather safe, rather bland, question I plump for is: "What is your family like?"

He takes a minute to think, and I like that he is considering his answer.

"They're pretty normal. Separate, I suppose, is the word I'd use for them. It's hard to think of my family all being together, grandparents and aunts and uncles, cousins. It used to be that way, but my parents are divorced now and my adult life has been spent seeing one relative at a time. It can be a lot."

The caravan springs into my mind, an image of us sitting round the TV together last night watching *Vera*. "That's sad. Is that why you moved to London?"

"No, no – I moved to London as a child with my parents when they were still married. They're both still there, but they split up when I was eighteen. It was like, hey Jak, you're an adult now, that's the end of family life as you know it."

"That's shit."

"A bit, but I'd already left home for uni and was generally happy. To them, waiting until I'd moved out was the least selfish option."

"Do you think they were unhappy together for long? Sorry, that's a terrible question. Don't answer. Shall we talk about something else? What football team do you support?"

He smiles. "It's fine. I told you to ask away. I never saw their unhappiness. They didn't fight or live obviously separate lives.

They were quietly dissatisfied with each other, I guess. In a way, sometimes I admire them for divorcing. Dad has a new girlfriend and Mum has a handful of good friends and her various projects. It worked out for them."

"That's good."

When I don't continue straight away, he takes his chance: "Can I ask you something now?"

"I can't really say no, can I?"

"You can. You don't have to tell me anything you don't want to. I'm just curious about something."

"It's fine. Go for it," I tell him. I'm still nervous about what he might ask, but I'm slightly less averse to opening up to him a little, given how honest he's been with me.

"Yesterday, when I asked you in the cafe whether or not you had a boyfriend, you said no. But I sensed there was more to your answer than you were giving. Am I right?"

"Oh." I consider how to answer but realise I'm not reluctant to give him an explanation. Why does it matter if Jakub knows about Lewis? "I don't have a boyfriend, but there is someone from home, someone I've known since I was child. I guess I was thinking about him when you asked. We're not together, but he means everything to me."

"Everything?" Jakub blows air out of his mouth. "That's a lot."

"I suppose so." I look out to sea and the horizon. We've walked past most of the beachgoers now and, apart from the distant squall of seagulls, it's so quiet.

"So you're, what, friends?"

"Yeah. He's my best friend."

"That's nice."

"What?" I ask when he's spent at least thirty seconds looking out to sea in contemplation, leaving me walking next to him, feeling foolish.

"No, I'm just thinking about what you said."

"I got that. Are you going to tell me what exactly you were thinking?"

"I was thinking, I don't have anyone like your friend in my life – no one I'd class as being *everything* to me. And I'm not sure I'd want that. I'm not sure I'd ever want to be everything to someone else either."

"Why not?" I ask, surprised. "Don't you believe in finding your soulmate?"

"I don't know. I haven't found anyone who comes close to 'soulmate' yet. Though I don't even know if I believe in the idea of soulmates, so I'm probably completely unqualified to talk about it. It just seems a lot." He pauses. "Is that what this guy is to you, then? Your soulmate?"

"I think so."

He nods. "If you even *think* he could be that to you, that he could be your Mr Everything, he must be pretty special."

"He is."

We carry on walking until we run out of beach. He tells me about his non-existent love life and his pledge to stop going on free dating apps for the rest of the year. He tells me two well-worn dating disaster stories and I share my best horror stories of dates gone wrong from the restaurant. The path back to the caravan is at this end of the beach, and I tell him that I should probably head back.

"Do you know, talking to you has been the nicest thing that's happened to me since I arrived," he says, when I say goodbye. "It's been the best thing that's happened for a long time, actually."

"It's been the nicest thing to happen to me too. I'm glad I met you, Jakub," I tell him, only realising once I've said it how true it is.

I walk away from him, not caring that I'm spraying sand up my wet calves, which is going to be a nightmare to wash off later. If I'd have lingered, I'm sure he'd have said more, tried to get me to agree to meet again. I've enjoyed being with him so much I'm not sure I'd have been able to turn him down a second time. But I know our time is up. I need to spend the rest of the holiday with my family and, before the day is over, I need to call Lewis again to make sure he's OK.

"Kelsey, wait." I turn to find Jakub walking quickly up the path to catch up to me. He also has sand all over his legs. "I'm not going to ask you out again or anything, but I'd beat myself up if I didn't do this."

I step back, sure he's going to try and kiss me, but instead he gingerly puts his arms around me, wrapping me in a light hug that he's pulling away from seconds after starting it, not giving me anywhere near enough time to put my arms round him too.

He looks at me after he's done it, an unsure smile on his face that reveals the single dimple he has on the left side of his mouth.

"Thank you. Meeting you has reminded me that there are

still perfect strangers out there. I'd started to worry I'd run out of chances, that I was never going to meet someone who I connected with. But then I come away to Wales, hang out with Henry VIII for a bit and my hope is restored."

"Glad to be of service," I say, trying to sound light when really I'm touched by what he's said.

"You're wonderful, you know? Really wonderful," he tells me, before turning and walking away, leaving me to watch him go.

thirty

Kelsey

I GET BACK TO THE CARAVAN TO FIND EVERYONE ASLEEP.
Mum is in our room with her headphones on and eyes closed.
Gran and Gramps's door is shut. It's twenty past twelve on a
Tuesday afternoon, and I have absolutely nothing to do.

*KELSEY: Hey, hope work's been OK. Nothing to report from Wales.
Wish I was back home hanging out with you. xxxx*

I will Lewis to reply, but my message sits there unread. If Gran
gets up soon, we can go out for lunch somewhere. I should get
in the shower and wash the sand away, but instead I stay on the
couch, ignoring the slightly funky smell it omits, and stay on my
phone, this time searching trains from Abersoch to Liverpool. It's
a stupid thought, and one I wouldn't act on – especially when I
discover there is no train from Abersoch to Liverpool, or from
anywhere less than fifty miles away – but I'm suddenly desperate
to be back home, to see Lewis again.

This shouldn't have happened with Jakub. I shouldn't have left
the beach with my heart racing, and I shouldn't have caught sight
of my pink reflection in the bathroom mirror when I got back to

the caravan. Now I've brought myself back under control, I feel silly and weak for losing my resolve so easily. Being with Jakub isn't what I need. I need to be back with Lewis. That's where my heart and mind belong – on his doorstep, trying to help him back into his life any way I can.

The best thing to do right now is to make myself a cheese sandwich, turn on *Loose Women* and try to forget all about Jakub.

"You woke me," Mum says, coming into the lounge and sitting next to me an hour after I turned the TV on.

"Sorry. Where did you go earlier? I tried to find you," I say, a little ashamed at the white lie.

"I needed decent Wi-Fi so I went into town. Being here, I've ended up stalling on any progress I'd made with my essay. It's not the same as home."

"No. No, it's not."

She looks at me in that way she sometimes does in Marks & Spencer, when she has news to impart and is weighing up how to tell me. "I was thinking, love, I might not be able to spend the week here, after all. It's an awful long time to be away from my studies. I was wondering if I might ask Gramps to drop me at a train station tomorrow, so I could head back. The three of you can spend the rest of the week enjoying yourselves without me stressing out."

I could tell her I've already checked the trains and she needn't bother, no one's getting out of this holiday unless Gramps drives us back himself – but doing that would be an admission I've thought the same. The thought that neither of us can stick out a week for Gran when she does so much for us is unbearable, so instead of being honest, I choose to be outraged.

"You can't do that. Gran needs us here. We're all staying, and that's that."

Mum's eyes widen in surprise.

"OK, OK," she says holding her hands up. "But what do you mean Gran needs us?"

Shit. "Nothing. She's a bit tired and needed a change of scene, that's all."

"Kelsey, your gran hasn't needed a change of scene her whole life, and she never complains about being tired. What's going on?" she asks, sounding alarmed.

I flounder around for a decent answer but don't have time to find one before Gran is in the room, laying a hand on my shoulder and giving it a squeeze.

"It's all right, love," she tells me. Then she speaks to Mum. "I found a lump. I've had a biopsy and I'm waiting for results. It might be nothing at all, so I don't want you to overreact. Your dad thought this break would help the wait, but it's not. I'm going to ask him to take us back this evening."

Mum's face has lost all its colour, and her unblinking eyes look huge. I can't tell if she's going to cry or run off or scream.

"For fuck's sake, Mum," she says, getting off the sofa, rushing towards Gran and putting her arms round her. "Why didn't you tell me?"

"I didn't want to upset you. Not with a cancer scare. Not after Martin."

Mum lets go of Gran and steps back from her, so she can look into her eyes. "Martin was unlucky. He waited too long to get checked out and a whole series of things went wrong after that. It doesn't mean the same is going to happen to you. You've got it seen to, that's the main thing."

It's actually the last thing either of us expected Mum to say, and Gran sneaks me a shocked look. Mum, calm in a crisis?

"And while you wait, you're not going home," she continues. "You're staying here with your family, where we can fuss after you and do enough crappy tourist things that you'll have no time to worry about the results. Starting with us all going out for a ridiculously priced afternoon tea. Isn't that right, Kelsey?"

I nod. "It sure is."

Gran starts to cry, and Mum pulls her back into her arms. "Thank you, Lorraine," Gran says.

It's the proudest I've ever been of my mother.

* * *

The holiday speeds up after that. True to her word, Mum puts her books away, doesn't mention her essay again and plans out our time, so we're so busy driving around to local beauty spots, trying our hands at pottery, attempting to fly kites on the beach and eating so much cake our clothes feel tight, that we're hardly in the caravan.

Gran is happy. I can see how much it means to her to spend time with Mum like this, for her to see Mum and I enjoying time together. For me, it's more bittersweet. Mum's held me at arm's

230

length for so long, I'd forgotten how much we got on. Memories come back to me of us baking on a Sunday morning in our pyjamas, of spending hours together in her little black Fiesta as she took me to netball when I started secondary school, singing Taylor Swift at the top of our lungs. We haven't made good memories in all the years since Dad died and there's a pain to making them now, after a gap of ten years.

But she's determined we're going to continue to make them. On Friday morning, Mum wakes me early to tell me how beautiful it is outside and that she's already woken Gran and Gramps to tell them to get ready for breakfast on the beach.

"We can go to that little cafe for bacon butties and sit at a table outside watching the day begin. It's a bit scruffy, but I'm sure I saw a sign saying it was 99p for anything before eleven. Won't that be nice?"

No, actually, it won't be nice. Since we parted on the beach, I've been on full alert for Jakub. Whenever we've gone into Abersoch, I've looked out for him, planning to duck into shops or lanes if I spot him. Whenever anyone has touted going to the beach, I've suggested going to the one on the other side of town with better views, instead of going to the one I know he and friends have been using. Today is Jakub's last day in Wales. I'm looking forward to spending the last couple of days of our holiday not worrying about bumping into him – and setting up outside Jan's this morning doesn't strike me as the best way to avoid seeing him before he goes.

Not that he wouldn't be lovely. I know he would be. And not that I wouldn't enjoy seeing him again and talking to him, because I know I would. But I don't want to think about him any more than I've already done, because nothing is going to happen between us. It's pointless.

"Won't it be cold?" I ask Mum, making a show of being chilly by rubbing my hands over my arms after getting out of bed. "Maybe we should go somewhere a little cosier."

"Don't be daft. It's not cold at all. Put on a jumper and you'll be fine," Mum says. "We're setting off in fifteen minutes. Your gran's looking forward to it."

"Fine," I say.

"You never were a morning person, were you? You just get ready. Once you're there, looking out at the sea, you won't want to come back."

I do as I'm told and walk down to the beach hoping Jakub and his friends have set off back to London first thing. I ask Mum to order for me, so I won't have to see Jan and risk her mentioning Jakub in front of everyone.

Mum and Gramps go inside, and Gran and I sit at the only picnic bench with the sun shining on it.

"What a view," Gran says. "Isn't it lovely up here? Oh, look! There's that boy you spoke to in the pub. Are you going to say hello?"

Jakub isn't playing football with his friends but walking on his own at the shoreline right beneath us. Course he is. As soon as Gran shouts "Coo-ee!" his head snaps up to where we're sat.

It's too late to hide, there are no escape routes – especially not now Gran is motioning for him to join us.

"What are you doing?" I hiss.

"I'm helping you out, love."

"You're really not," I whisper, as he approaches us.

"Hey, you," he says. His voice, his wide smile, ooze so much warmth, I know Gran will be smiling smugly next to me. "How funny to see you this morning. I'm just taking a final walk before we set off. I'm all packed but the others haven't even started yet. It's chaos in our lodge."

Gran over-laughs and stands up. "Well, isn't this a bit of luck? Come on, Jakub, you take my place here. I'm going to nip inside and see where my breakfast has got to."

Please don't wink, please don't wink, please don't wink.

She winks at us before leaving us alone.

Jakub does as he's told and takes Gran's place, only his thighs are so wide, he ends up brushing up against my leg. I shuffle down the bench, but there's not much room left.

"It's not really luck we bumped into each other," he says. "I was kind of walking up and down hoping to see you again before I left. In fact, I've been looking for you the last few days."

"Oh." I try to stay calm and hide the fact my heart is pummelling against my chest. He's being nice, that's all. I can handle one more conversation of nice before he leaves, and then I never have to see him again.

"That's OK," he says. "I know we said goodbye, but I wanted the chance to speak to you again, to say thanks for turning this week into something I really needed."

"You already told me that, remember?" *You also told me I'm wonderful*, I think to myself. "But you're welcome. Again."

"Can I be honest?" he asks, and my heart speeds up even further.

I manage a nod.

"This is going to sound weird, I know it is, but I'm going to say it anyway. I know this hasn't been a holiday romance in any way, but it kind of feels like that to me. A one-sided holiday romance, I admit. But, even so, I'm glad it happened. I'm pretty sure you won't, but if you ever did find yourself in a position where you might want to make it less one-sided, that would be great. Can I give you my number, just in case?"

"Jakub, you're lovely, and it's been nice meeting you too, it's just—"

"You've no space?" he offers, looking at me with those kind, piercing blue eyes.

"Exactly," I say, although that's not exactly right. I have space – I've had space for a long time. But I still can't fathom anyone other than Lewis filling it up.

"I get that, and I know it's probably pointless, but it would make me feel a tiny bit better if I knew you had my number, just in case anything were to change."

He holds out a piece of paper, folded in half. I open it to find his name, a number and a kiss underneath. I can't help but smile at how old-fashioned and organised he is.

"How long have you been carrying this around?"

"Ever since I last saw you."

My lips twitch up even further. "I'm glad you found me to give it to, then."

"Me too. Have a safe journey."

As soon as I hug him, I realise it's the last thing I should have done. This time, he hugs me tightly, his arms wrapped around me, and I'm entirely pressed against him. I breathe in the smell of him and, when he pulls away, I look up at him for a second before moving my lips up to his.

thirty-one

Lewis

TWENTY-FOUR YEARS OLD

HE WAS OVER AN HOUR LATE WHEN HE KNOCKED ON THE
bungalow door and braced himself for a telling off.

His new, swish job back in Liverpool had been so all-consuming
since the day he started that being late, cancelling plans, even
forgetting plans altogether, had become traits fixed onto his
personality. Much as he hated them, he loved the job. He loved
the complexity of the coding work he was doing, the seniority
he was given in the new company, the passion of those working
with him. Being completely unreliable in his personal life was a
downside he could only hope he'd get on top of with time.

He was so tired, he'd wanted to ask Kelsey if they could
change theirs plan so they could meet on the Sunday for some
food or a walk, rather than him rushing around on a Friday night
before he had to be out again with people from work. Only, when
she'd rung this morning to check he was still coming, there was
a nervousness to her voice that made him worry something

was wrong. He said he'd be there at half five.

Half five was never realistic, though. Lewis never actually stopped work at five and his colleagues knew it. He was still on the phone at half past. By the time he'd got ready for the night out and had half-run, half-walked over, he was desperately late.

"Here you are," Kelsey said, answering the door and throwing her arms around him, dragging him in by his neck.

"Easy there," Lewis said, pulling himself free. "I'm so sorry, Kels. You know what it's like."

She waved her arms, batting his apology away. "Of course I do. But you're here now. Come on, let's have a drink." The slur in her voice told him it wouldn't be her first. She took his hand and led him down the corridor to the kitchen.

"Where is everyone?" Lewis asked, following behind.

"Bingo. We've got the whole place to ourselves tonight," she said, her voice swaying as much as her body as she walked, grasping Lewis's hand tightly.

Lewis was glad she wasn't looking at him to see his colour rise at her attempts at flirting.

Until three months ago, Lewis had been in London and there'd been no flirting between them whatsoever. After his internship, he'd been offered a job at a prestigious technology company and had made the decision to put off returning to Liverpool a little longer. He'd loved it. The apartment, the long but satisfying daily routine, the nice clothes, the pride in doing a good job. It was hard to come away, but at twenty-four he'd started to long for something else. He'd handed in his notice and decided to head for home.

Perhaps that something else was Kelsey. Kelsey was still at home, still living with her grandparents and working various jobs, trying to find something she liked enough to want to pursue. She made it clear she couldn't have been happier with Lewis coming back.

Finally, they seemed to be in the same place. Both of them were single, they both spent more time talking to each other than anyone else, and they both wanted whatever life was meant to bring them next. The time they'd spent together since he'd come home had been charged with a nervous energy. Their conversations were punctuated with long gaps where each waited for the other to say the thing that would move them on, but neither did. Hugs became questions that remained unanswered. Saying goodbye and waiting to see if it really was a goodbye or if, finally, something would happen was excruciating. But changing things felt so big that neither was able to make the first move.

Until Kelsey opened the door to her empty bungalow and pulled Lewis inside.

"Wine?" she asked, and he nodded. She filled up their glasses to the brim and handed him one.

"Cheers," he said. After a few sips, he said, "I should go easy. Got to be on my best behaviour tonight."

"No, you don't," she said. "I think your best behaviour is part of the problem."

He baulked a little at Kelsey's flirting. He was so unused to seeing this side of her, but he knew one of them had to start it if they were to move any further forward. Honestly, he was glad it was her, not him.

"Not with you," he said, laughing a little nervously. "With work. I'm out in Chester tonight, remember?"

"Can't you cancel?"

"I can't. Not tonight. I'm only calling in to say hi," he said.

"But I've not seen you all week."

"Sorry," he said. "How about we spend the whole day together on Sunday? Roast, walk, a few films, the works. Sound good?"

"It does." She gulped down most of her wine, before edging along the worktop and stopping right next to him. "If you're not here for long, I guess I best get on with this before I lose my nerve."

Without hesitating, she turned her face up to his and kissed him. It took a moment for Lewis to register how the kiss felt, because at first, all he could think about was how he was finally kissing Kelsey Bright. The moment he'd dreamt of since he was a teenage boy was happening, and it was her who kissed him!

But then she bit his lip, and he was suddenly aware of everything. Her arms were clamped around his, so he couldn't pull her close, couldn't run his hand through her hair like he imagined. She tasted of wine, and she was leaning against him, as if she needed him for balance. The kiss was hard, almost ferocious – the kiss that he'd always presumed would be gentle and intimate.

He pulled back.

"Come on," Kelsey said, taking his retreat to mean something else. "Let's go to my bedroom."

"No, I, erm . . . I don't think we should."

He hated to see the hurt on her face he'd caused, but there was no other choice but to cause it. He'd wanted that kiss. They could never have that moment again, and he would always know from now on how wrong it felt.

The kiss itself wasn't great. But that wasn't what was causing the sinking feeling in his stomach instead of the flipping sensation that should have been there. He almost couldn't believe it, but there was no getting around it. He'd kissed enough people to know what felt right and what didn't, and his body was telling him he didn't want to be kissing Kelsey.

He'd loved her for so long, he'd imagined the kiss to be a moment when everything finally slotted into place. He hadn't expected this moment to be one of the most crushing of his life, the moment he discovered whatever this love was between them, it was not *this*. Every time they'd missed each other before it had felt like bad timing, but he saw then it wasn't. It was one or the other keeping them as friends, keeping them where they were meant to be. This moment wasn't meant to be in their story, and he was shocked at the mistake.

"Why?" she asked, backing away from him. "I thought—"

"I'm just so late," he lied, shying away from a truth that would only hurt her more. "I should go. Call you tomorrow, OK?"

thirty-two

Kelsey

THE TOUCH OF MY LIPS AGAINST HIS, MY FINGERS RUNNING through his thick hair, the warm pressure of one of his hands on my back, the other finding my face, a finger tracing the contours of my jawline. My stomach responds, whirling at his touch. Jakub's lips press harder and for a moment I press back, contemplate pulling him closer. My brain races into gear, and I pull away.

"I'm sorry," I say. "I shouldn't have done that."

I get off the bench and move away, suddenly needing as much distance as I can get from what just happened.

"Yes, you should have." He's smiling, and there's an undone expression on his face, a look I've caused, that makes me want to go back to him again. I take a step back.

"It was a mistake, I'm sorry."

There's a glimmer in his eyes that tells me he's hoping I'll change my mind. I'm forced to go on.

"That should never have happened."

Hurt widens his eyes now. Guilt hits me, but it's nowhere near as strong as the guilt I feel when I think of Lewis back in his house, alone. I know we're not together, that doing this is not cheating on him, but that doesn't stop it feeling wrong. Wrong because my focus is meant to be on Lewis, wrong because my heart is full of him, and there shouldn't be space for this.

"But it did happen. And I'm glad." He watches me for a moment, before asking, "There's not even a small part of you that thinks that was a good idea?"

That's the problem. In that moment, *every* part of me thought it was a good idea. But he's leaving today, and I'm going home soon, and there's Lewis, and it's the last thing that should have happened. I can tell Jakub wants this moment to be huge, to be defining. But I need it to become as small and insignificant as possible.

I stay silent, and the awkwardness grows between us.

"OK," he says eventually. "Mistake. I get it."

"My family are going to be out any second . . ."

"Right. I'll go then, shall I?"

"Yes." I make a point of staring at the horizon, not facing him again in case he reads a different story on my face.

"Right. Goodbye," he says, when he finally realises this is over.

I keep looking ahead until I'm sure he's out of sight. Then I look down at my hand, where I'm clutching the piece of paper with his phone number on it. I contemplate tearing it up and letting the wind take it, but there's something about the slope of his handwriting, the care he's taken over writing my name, that stops me. I put it into my hoodie pocket and turn back to Jan's, desperate to get back to the day I'm meant to have.

Mum is standing by the door holding two paper coffee cups and grinning. "Didn't I tell you a holiday romance was exactly what you needed?"

"What? No, that was nothing."

She ignores me and emits a girlish squeal. "Kelsey! He's bloody gorgeous. Go you."

"No. Not go me. It should never have happened. I told him that."

Her mouth falls open. She couldn't look more taken aback if she tried.

"Please do not tell me the reason you pulled away from that gorgeous man, who is clearly mad about you, is anything to do with Lewis."

I don't answer, and she shakes her head.

"For God's sake, Kelsey. What are you doing?"

I feel my defences going up at the question. "I'm not doing anything. I'm going to take that coffee from you and go back to cheering up Gran like we planned."

"You've just let that man walk away from you without so much as a second glance, and you've done it for what? Wake up, Kelsey. Nothing's going to happen with you and Lewis. Lewis clearly knows it, and you're the fool putting their whole life on hold for a fantasy."

"That's *not* what I'm doing." There's a bite to my words, the anger in me rising. "So what if it I'm focused on Lewis right now? After all he's been through, I'm pretty sure most people would see that as a nice thing."

"But you're not just helping him, are you? You forget how well I know you. You're still waiting for it to all turn out the way you want it to. That's what this is about."

It's like the kiss with Jakub has loosened everything inside me. The things I've pushed so far down, so deep inside me I've been able to pretend they aren't there, are now whirling to the top and I've got no control over it.

"Would that really be so bad?" I ask her. "Is it really the worst thing in the world for me to hope that one day Lewis gets to the point where we can be together?"

"No," Mum says, "not if I thought for a second it would happen. But it's not going to, Kelsey. Can't you see that if you were meant to be together like that, it would have already happened?"

"That's not true. The timing's never been right before, and just when it was the right time, this awful thing happened to Lewis. Maybe I do believe that one day it will all work out. I'm not going to let you make me feel like that's wrong."

"Timing," Mum says, her voice low now. "That's crap." She's shaking her head at me again, like she's disappointed in me. As if she has the right. An hour a week in fucking M&S does not give her the right to tell me what's going on in my own life.

"I'm not listening to this," I tell her, turning away and walking towards the path that will lead me back down to the beach.

"Fine," she shouts after me. "You keep going the way you are, but let me tell you, Kelsey, you're going to end up all alone if you do."

I whip back round to face her. "I am alone!" I shout. "Can't you see that? I'm already alone. I have been for years. Sorry if you hate the idea that Lewis is the person who gives me hope that it – that *this* – won't last for ever. You've got no idea what you're talking about. You don't know me well enough to comment on my life, Mum. So don't."

I take the path down to the beach before Gramps and Gran come out and Mum can tell them what I said. I've never spoken to Mum like that before. She's been so fragile to me for so long, I've never dared add to her load. I've been quiet and good and have minimised my shit for her sake. But I couldn't keep it up. Not today. Not with what she just said, and not after saying it straight after Jakub left. My mind was already too full to keep anything else inside it. Before we speak again, I need to keep walking and I need to regain myself.

But it's not just anger I'm feeling. It's that kiss. I walk quickly, hoping the movement will push out its lingering traces, but my body fails me. The phantom of his touch hovers over me, my lips still feel the pressure, and it's not exertion that makes me feel the beat of my heart radiating from my collarbone to my stomach.

I walk and walk and walk, but nothing fades. Not Mum, not Jakub. Eventually, I give up and sit down in the sand, the cool damp of it seeping through my jeans.

I need to go home. Back with Lewis, where everything makes sense. That's where I need to be.

thirty-three

Kelsey

I DON'T BOTHER TO GO INSIDE THE BUNGALOW WHEN we finally arrive back from Wales on Sunday afternoon. As I fling the car door open and jump out, I tell Gramps to leave my suitcase in the car and I'll get it later before setting off on foot towards Lewis's house.

Once I returned to the caravan, I was sure I'd open the door to find Gran and Grampssitting on the couch ready to tell me I was out of order, or to interrogate me about the kiss I expected she'd have told them all about. But Mum had chosen to keep it all to herself, and I chose to do the same. We carried on as though it had never happened. I was unbelievably grateful at first. But my brain insisted on replaying both the kiss and the argument so much, by the end of the holiday I wondered if it would have helped to talk about it, to get it all out in the open and properly move on.

The rest of the holiday passed with Mum and I focusing entirely on Gran. We tried so determinedly to fill the final rain-soaked forty-eight hours that yesterday afternoon, Gran begged us to give her a rest and let her read a magazine for twenty minutes without being disturbed. She told us her face was beginning to hurt from all the smiling and she'd like not to be stared at while she caught up on the latest celebrity gossip, and we were to do something, *anything*, as long as it didn't include her.

On a different trip, there might have been outrage at the nine o'clock checkout time from the caravan, but this morning, we were all ready at half eight with the fridge emptied and our bags packed. We didn't stop at the services on the way home, Gramps insisting on getting back. With all of us knowing each mile brought us closer to reality and finding out Gran's test results, the three-hour journey was miserable.

Now home, Gran needs her space. I don't want to be standing next to her while she fretfully checks the post and listens to any messages left on the landline answering machine. If there's terrible news, her and Gramps should hear it first. If I'm with them, their first thoughts will be how to comfort *me*, how to help *me* make sense of it, and I don't want that. The prospect of waiting for results must have been on her mind too, as when I said I'd go check on Lewis after we dropped Mum off, there were no objections.

He doesn't know I'm coming, and it's only when I start walking up Ellcott Avenue I wonder if this was the best idea. We're fine. Apart from that one phone call when he was short with me – which he later said was nothing to do with me but to do with a work problem and a colleague who was an arse – we've been chatting like always. In fact, the last few days I've even gone to my phone to find messages waiting from him, but it's not like I'm skipping back to him refreshed after the break. I can't stop thinking about Jakub and feel queasy with guilt not only for having that kiss but for not telling Lewis about it. That's the sort of information friends would usually share with each other.

But I'm here now, and the holiday is over. Determined to forget about Jakub, to not let Mum's words get to me, I stride up the street to his house.

Once in front of it, I'm met by a sight I'd never have expected. Sitting on the doorstep, leaning against my blue plastic box and speaking into the open letterbox, is Lana. She doesn't hear me approach, and is so involved in her conversation that I'm standing right behind her when I say, "Hi?"

I make her jump, and she turns round, her hand against her chest. When she sees me looming over her, she smiles.

"Kelsey! Hi."

"Hey, Kels," Lewis says from behind the door. I try and gauge his feelings from his voice, but I can't make it out.

"What's going on?"

Lana, noticing the concern on my face, laughs. "Oh, no, don't worry. It's all good. Lewis and I have just been getting to know each other since you've been away. I knocked on his door with some mail for him that had come to my house by mistake and we got chatting. Or rather, I chatted to him for an hour straight about all the things going wrong in my house since I moved in, and Lewis was kind enough to listen."

"That's completely true," Lewis says, and he laughs too.

I look down at Lana, who is smiling up at me, her face completely made up, her hair straightened and glossy, her leisure wear fitting her curves beautifully. Looks like I'm not the only one of us holding things back. In all the phone calls and texts this last week, Lana's name hasn't come up once.

She's waiting for me to say something, so I oblige.

"That's great," I say through gritted teeth. But as soon as I say it, despite my jealousy, I know it's true. It was only weeks ago that Lewis had removed himself from life so much that he couldn't even talk to me. Only weeks ago that Lewis was living a lie, that he was 'living his best life in New York'. Now he's at his door, talking to Lana, making new friends. It's huge progress and, rather than begrudging her being here, the sight of Lana on his doorstep brings a swell of pure joy. "I'm so pleased you've met."

"So how was Wales?" Lewis asks.

I drop down to the step, so I'm sitting next to Lana. "It was fine. Nothing much to report."

I can feel my cheeks blazing and turn to Lana to see if she's noticed, but she's facing the door, her attention not on me.

"Well, that's the update we were looking forward to," Lewis teases, and Lana barks out another laugh.

"Was it a nice place at least?" Lana asks.

"Yeah. Not the caravan, but it was good to be by the coast, to see the horizon."

"Ah, the horizon. Kelsey has a slight obsession with seeing the horizon," Lewis explains. "I've never known anyone notice it as much as she does."

"That's because I live in a city. Seeing the horizon doesn't happen that often."

"I completely agree," Lana says. "There's nothing that calms me and brings me back to what's important in life more than looking out to sea. It's been ages since I did that. Maybe that would put my dodgy boiler and cracked tiles in perspective. Speaking of which, I've got a plumber coming round shortly. I'll leave you both to it. Glad you're back, Kelsey. See you soon, Lewis." She unfolds herself effortlessly from the doorstep. She gives me a wave as she crosses Lewis's small patch of lawn to get to her house. I wave back and wait until she's inside before turning back to the letterbox.

"I can't believe you're talking to Lana now. That is brilliant."

"It's been a few five-minute chats, Kels. Let's not get carried away."

"Maybe, but it's still great. And have you told her about your situation?"

It's not been my place to tell her, not my place to do more than offer her a friendly wave when I see her, but I'm sure Lana must have been curious about what's been going on with her neighbour.

"She knows the script, yeah."

"That's really great, Lewis," I tell him again.

"I suppose so," he relents. "She's nice. A bit lonely, I think."

"Yeah, I got that too. Maybe I should invite her out for a drink one night."

"That's a nice idea," he says, before following it with what is definitely a chuckle.

"What?"

"Just you. Not content on fixing me, you're now moving on to my neighbours."

"Am I being too much?"

"No, no," his voice softens. "You're never too much. You're just very caring."

I smile at that, at the ease in which Lewis has always been able to sprinkle compliments into his conversations. "So, you've been all right then, since I've been gone?"

"Yeah. I've been fine, but let's not talk about me. I want to know how you are. Has your gran heard anything yet?"

"Not as far as I know. I came straight here after getting back, so there could be news when I get home."

"Whatever happens, you know you'll get through it, don't you?"

My throat closes up at the thought of what 'it' might be. "Yeah," I manage to get out.

"I'm sorry it wasn't the best holiday, Kels," he says.

An image of Jakub standing on the beach suddenly appears in my mind. For the first time, I wonder if keeping what happened from Lewis is the best idea after all. What if I do tell him – tell him that I met a man who found me wonderful, who I ended up kissing, who I ended up hurting. What if telling him makes him realise he loves me, what if him realising he loves me is the one thing that pushes him into getting help for his agoraphobia, what if getting help for his agoraphobia goes so well he's able to open the door and let me in?

"No, it wasn't the best," I say to him, choosing to erase Jakub

251

now, to leave only an empty beach and a clear view of the horizon behind in my memories. I remember Melissa's advice. Focus on the here and now. I'm not meant to be doing 'what ifs' any more.

"Such a shame," Lewis says. After a pause, in a softer voice, he adds, "I'm really glad you're back, though."

"Me too."

I lean my head back against his door and close my eyes.

Maybe I'm not quite ready to give up on 'what ifs' altogether. I'm here, and he's here, and we're talking, and as long as that keeps happening, there's always going to be hope.

thirty-four

Kelsey

DAYS PASS WITHOUT GRAN HEARING ANYTHING FROM the doctors. *No news is good news,* we all tell her – even Mum, who pops in for a cup of tea no less than two times in the week – but I'm not sure that's true. It was difficult enough for her to take her mind off the results when we were away, and now she's back, the wait is even more painful for her. I can't help but think that, whatever the news, it would be better for her just to have it.

When I have to go to work late Friday afternoon for the busy evening shift, she looks more tired than I've ever seen her. I tell her that with the weekend coming, it's a chance for her to try and take her mind off the results for a couple of days. She doesn't answer, just closes her eyes – as fed up with listening to the same pointless advice as I am of giving it.

Stepping through the glass front door into Ilk, my first sight is of Dessie scowling at Joy, who is scowling right back at her from the other side of the restaurant. The atmosphere is so tense it's a wonder the customers are eating and drinking away obliviously, rather than sitting in silence to witness a stand-off as epic in proportion as Harry Potter and Voldemort.

"What the hell is going on there?" I ask Tom, who has his back turned to the front door, looking as though he is waiting to make sure there isn't an all-out fight.

He turns to me, his eyes rolling so hard that his botoxed forehead produces a wrinkle.

"You would not believe the drama these two have caused today."

"What's happened?"

"You know that guy Joy started seeing?"

"The one from her course?"

"Yes. Well, turns out he came in here to see her one evening and found Dessie working instead. The snake asked Dessie out then and there – and has continued to see the both of them at the same time."

My mouth falls open in shock. "What the hell. How did they find out?"

"The absolute cretin only came in this afternoon when they were both working. It was terrible, Kels. Now Dessie and Joy won't speak to each other, and Joy keeps on going to the ladies every two minutes to cry. Don't suppose you can try and sort them out, can you?"

"What do you want me to do?"

"You're great at this. If ever there was someone to put an optimistic spin on a two-timing love rat, it would be you."

I narrow my eyes at him. "Charming. Fine, I'll try."

"Oh, Kels," Joy cries five minutes later, after I've swept her off to the ladies again and closed the door firmly behind us. "I really liked him. Why did Dessie have to ruin everything?"

"You know it's not Dessie's fault," I say. "It's the prick who two-timed you."

"I know," she sulks. "But still, why did it have to be her? I just know if he decides to choose between us, he's going to pick her."

"Then let him, and let Dessie be the one to tell him to go to hell. Both of you are far too good for him, and you're too good friends to let him come between you."

"Yeah, I know that. It just bloody hurts that the best thing to happen to me for years wasn't even real." She starts to cry again.

"It was real. Whatever you felt, that was real, and that's why you're upset now. Dessie's just the same. Why don't you talk to her? Let her know you don't blame her."

"I will," she sniffs. "Not yet, but I will."

"You're going to be OK," I promise her.

I pass her a paper towel, and she sets to work wiping off the mascara from under her eyes. I stay with her until she's stopped crying, watching her resolve strengthening.

"I wish you were always around like this," she says. "You can be a really good friend when you want to be."

She doesn't stay for a reply and heads out the door. I look at my reflection and ask myself what I see. I thought a good friend was exactly what I had been these last few months – but can I call myself that if it only applies to one of my friends and not the others? Joy's words hurt, but it's only because there's so much truth in them.

Ashamed, I turn away from myself. That's not the kind of person I want to be. Wanting to prove that I can do better, I decide to go straight to Dessie and have the same conversation with her. Only, when I open the door into the restaurant my feet stop, fear rooting me to the ground.

Gramps is standing talking to Tom at the front desk. His face is ashen.

"Isn't that your Gramps?" Dessie says, coming towards me. I catch her and Joy exchange a worried glance. When they texted midway through my holiday to see how I was getting on, I told them about Gran's biopsy, and they've been brilliant at checking in on me ever since.

"Yeah."

"You should go and see what he wants," Joy says, pushing me gently in the back to get me moving.

But I already know what he's going to say. There is only one explanation why Gramps is here, only an hour after I left the bungalow, and I can't go and hear it. I want to turn back and run down to the toilets, to shut myself away, only Joy is behind me, and Tom has turned round and is now pointing straight at me.

Slowly, I weave past diners until I'm in front of Gramps.

"Is it?" I ask, in a shaky voice.

He nods, and his eyes fill with tears.

"I'm so sorry," Tom says to us both. "Why don't you have a moment in my office."

I lead Gramps into Tom's cubicle of a room, which is nothing more than a converted cleaning cupboard, but at least there's a door I can shut behind me. I give Gramps a hug and feel my hot wet tears soaking through his jumper.

"This is why I came," he says, pulling back from me. "I know it's awful, Kels. I'm devastated too. But your Gran needs us to be strong. When the doctor rang, her first words were to ask how she was going to tell you. I know life's dealt you a tough hand, kid, and I know this is more of the same, but you can't show your Gran that. We all need to be there for her, OK?"

I nod. "I know. I will be. Do you want me to come home?"

"No, no. The news has knocked it out of her. She's gone to bed already. You stay here, and just be ready to offer her the love and support she'll need in the morning."

Once Gramps has told me about the operation she'll likely need, the course of treatment that may come after and how we all must wait until Gran's appointment with the oncologist to find out more, I stop asking questions, sensing how tired he is, too. He kisses the top of my head and starts to leave. Before he lets himself out of Tom's cupboard, he pauses and turns to me.

"Are you going to be OK? I know how hard this must be for you, love."

I give him the bravest smile I can. "Don't you worry about me. I'll be fine. But what about Mum? Does she know?"

"She does and she's being remarkably strong and practical about it all. I think she's going to be a real comfort to your Gran over the coming months. Just like you will be."

"That's good." I don't know how much I believe she's being strong about it, but I'm relieved Gramps and Gran do. I make a promise to myself to call her and check she's really OK. "Go on, you get back to Gran."

"I will. But if ever you're not fine, you let me know, all right?"

I nod in agreement.

"I'll see you soon," he says, before letting himself out.

The second the door shuts, I drop on to the leather office chair and bury my head in my hands. I'm not fine at all. My chest is so tight it hurts, and there's nothing I can do to stop the tears from rolling down my face and onto my uniform.

My poor, poor, beautiful Gran.

I don't know how long I'm lost in my upset. I only look up again when there's a gentle knock on the door and Tom enters the office. I do my best to brush the tears from my face.

"Honey, I'm so sorry. What do you want to do? Do you want to keep working or go home?"

I can't go home. The reason Gramps came to tell me tonight was to prepare me for seeing Gran, but I'm nowhere near as in control of myself as I need to be when I next see her. But the idea of serving carbonara to strangers and laughing at their jokes all night seems equally impossible.

"Would it be OK if I went home?" I ask, hoping the lie won't bring too much colour to my cheeks.

"Of course," Tom says. "You go. Joy and Dessie can share your section of the restaurant. Who knows, it might even help bring them back together."

"Thanks, Tom."

I walk out of the restaurant in a daze and get all the way to

Lewis's house without paying any attention to my surroundings. My brain is too overwhelmed to register anything else.

When I get to his front door, I'm shivering all over. Once I'm sat on his doorstep, I open the plastic box, take out the blanket I put in there and drape it over myself before knocking on the door.

There's no answer. I knock harder and open the letterbox flap to call his name.

"Lewis, are you there?"

I hear him rushing down the stairs and take his place on the other side of the door. As he sits down, I see a flash of a green jumper and denim jeans, a classic Lewis combination. It's such a comfort to be with him, to know I've reached the person I need to be with, I begin to cry with relief.

"What's happened, Kels?"

Relief turns to pain as I tell him why I'm here. "It's … it's Gran."

It's harder than I thought it would be to say it out loud. When Dad was ill, no one liked to use the correct words around me. I think they were trying to protect me from the reality of what was happening, but I remember finding it infuriating at the time. Mimi, Dad's mum, would only call it 'Dad's problem'. Never 'cancer', never 'his tumour'. It was like saying the words out loud would make it all so much worse, so they opted for a plan of playing it down and giving me the surprise of his death instead of giving me the hard truth.

Much as I'd wished they would just say it back then, the fear around the word must have stayed with me, because now I find it is thick like treacle, sticking in my throat. But for me to handle this, I'm going to need Lewis, and I have to say it.

"She's got cancer."

"No . . . I'm so sorry."

"I'd spent the last few weeks telling her it wouldn't be that – that it would be something else – but I was completely wrong. Oh God, Lewis, what if she—"

"Don't think like that. You're a long way from that, so don't even think it."

"I can't help it," I say, before I'm completely overtaken by the pain of it all and huge sobs take over my body.

"It will be OK," Lewis says from the other side of the door. "It will all be OK." His voice is filled with emotion, and when he sniffs, I know he's crying too.

The sobbing has left me slouched on his step, but I sit up now at the sound of him mirroring my pain. His life is so bound up with mine, there's nothing that would hurt me that wouldn't hurt him too. He has always felt my pain and he's always known how to take it away, ever since that first night I came into his house and he gave me *Family Guy* and bad jokes.

I take a few deep breaths so I know I'll be able to talk again, and wipe the tears off my cheeks and my chin.

"Lewis? Please could you let me in?"

The sound of him shuffling about escapes from the open letterbox. He doesn't answer for what feels like for ever.

"I can't." His voice is small. "I wish I could, but I can't."

"I wouldn't ask you unless I needed you to. Please, Lewis. I really, really need you."

260

"Don't do this. Don't ask me to let you in. I can't."

His reply is such a gut punch, I gasp at the pain of it. But no matter how winded I am by his rejection, I know I won't ask again. There's so much pain in his voice, it kills any notion of persuading him to change his mind immediately. Much as I'm hurting, he's hurting too, and this is only hurting him more.

"I know," I tell him. "I know."

"I'm sorry."

"Don't be. You've got nothing to apologise for. You've listened to me; you've said all the right things. You've done nothing wrong, Lewis. OK?"

We sit in silence for a few minutes before I stand up. I was so sure this was where I was meant to be tonight, but now I'm here I just want to be at home. I want to be near Gran, if she needs me. I want Gramps to know I'm going to be OK. I want to climb into my bed and think about how I'm going to cope with the long months that are coming our way.

"I need to go home. I'll see you soon," I tell Lewis, before walking away.

thirty-five

Kelsey

I TAKE MY TIME OPENING THE FRONT DOOR AND SHUTTING it again as softly as I can. There's no one in the lounge and Gran's bedroom door is shut. There's light coming from the kitchen, but I don't go to it. Gramps wanted me to be ready to be strong when I returned, and he'll see straight away I'm nowhere near there yet. I head straight to my bedroom and shut the door behind me.

I climb into bed still wearing my uniform, and turn on the TV, not caring what's on as long as there's some noise to keep me company. Automatically, I get my phone out of my bag and bring up Lewis's number. He'll spend all night talking to me if I ask. I could fall asleep with him on the other end of the phone if I needed to. On another night, I'd already be pressing on his name. But I know if I ring him now, the conversation would be tinged with the upset of what happened earlier.

I scroll through my contacts, trying to think of anyone else who could help. Joy, Dessie and Tom are all working. I know I need to call Mum, but that's a call that will pull us back to the fear and pain of my teenage years, and I can't do it tonight.

Before I give myself time to consider what I'm doing, I go over to my laundry basket in the corner of my room and begin to sift through clothes until I pull out the jeans I was wearing when I last saw Jakub. I pull out the piece of paper with his number on it from the back pocket.

I never expected I'd be typing his number into my phone a week after seeing him, but I've got to do something to escape from the thoughts swirling round my brain – about Dad and Gran's diagnosis, and all the terrible 'what ifs' that might be in our future. I not only add Jakub as a contact but press the green button without hesitation and call him.

He picks up after the fifth ring, and wherever he is, it's somewhere loud because he has to shout into his phone. "Hello?"

"Jakub?"

"Yeah, who's this?"

"Hi, Jakub, it's—"

"Kelsey? Wow, hi. Hang on a sec, will you?"

I listen to the sound of him opening a door, asking someone to let him past and the music fading, all the while thinking I should hang up but never doing so, until he's back on the phone.

"You still there?"

"Yeah."

"It's so great to hear from you. And a little surprising," he says, laughing. "After the way we left it, I thought there was no chance you'd call."

"No, I wasn't going to. I probably shouldn't have. It's just, my Gran . . . she got some really bad news today. She's got cancer.

I needed to talk to someone, and because you met her, you'd be able to picture how lovely she is when I told you."

I'm crying again, the upset too great to be contained, and I hold the phone away from my mouth while I try to stop.

"Your poor Gran," Jakub says, sympathy replacing the amusement in his voice. "I'm so sorry, Kelsey. Is there anything I can do?"

"No. Nothing. I should leave you to your night. I guess I just wanted to tell someone. I hope you don't mind me calling."

"No, I'm glad you did. You can call me whenever you want." He sounds achingly sincere.

"I'll be fine in the morning. I'll see Gran, and I'll be strong for her. I'm just not quite there yet."

"OK, but if ever you're not quite there yet again, you call me, OK? Anytime."

"Thanks." I should leave it at that but, before I can think about it, I find myself adding, "It's nice to hear your voice again."

"Yours too. Every time I hear the Liverpool accent now, I think of you. I found this really old soap called *Brookside* on YouTube that's set there, and I've grown strangely fond of it. Have you heard of it?"

I burst out laughing. "Er, yeah. I only grew up with it. I'm glad you like it. Keep watching, that's my advice."

"Oh, I will."

I smile into the phone. "Thanks, Jakub. You've helped."

"I'm glad. Goodnight, Kelsey."

* * *

264

The next morning, I wake with a start. I sit up, aware that there's something important for me to remember, but it takes my brain a few moments to shift the fog. When Gran's diagnosis comes into focus, I fall back onto the pillow.

The bungalow is silent. I can't hear any traffic outside, only the lacklustre caw of a crow nearby. It must be early, and I hope Gran is still asleep. Turning onto my side, I reach for my phone to check the time and see two messages. The first is from Lewis. The second is from Jakub.

I press Lewis's message, sent at 2.43 a.m.

LEWIS: I can't sleep thinking about earlier. I hate that I couldn't be there for you the way you needed me to be. I know you said I don't need to be, but I am sorry. If you're able to, please come round in the morning.

I feel terrible that I've caused him a sleepless night. I should never have asked Lewis to let me in last night, never put him in that position. I went to his house wanting my best friend, and he gave me that. It was stupid to ask for more.

I come out of his message and there, on the screen, is my next mistake. Jakub.

JAKUB: If you ever need anything, let me know. We might not know each other well, but I really do care about you. Speak soon, J xxx

Ugh. My stomach roils with regret. I was meant to leave Jakub on that beach in Wales. That was the simple choice, but now I've made it messy. He has my number, and he knows I'm upset. He's not the sort of person who will leave the phone call at that. I'm pretty sure 'speak soon' isn't an empty saying to him – he means it.

I roll out of bed, pull my hoodie over my pyjamas and walk out of my bedroom, leaving my phone and messages where they are. I'll go and see Lewis this morning and make things right between us again. I'm not so sure what I'll do about Jakub.

The hallway is dark, and I walk towards the half-light coming from the lounge. I'm itchy with tiredness and plan to lie on the couch with the TV on in the hope I might forget about the mess I made of everything last night and fall asleep. Only, when I get to the couch, I find it already has an occupant: Mum.

I go to the front of the couch and kneel in front of her – smelling for alcohol, checking she hasn't choked on her own vomit. I tried to avoid it last night by not calling her but seeing her here has plunged me back to being fifteen all over again, to the days after Dad died when it was just Mum and me, the suffocating air around us black with grief.

But I don't smell alcohol. And rather than her face being caked with sick and saliva, she actually looks quite nice, with lip gloss on and a smudge of blusher on each cheek.

"Kelsey, what *are* you doing?" she asks, opening her eyes and sitting up quickly, without wincing at the movement. She's dressed in an unrumpled jumper and a pair of jeans. Both clean.

"Mum?" I search her face for a reason she's here, and her clear eyes look back at me.

"You don't need to worry," she tells me, guessing my thoughts. "I'm OK. It's going to be OK. I didn't want your Gran to wake up without me here, so I came round about an hour ago – only I forgot everyone in this household spends the morning in bed."

"It is only six, Mum."

"Well, anyway. I wanted to make everyone breakfast and for us all to come up with a plan of how to fill the weekend. The next few days are going to be very hard for Gran. It's natural that her mind will go to the worst-case scenario, but we've got to remind her that it's just a diagnosis at this stage, that there's every chance she'll get better, that knowing is a good thing. Once she's seen the consultant and there's a treatment plan set up, she'll feel much more able to cope."

"I agree," I tell her, amazed at her calm demeanour and practical ideas. I look down at our hands intertwined and feel her now squeezing mine.

"I'm glad. Now, do you think you'll be able to sort work out so you can be around this weekend? It will be good for us all to stick together."

Work isn't even a consideration. I know I can ring Tom and he'll get my shifts covered. What I'm not sure about is if I can let an entire weekend go past without seeing Lewis after last night, without making sure he's OK.

"I was going to see Lewis this morning," I tell Mum, not meeting her eye.

"Can't you call him? Your family need you. You know there's no one else Gran would rather have with her than you." If there's hurt in that sentence, she's careful not to show it. My eyes meet hers and I'm amazed to see there's no judgement in them, no upset. Just strength. There's no way Gran's diagnosis won't be hurting Mum, no way she won't be falling back in time, like I have, to Dad having cancer – saying the same reassuring words to Gran she must have said to Dad – and the months that came after it. But she's still here.

I do something I never do then. I give my mum a hug.

"I'll stay," I whisper into her ear, and she hugs me back.

thirty-six

Kelsey

"AM I FORGIVEN?"

"There's nothing to forgive," Lewis tells me.

"I shouldn't have left like that. I wish I could have come round earlier than this to apologise. I wasn't mad at you, you know. For not letting me in. I'm sorry if me not coming round made it seem like I was."

It's Wednesday, five whole days after I walked away from him. I wanted to see him earlier, but there hasn't been a right time. There have been a few narrow chances to see him – between being with Gran, going with her to the hospital yesterday, and taking the early shifts to make up for my absence over the weekend – but I've been so tired, I've not been able to force myself into the cold, relentless rain that's fallen since Friday to make the journey to see him. Today, even though I was woken by the cackle of more raindrops against my bedroom window, I knew I didn't want another day to go by without sitting with him, putting things right.

Now, umbrella balanced against my shoulder, sitting on a plastic bag on the doorstep to stop my bum getting wet, I've said what I needed to say. I immediately feel better for it.

"Please stop apologising," Lewis says. "I'm just glad you're here. How's your Gran?"

"She's doing OK. Mum was right, once she saw the consultant she started to feel more in control of things. She's going to need an operation and a course of chemo, but the cancer hasn't spread and the consultant is hopeful it will be enough. I've left her writing a list for Gramps of all the things she'll need in hospital, even though the operation's not been booked in yet, and I'm to go to the library after seeing you to nab all the best books for when she's recovering."

"That sounds like the Gran I remember. She does love a list. So you're OK, then?"

"Yeah. I wasn't, but I'm getting there. Mum has been amazing. She's been the one that's held us all together."

"That's great. I bet you didn't see that coming, did you?"

"Nope."

I'm about to make a joke at my mum's expense when Lewis coughs, clearing his throat in that way he does before he broaches a subject that's difficult.

"I'm glad you haven't been back for a while, actually."

"Oh. If you don't want me here . . ." I start, hurt at his bluntness, but he interrupts me with an apologetic laugh, as though he's just heard what he's said.

"No, not like that. Sorry. I mean it's given me time to think about that night you came round, how I reacted to you telling me about your Gran. I wish I could take that night back. I wish I could

270

have opened the door when you asked me to and put my arms around you like you needed." He pauses. "I'd like to do that now for you, if you still want me to."

I stand up, my heart pounding so much I feel a little sick. I can hear him moving on the other side of the door, I can hear a bolt being drawn back, the turn of a lock . . .

"Lewis, stop!"

I hardly know what I'm saying – all I know is that this feels wrong. Lewis isn't opening this door because he's ready. He's doing it because of his guilt at not offering me what I asked for. The one thing I promised I wouldn't ask from him in the first place.

"What?"

"Just wait a second. Let's talk about this," I say. "Sit down again. Please."

I return to my plastic bag, and after a few seconds the lock clicks back into place and I see his legs as he sits back down on the hallway floor.

"What's going on, Kelsey? I thought you wanted me to do that."

"Were you ready to do that?"

"You need me, and I let you down. I want to be there for you. Properly. Not from behind this bloody door," he says, his words sharp with an anger he's turned on himself.

"That's not what I asked. Were *you* ready to do that?"

"I don't know," he answers, quietly now. "Probably not. But I want to be ready. So much. You need me, and I hate not being able to let you in."

"I know. But I'm OK, I promise." It's only once I say it that I recognise the truth of it. I am OK. I'm devastated about Gran, but I'm handling it. Since finding out, I've been surrounded by family, and by Tom, Joy and Dessie. After that first night of finding out, I haven't been on my own at all unless it was through my own choice. The people in my life have worked hard to get me through this last week. Dessie and Joy have been texting constantly and have taken me out to Starbucks twice. Tom has been amazing at work, giving me the easiest jobs and long breaks where we've sat together and he's plied me with free food. I've *wanted* Lewis, but I haven't *needed* him.

Suddenly, a memory of Jakub appears. Us standing on the beach, and him saying what a lot of pressure it is to put everything on one person, to rely solely on that one person to give you everything you need. Perhaps he was right. I know Lewis can help me get through the next few months, to deal with everything that happens with Gran, but I don't *need* him to. For this, I don't need him to open his door, not if he's not ready.

"Really?" Lewis asks.

"Really. Like I say, Mum's been amazing and my friends at work have been so kind. I've got people looking out for me, so please don't feel like you need open that door for me. Only let me in when you're ready, OK? If it's helping you to stay in there, to deal with what happened to you, you do that. No pressure from me."

"Wow," Lewis says, and we both laugh. I can hardly believe I've just said that either.

"Can I ask you something, though?" I say. "*Is* it helping? You staying in the house?"

He takes his time to think about that. "I don't know," he says, eventually. "I'm hardly having a rich and full life in here. Not unless you count watching every boxset going on Netflix. But, right now, there's not really another option. Me staying inside is about control. When I'm in here, alone, I can control everything. There's nothing that can surprise me, no situation that isn't of my own making. That's what agoraphobia has been for me. I always thought it meant you were scared of being outside, but it's what happens when I'm outside, the fear of feeling anything close to how I felt those few times I went out after the attack, that terrifies me. Inside, there's none of that. You stepping inside this house and bringing all your life with you means giving up a bit of control. I would have done it, I honestly would, but it would have been hard."

"I'm so sorry, Lewis." I realise I haven't asked him enough about this, about how he is feeling. "You've been through such a huge trauma. It's going to take time to heal from that."

"Thanks. And, yeah, that's what Lana says too. She pointed out that we all have this terrible tendency to think that we can – we should – bounce straight back from everything that life throws at us, but it's not true. We need time to heal, and we need to give ourselves that time."

"Lana said that?" I'd presumed Lana and Lewis's conversations were more about neighbour gossip and what days the bins were being put out.

"Yeah. She's, erm, she's been great. She has this calm way about her, a way of looking at things and making sense of them, you know?"

"Right." There's absolutely no place for jealousy in this conversation, but, much as I try, I can't get rid of it altogether. *Calm* Lana. Lewis must see her as my pole opposite. "She's right," I say, pulling myself together. I remind myself to be glad Lewis has Lana. Haven't I just been telling Lewis how much it's helped me having other people around? "You've got to heal."

"Thank you, Kels." I hear him sigh. "Honestly, I didn't see today going this way. I thought I'd be the one comforting you, but here you are making me feel better. I'm so glad I've got you."

"I'm glad I've got you, too." After a moment, I add, "But I'm completely dripping here, and this umbrella has about two more minutes until it completely collapses. See you tomorrow?"

"I'd love that," he says.

thirty-seven

Kelsey

"SORRY KELS, I'VE GOT A MEETING COMING UP AND I'VE done bugger all so far today," Lewis tells me when I arrive the next morning. I'm about to protest, to ask why the hell he didn't text and save me a trip, when he follows it up quicky with, "Mum's here though, and she wants a chat with you, if you're free. You can go into the garden rather than sitting here, if you like."

"Really?"

"Yeah. I'll be upstairs. Might as well sit at a table than on the doorstep. I'll go and find her and get her to let you in the back. Speak later?"

"Sure."

It's strange to know that Melissa is in there right now, while my boundary is so clearly marked. It makes me wonder how many other times she's been in the house while I've been sitting on his doorstep.

"Hi, Kels. I'll go round and open the gate," she says, as she passes through the hallway. I feel strange – like an outsider, someone who is lingering on the periphery – but I quash it by telling myself Lewis letting me into the garden is a pretty big step forward, one that he seemed to have no trouble making.

I don't want to get ahead of myself, but it's hard not to notice the progress he's made recently.

I go round to the gate, which is at least eight feet tall and as wide as two regular gates. It's not made from wood, but from steel. By the side of it is a keypad I've never noticed. He's got this place set up like a fort. Living here isn't just about him having a place he doesn't need to come out of – it's having a place that no one can get into. How big a deal it is that I'm being let in now hits me all over again.

"Come through," Melissa says after she opens the gate, and I follow her down the side of the house and into a huge garden. A line of poplar trees at the bottom block out any view and a lot of light, and lining each side of the perfectly manicured grass are conifers, which have been allowed to grow to the height of the house. Despite its impressive size and the immaculate lawns and patio area – which has a beautiful round wooden table with eight matching chairs under a wooden awning – the space is claustrophobic and, in this weather, a little depressing.

I turn back to the house and look in the bifold doors to a huge kitchen with dark grey units and a white marble island, copper lighting and handles giving it warmth. It's a beautiful room, and it more than makes up for the garden. I hope he spends hours in that kitchen, music on, cooking meals on the huge range, an open bottle of wine on the worktop.

"This is beautiful," I say.

"Isn't it? Sit yourself down. Do you want a coffee?"

"Yes, please."

She opens the bifold door just enough to slip inside and shuts it after her. I spend the time waiting for her to come back peeking into the other two windows on the ground floor. The back of the house seems to be one huge room, with a dining area leading off from the kitchen and a snug lounge at the end with a massive TV on the wall. It's all beautifully decorated and very expensive-looking.

Melissa appears after a few minutes with two steaming mugs of coffee.

"This is nice," she says, coming to sit next to me. "It's been a while since we had a catch-up. I wanted to say I'm so sorry about your Gran, love."

"Thank you."

"I've got to say, you seem to be handling it remarkably well."

"I don't know about that," I say.

"You are. You're stronger than you give yourself credit for – than perhaps we all give you credit for." She smiles at me. "Lewis told me about yesterday. He said he was going to let you in, but you told him not to. I don't mean this to come out the wrong way, love, but I was surprised when he said you'd told him to keep the door shut."

I feel heat spreading from my nose outwards, across my cheeks. Is that really how I come across – so desperate for Lewis to let me in, I'd hurt him in doing so?

"I want to be further back into his life," I say, "but not until he's ready to have me."

"That's good. I wasn't at all sure how you were going to handle this, but you're really helping him." She reaches for my hand. "I'm so pleased you're here."

"Me too. I'm glad you think I'm helping. I wish I could do more."

"I know, but it's hard to know what else to do. I tell him every day that he should speak to someone, he should get the help he needs to find a way to cope and to get back into the world, but we both know he won't until he's ready to."

"No. Back in school, the panic attacks . . ." I say, recalling the time. "He just carried on, didn't he? I don't know if I really appreciated the severity of it. Seeing him now, I've been wondering about that – about how bad it really was for him, the panic attacks and then going off to university all alone. I knew he was a little reluctant to go, but I pushed him, thinking it was the right thing for him . . . but now, I don't know."

"I've been thinking the same, too. Given what's happened, it's hard not to remember him then," Melissa replies.

"Yeah." I nod. "It makes me think about how easy it is to put things in the past, like it's a cupboard you can shut, only those things aren't really shut away at all – you still carry them round every day. He was vulnerable back then, wasn't he? I didn't see it enough."

"Nor did I," Melissa says. "Sam did, though. I'm certain that back then he saw himself as the one with everything, and Lewis, who was ill with stress and fawning after you, as someone to be pitied. He must have hated seeing Lewis become so successful, rich and happy."

I'm thrown by the random mention of my ex-boyfriend. The colour suddenly drains from her face, and before I can say more, she stands up, collecting my still full cup of coffee, splashing large drops onto the wooden table.

"I should get back to it."

"Why did you bring up Sam?" I ask, confused at the mention of him alongside the abrupt change in her manner. There was hatred in her voice as she spoke of him, and Melissa doesn't hate. Not unless she has very good reason to.

"No reason."

"No. Why Sam?"

After a few long seconds, her tense shoulders fall, the wind goes out of her, and she folds herself back into the seat.

"He didn't want you to find out."

"Find out what?" I ask, but my pounding chest and tremoring hands tell me I already know. I need to hear her say it.

I'd accepted Melissa's explanation for why Lewis didn't want to tell me about his attacker without question. It made sense to me that he didn't want to think about who did this, wanted to shrink that person by depriving them of a name, of a personality. So, I left it. Not once did I consider there was more to it, that there was a deliberate reason he didn't want me to know.

"It was Sam. He was the one who attacked Lewis that night."

His name is like a punch to my gut.

"But . . . Lewis said he'd been attacked because he helped a girl who was drunk, and the boyfriend didn't like it."

"That's true," Melissa says. "But the boyfriend was Sam, and the reason he didn't like it was because the person helping was Lewis."

"I can't believe this." I stand and begin to pace, the mixture of shock and anger and sadness sending too much energy through my body. "Why tell me everything else but keep this from me?"

"I know you might not believe it, but he was looking out for you, Kels. He didn't want to bring you into this any more than you needed. He was trying to be selfless."

"Lewis has a habit of telling himself he's being selfless when actually what he's being is selfish and cruel to me," I say, before I can stop myself. "He lied to me, decided what I could and couldn't know. And so did you. I thought we'd come so far, but we haven't at all. He might as well still be pretending he's in New York."

"That's not fair."

"I think it is," I tell her. Then I walk towards the gate and let myself out.

thirty-eight

Lewis

TWENTY-FOUR YEARS OLD

NOT EVEN THE DEAFENING HOUSE MUSIC AND THE thumping of his head that six pints had given him could rid him of the guilt. What was he thinking, leaving Kelsey like that? He should have stayed with her, made sure she was OK, fed her Oreos to soak up the booze until she was ready to talk about the kiss. He should have been honest with her and told her how he felt. It would have been the most painful thing he'd ever had to do, but she deserved to know the truth. It wasn't right to let her go on thinking this was the start of something, when it was really an end. Somehow, he should have found the words to tell her he loved her more than ever, but not in the way she wanted.

But he wasn't doing any of that now, because instead, he was here, in a packed club in Chester, where everyone was off their faces on drink and drugs. He'd managed to smile through the beers and chat in the nice, trendy bars they'd been in, but he couldn't pretend to be anything other than miserable in this dive

281

of a place. He'd been here an hour already, standing alone by the bar, watching Matty and Kyle disappear to the toilets every two minutes before starting to jump around on the dancefloor, and he couldn't stand it any more. Spotting Matty drifting towards the end of the dancefloor, he took his chance. He weaved in among the crowd to reach him, but before he could tell him he was going home, Matty lunged towards him and gripped him in a bear hug.

"Yes, Lewis! You ready to help me out?"

Lewis remembered some vague promise about being Matty's wingman if he saw some girls he wanted to chat up. He was surprised that his supervisor, usually so responsible and quiet, was like this on a night out, and he wondered how he would handle the nine o'clock call they had booked in for the morning after.

Lewis managed to break free from him and had just started to tell him he was off, when he was pushed from behind. He spun round, ready to bollock whoever it was, but found the guilty person was a slim girl with unfocused eyes who seemed unable to stay on her feet. The slurred word she was saying must have been sorry, but it was too hard to hell. He looked around for her friends, but she appeared to be alone.

"Come on," he said, abandoning Matty and turning his attention to the girl. "You look like you could do with some water."

He helped her over to the bar and, with a hand loosely round her waist to stop her from falling, he ordered a pint of water.

"What the fuck do you think you're doing?" came a voice from behind. When he turned round to explain, he couldn't help but smile at the coincidence. Puce-faced, vein throbbing in his neck, was Sam Partington, Kelsey's ex-boyfriend. They hadn't seen each other since Lewis had left for university at eighteen and Kelsey had broken up with him shortly after. Now, here they were at a random dingy club in Chester.

"Sam! No way. How are you?"

"It's you," Sam said, flatly. "What the fuck do you think you're doing with my bird?"

Lewis looked down at the girl next to him, reluctant to take his hand away from her waist in case she fell. "I was just helping her get a glass of water. She had a bit of a tumble on the dancefloor."

Sam turned to his friends and began to laugh. "Bit of a tumble," he mimicked, and the friends dutifully laughed. "Forgot you were a posh twat now. Look at you with your shirt and your chinos. You're in a fucking club, mate."

"Yeah. Well, nice to see you too."

Lewis was happy to leave it at that now that Sam had given him a reminder of what he was really like – nothing like the decent and gentle act he'd put on for Kelsey. Walking away, Lewis felt gratified that he'd never fallen for it. But Sam didn't seem in any hurry to part from Lewis.

"You still knocking about with Kelsey? Still trying to get her to shag you?"

He stopped walking at that and spun back to answer. The smug expression on Sam's face was infuriating.

"We're still friends, yeah. I'm sure she'll be delighted to hear I bumped into you. Oh, but then again, maybe not. Wasn't she the one who dumped you?"

Sam charged at him, pure hatred on his face. Lewis braced himself, but his friends grabbed Sam's shoulders, pulling him back.

"Not worth getting chucked out for," one of them said.

Lewis's stomach bottomed out as he watched Sam fighting with his anger, unsure whether he would try again. But all of a sudden, the anger disappeared and Sam smiled at him.

"Good to bump into you, mate. Look forward to seeing you again," he said, before he abruptly turned and walked off, leaving his girlfriend at the bar.

Lewis stayed to make sure she drank the water, and only when her friends had finally come to find her and promised they'd make sure she got home safely did Lewis think about leaving. The exchange with Sam had left him uneasy, and all he wanted was for this night to end so he could get back to Liverpool and to Kelsey.

Stepping out into the cool night air, Lewis shut his eyes for a moment and took in a deep breath. Just then, a whistling noise to his right made him turn, and out of the shadows of an alleyway, Sam and his two friends emerged.

"Hello again," Sam said.

thirty-nine

Kelsey

"I WISH YOU'D BE ANGRY AT ME. YOU MIGHT FEEL BETTER IF
you call me a prick."

Lewis is trying to make me smile, but I don't give him the
satisfaction. It's been three weeks since Melissa let slip about Sam,
and nothing has changed. I'm still coming to sit at his door most
days. We're still talking and he's still trying to be funny. Gramps
still bakes for my visits, and we still eat blondies or cheesecake
or muffins and marvel at how good he is. Lana comes and goes,
sometimes joining us, and I still push down the same jealousy
that I feel whenever I listen to their easy banter.

Nothing has changed, but everything has – because I can't get
over the fact that Lewis's attacker was Sam, and Lewis didn't tell
me. He gives me his reasons, and I try to understand them. He
didn't want to make me feel like I was a part of this, and he hated
the thought that I might feel guilty because it was my ex who did
this to him. He didn't want me connected to any of it. The way he
saw it, the only way he could have me back in his life was if I could

step away whenever I wanted, and he didn't think I'd be able to do that if I knew Sam was his attacker. He didn't want me to feel in any way that I was bound to him because of what happened.

I listen to these reasons one day and then ask him to tell me again the next, because, noble as he thinks he's being, it's bullshit. After all the lies he told about New York, he had a choice when I came back into his life about how to proceed and he decided to keep lying. That hurts more than thinking he was away for a year. It hurts more than him telling me we won't be together. He weighed up his options, and still thought I wasn't able to handle the full version of events.

I am not only angry but insulted that he made decisions about what I could and couldn't handle – that we still haven't been at a point where we're open with each other because he's chosen to keep this huge detail of what happened to him from me. I'm seething with the pain of it all. But I can't show him that. If I still want to help Lewis, showing him how I really feel is only going to push him further inside.

I can rage at Sam, though. I want Sam to feel every molecule of fury I have for him. I keep imagining visiting him in prison. I'd sit opposite him and not look away, making him face up to what he's done. I like to plan withering lines I could use to make him feel the pain of what he did, cruel barbs that he would carry back into his cell. But for Lewis's sake, I know I never will. I have to be content with hating him from afar.

"I don't want to call you a prick," I tell Lewis. "I want to understand why you didn't tell me."

He's been so patient, repeating the same reasons over and over again, but today I hear a sigh of annoyance.

"I know you do, and I wish I could make you see it the way I do. Misguided as it might have been, I was trying to do the right thing."

"I know."

We're about to fall into silence when he asks, "Aren't you doing the lunch shift at work?"

I check the time on my phone and push myself up off his step. "Shit. I need to go. Speak to you later?"

"Sure," he says, and I pretend to myself I didn't hear another sigh.

* * *

It's cold out, and I burrow my face down into my scarf as I wait for the bus. When it arrives, I step into a sea of woollen coats and laptop bags. I sit next to a man doused in aftershave, and I read the BBC news headlines alongside him on the phone he holds out far enough for me to get a good view of. The morning bustle of the city only quietens when I reach the docks and I breathe in the cold air coming off the Mersey.

Ilk isn't open for another half an hour and the only person around is the barman, John. I say hi before going down to the toilets to get ready for the day. When I drop my bag in Tom's office fifteen minutes later, the office chair swivels round and Tom comes into view, curled up on it like a cat.

"Have you slept there?" I ask, shocked at how dishevelled he looks.

"No," Tom grumbles. "That was the plan, but I haven't managed to."

"What's happened?" I ask, already sure I know the answer. Henry.

"I told him no," Tom says. "Last night, he asked me to move in with him and I told him no. He wasn't even looking for an answer there and then, but it just came out. I told him it was too much to upend my life, that moving in with him would make it too hard to get here for work and I'd have to find a new job. I asked if we could keep going as we were, but he said he didn't want that. We broke up, Kels."

He starts crying and I go towards him, crouching down and putting my arms round him. "Oh, Tom. It was the right thing to do. You love your life. You couldn't give everything up for him."

"I know that. Doesn't stop it hurting though."

"I'm sorry. Is there anything you want me to do?"

"Can you open up for me? I wouldn't ask, but no one can see me like this. And don't tell Dessie and Joy. They're both working this evening, and I'm not ready for them to gloat yet."

"They won't gloat," I tell him. It's true, but it doesn't mean they won't be delighted. They were both so angry at Henry for trying to change Tom, I wouldn't put it past them to open a bottle of champagne at the news. "I won't say anything, though. And I'll go and open up as soon as I've brought you a coffee and a pastry."

"Thanks, Kels. I knew you'd understand."

"I do. You love him. It's the hardest thing in the world, letting go of that. Let me get you this pastry."

I've been so exhausted recently, I'd hoped for a quiet morning. But with Tom out of the picture, I spend hours running around, welcoming customers and showing them to their tables before going on to serve them. John has to come out from behind the bar to help me. The complaints we accrue between us for our slow service would make Tom explode if he were out here. Not a good shift for tips.

It's only in the half-hour lull between our brunch menu finishing and the lunch menu starting that I'm able to stop for the first time. I go behind the bar to help myself to an orange juice and am just starting to drink it when the door opens again, and another customer comes in. My first instinct is to duck down behind the bar and wait it out until he goes, but it's too late. He's already seen me and is bounding across the restaurant, a handful of customers watching with their mouths open.

I thought he looked incredible when he was wearing that tight T-shirt from Jan's and shorts, but Jakub in a suit is another level entirely. He looks so sleek he could have come here straight from shooting an advert for a designer aftershave, and he's walking towards *me*. Me with my bouffant hair from the wind earlier and my sweaty face and stains on my apron.

By the way he's smiling at me, I can tell this is all going according to plan. I bet he's got a sexy opening line all worked out.

I pre-empt it by blurting out, "What the hell are you doing here?"

A flash of surprise crosses his face. We've spoken at least a half dozen times over the past few weeks, our last conversation only a couple of days ago. After me calling him about Gran that first night, he's taken to checking in on me. It's been surprisingly comforting to have him to talk to. Sometimes, it feels too much to put all the stuff with Gran on Lewis, considering everything he's going through, and since finding out about Sam, it's almost felt like we're at our limit of problems to deal with. With Jakub, it's easier. He has this tendency to keep the conversations about me. I might ask him about his day or his own family, but I'll often come off the phone an hour later having pretty exclusively talked about how I'm doing. An hour into our last conversation, after I'd cried while telling him a story about how Dad once took me camping when I was ten and ended up checking us into a Marriott three hours later because we both hated it so much, I told him how glad I was he'd called. So I guess I can understand why my greeting right now might not make the most sense to him.

"Hi," he says.

"Hi. What are you doing here?"

"I'm here for a few meetings, and I thought I'd take the chance to see you. Is that OK?" he adds, his bravado failing him.

"Yeah. It's really nice to see you. Only, I'm working." It *is* nice to see him. I'm taken aback by how nice it is. I didn't think I'd ever see Jakub again, and it's only now he's here in front of me it hits me how pleased I am that we stayed in touch. But it's the wrong day for this. My day and my mind are too full to find any more space to discover what him being here is really all about.

"I can see that," he says. "I've got work too, but I thought I might grab a quick coffee with you and see if you were free tonight."

"I'm sorry, I can't. I'm covering for my manager, and don't have time to stop."

As if on cue, Tom comes out of his office. The transformation from the devastated Tom I left a few hours ago to the one who is now smoothing out his shirt as he strides over to us is remarkable. It's amazing the power a hot man can wield.

"Jakub, this is my manager, Tom," I say, once Tom has joined us at the bar. "Tom, this is Jakub."

"Manager and friend, thank you very much. Lovely to meet you, Jakub," he says, shaking Jakub's hand. "We've heard so much about you."

"Really?" Jakub asks.

"Oh, yeah. Kelsey's told us all about the holiday, the rugby ball . . ."

"Oh God." Jakub grimaces before laughing.

"So, what brings you here, *Jakub*?" I give Tom a death stare to tell him to cut it out, but he's determinedly not looking at me.

"I was just saying to Kelsey, I'm here for work until tomorrow. I was hoping to have a coffee with her but she's busy, so now I'm hoping she'll say she's free tonight."

"Nonsense. You can have a break, Kels. I'll man the fort. You two catch up. And if you want to come back later, I'm sure I can sort out some drinks on the house for you."

"That's great! Thanks." Jakub turns to me with a big smile on his face.

"No, I can't have a break, actually," I tell them both. "I don't *want* a break, in fact. I've got a busy day ahead and, I'm sorry, Jakub, but you turning up without any warning doesn't work for me."

"I'm sorry," Jakub says quietly. "I thought—"

"You thought wrong then," I tell him, before going round to the other side of the bar and walking towards a group of four customers who have walked in.

Jakub sits by the bar talking to Tom for another five minutes, before he walks past me on his way out.

"Sorry, Kelsey. I should have called first. I wanted to surprise you. I didn't think it wouldn't be a nice surprise."

"Jakub, wait," I call after him. I don't want him to leave. A small part of my brain is screaming at me to start over – to tell him it's wonderful to see him and jump at the chance to be with him again. The part of my brain that is all-too-aware of how my heart sped up as soon as I saw him, and how taken aback I was again by how lovely he is.

At the door, he turns round to look at me.

I meet his eye but don't smile. I can't.

He stares back at me for a few moments before turning and walking out, his head shaking as he does.

"Everyone ready to order?" I ask, turning back to table I'm waiting on.

Tom waits until I've put the order into the kitchen before he taps me on the shoulder and says, "A word, please."

I follow him back to the office, sure I'm going to be told off for failing to mention quite how gorgeous Jakub is, but I'm met with something entirely different. His eyes are wide, and his mouth is turned down like he's about to cry.

He pulls me into a hug, squeezing me until it's almost painful.

"It's OK," I say. "You'll meet someone else. I know you will."

"Oh, Kels. This isn't about me. What *are* you doing?" he asks, pulling us both down to sit on the chair, which can only really hold one of us comfortably.

I'm thrown back to the argument outside Jan's with Mum, after she saw me kissing Jakub and asked me exactly the same thing. "I'm not doing anything."

"An absolutely stunning man has just come to see you, he's stood in front of you and had the guts to ask you to give him a chance, and you've let him walk out the door. I repeat, what are you doing?"

"Maybe I'm not as powerless to good-looking men as you are," I say, nudging him playfully, but he's clearly not in the mood to joke.

"Bullshit. Even if he didn't look like that, he was nice. Like, really nice."

"Yes, he's nice. Now can we get back to work, please?" I ask, trying to shuffle away from him so I can stand up, but he puts his hand on my arm.

"No, not until I've said this to you. You're stuck, Kelsey. I've never seen it more clearly than I just have back there with Jakub. You're completely stuck. Working here, living at home, turning down everything that comes your way. You might think this whole just-friends thing with Lewis is working, but it's crap, and we can all see it. You still believe you're going to end up together. You cling to Lewis like he's your whole future, but he's not."

"That's not true. I don't cling to Lewis. What's going on between us right now is far more complicated than you make it sound, and you know that."

"No, Kels, it's not," he says gently. "Please listen to me, because I know what I see. Henry and I have broken up because we knew we weren't going to work together. It hurt like hell because I cared for him, but it was better to have the hurt now and get on with life than wasting years of it on something that wasn't going to give me everything I wanted."

I let out a laugh of despair. "Oh my God, please tell me you're not comparing what you had with Henry with me and Lewis."

"Maybe not exactly, no," he says defensively. "But I know what I saw with Jakub, what you just turned your back on, and I'm worried about you."

"There's really no need to be, OK?" I give him a smile to try and show him how fine I am, how wrong he is.

Tom gets off the chair and holds his hands out for me, in a sign of peace. An argument would be easier to handle than this concern, but I'm not going to get one from him.

"Look, it's your life. You do what you think is right, but make sure you really are thinking about it. That's all I ask. Make sure you're certain whatever's going on between you and Lewis is right for *both* of you. Because you're giving up an awful lot for it."

forty

Kelsey

I'M EXHAUSTED BY THE TIME I GET HOME IN THE EVENING, but my mind is whirring too much to crawl into bed and try to forget about the day. Despite my best attempts, what Tom said has clung to me, and the best way to get rid of his words is to talk to someone about them, to have someone help me peel them away by telling me how ridiculous they are. I look for Gran, but Gramps tells me she's out with Mum at Sainsbury's, buying some essentials for her hospital stay.

"That's good," I say.

"It is," Gramps replies, giving me his raised left eyebrow glare, the most powerful and least-used warning expression in his armoury. I've not seen that one for a good while.

"I know," I tell him. "Really."

I'm fine with Mum taking over. Gran is happy that she's around, that she wants to help, and I am too. Only, now I've nothing to do but try and get what Tom said out of my head on my own.

"Are you sure you're not free tonight?" I ask Lewis when he picks up the phone. I won't tell him what Tom said, but at least being with Lewis might help me prove him wrong. If I'm lucky, I'll go over, and there will be another glimmer of something that gives me hope there's a future together still out there for us.

"Positive."

"Sure?"

"Yes. I've got a ton of work this evening. Even if Dua Lipa called round wanting to chat, I wouldn't be able to fit her in with this packed schedule."

"Interesting. Let me ask you this: hypothetically, if you did, perhaps, happen to have a spare half an hour tonight and could only see one of us, who would you choose? Me or Dua Lipa?"

"Oh, Kelsey. Like you don't already know the answer."

"Dua Lipa." We say at the same time, and I grin.

"You're my first choice tomorrow, though. See you about eleven?"

"Sure."

When I hang up, I notice a missed call from Jakub and my voicemail has a new notification. I consider putting my phone away and ignoring him, but eventually give in.

"Hi. I'm sorry for dropping in on you like that earlier. I really am here for work, by the way, and I really am leaving tomorrow. If you're not free later, that's fine, but if you are and fancy keeping a lonely traveller company, I'm staying at The Titanic and it would be great to meet for a drink. Or I could come to you? Whatever's best. Let me know. OK, bye, bye, bye. It's Jakub by the way. Bye. Bye."

Once the message has finished, I listen to it again. With his

Polish accent and low, gravelly tone, he has the best voice for leaving messages. He could easily have his own podcast giving an insightful window into the world of banking, or he could talk about the weather. It wouldn't really matter.

His offer is tempting. Night after night sitting with nothing but my own thoughts for company is becoming painful, and it will be all the more so tonight, thanks to Tom. I could do with a distraction. Seeing him would also give me a chance to apologise for being crabby to him this morning. If he's going tomorrow, tonight is my only chance – and I'd rather him go back to London with a nice memory of me than a sour one.

"Going out, Gramps," I shout in the direction of the lounge.

I text Jakub on the bus to let him know I'll be in his hotel bar in half an hour and immediately receive a thumbs up.

It's only when I get to the hotel bar and take off my coat, I take note of how swanky the place is and how underdressed I am. It's a beautiful space, all low lighting and dark colours, the rose gold light fittings and candles on each table beacons of warmth. It's a place to lose yourself in for a few hours, somewhere to feel special.

On the tables that are taken, there are a variety of delicious looking cocktails and glasses filled with expensive wines. Most of the women are wearing thin dresses or silk shirts. I spot at least three men in suits and, as I look round, I'm deflated to discover I'm the only person in the building in knitwear. Jakub will most likely come down in his suit and immediately fit right in, while I'll be left in the role of his frumpy friend. At least my hair is freshly washed and curled, rivalling the blow-dried locks of the nicely dressed women. After I take a seat in a booth in the corner, I scrunch up the waves at the bottom of my hair and pat down the top.

Jakub keeps me waiting for nearly ten minutes, but all is forgiven as soon as I see him and discover he's gone for a woolly jumper of his own and a pair of jeans which have seen better days. I wave him over and he slides into the booth next to me.

"Sorry," he says, after looking around at the customers himself. "All I brought with me was my suit and my scruffs. Should have gone for the suit."

"I'm glad you went with the scruffs," I tell him. "We match."

"Hardly," he says. "You look great. As always."

I don't know what to do with the compliment, so I push past it and ask him what he wants to drink.

"Would it be tragic if I said a Diet Coke?"

"Not at all. The cocktails look incredible, but a Diet Coke is exactly what I want too."

"I'll get them. You stay here," he says, and slides back out of the booth. I watch him as he leans over the bar to speak to the waitress, watch how she starts smiling at him and doesn't stop until she's poured our drinks, taken his payment and moved on to her next customer. I bet all his days are like this, filled with pleasant interactions and easy smiles. I hope they are. He's too nice to be unhappy, and yet it's there, underneath his smooth surface, a vulnerability that ever so often shows itself in the drop of his mouth or a gaze that's held a little too long.

As soon as he gets back, I launch into the speech I prepared on the way over. "I'm sorry about earlier. I was rude. I had a lot on today, and I might not have shown it earlier, but I *was* pleased to see you. Sorry if it didn't come across like that."

He places a hand on mine and waits until I'm looking at him before giving me a sad smile, not at all like the kind he gave to the waitress.

"It's fine, Kelsey. You're not interested. I get it."

I could leave it at that. It's been nice having Jakub to talk to recently, but it could stop easily. A few calls I don't answer, texts that I don't read, and I could end our burgeoning friendship easily. It would be the simplest option, only I know he deserves to know the real reason. I start to tell him about Sam being Lewis's attacker, and how difficult it's been dealing with the change from his attacker being a stranger to his attacker being my ex-boyfriend.

"I'm so sorry, Kelsey. I wish you'd told me."

"I should have, but you've been so good talking to me about Gran, it felt too much to share that with you too."

"OK. But, just so you know, there's no limit on what you can share with me. If I knew what was happening with Lewis, I wouldn't have barged in today presuming you could drop everything for me. I'm sorry."

"No, it was nice of you to come and see me. I'm glad you did," I say, honestly.

"You are? Well, that makes me feel less foolish." He takes a sip of his drink. "So, what's the plan with Lewis?"

It's such a simple question, but I don't have an answer. *Keep going the way I am until he realises we're better together than apart* doesn't seem to cut it any more. *Keep helping him until my help allows him to fall back in love with me* was the real plan, but that's not something I feel comfortable saying out loud.

"I don't know. Right now, I can't even begin to think about that."

"Then don't. We're only together for a little while, and I might be wrong but I think we could both do with making the most of that and having a nice night."

He's right. Tonight, I want to feel happy. I'm sitting here in the nicest bar I've ever been in with a kind, handsome man who makes me feel completely at ease, and my heart is telling me to allow that in.

"I agree. I'm ready for a night off my stuff, which, to warn you, is going to mean lots of talking about you."

"Now I'm worried."

"Don't be. I'll go easy on you." I lean back into the luxurious cushion of the booth seat and settle in. "Let's start with how your trip has been so far."

"Boring," he says. "Apart from the bits where I've seen you, obviously."

"Obviously."

"I've been stuck in meetings. I had big plans to see the sights, and I've not done a single touristy thing."

"What did you want to see?"

"The museums, the docks, the Liver Building, Anfield."

I nod. "Well, what are we waiting for? Maybe not the museums, but you could still see everything else. Come on," I say, before picking up my glass and downing the Coke in one.

"What?"

"I'll show you around. It won't take long. I can't have you going back to London having only seen hotels and meeting rooms."

Grinning widely, he follows my lead and we stand up together.

"This way, sir." In full-on tour guide mode, I take his hand and lead him outside, but when we stop on the street and he looks down at me, that decision begins to feel dangerous. We're so close to each other and looking up into his eyes reminds me too much of being on the beach with him in Abersoch, of that urge to kiss him.

"Come on, we'll go to the front," I say, dropping his hand and marching off.

"Wait up."

"It's getting dark. We should get a move on."

"If it's not a good time, we could always go back to the bar. Of all the things I wanted to see in Liverpool, you were number one. So I'm happy to just go back, if you'd prefer."

I stop on the street. "Why?" I ask. I don't get it. Yes, we've been getting on well, but I can't see a point when I'd given him any hint that there might be more between us than a long-distance friendship. "Why are you so keen to see me?"

He holds his hands up. "OK. *Maybe* these last few weeks I've let myself hope a little that something romantic might happen between us somewhere down the line. That the kiss we had really did mean as much as it felt like it did at the time."

Pushing past the stomach flip caused by him talking about the kiss like that, I go for the obvious question, the one anyone standing in front of Jakub hearing him say stuff like this would be mad not to ask. "Out of everyone you could have, Jakub . . . why me?"

He looks at me levelly. "You're joking. How could I not? Kelsey, you're funny and you're beautiful, and you might be going through a hard time right now, but you're so strong. Look at the way you've handled everything with your Gran."

I'm not used to people flinging compliments like this at me and, touched as I am he's saying all this, it's hard to believe.

"Thanks. But I don't feel strong. I feel a bit of a mess, to be honest."

"I'm sorry," he says, squeezing my hand, and he's so genuine, so caring, I have to swallow down the lump in my throat. "I realise that we're not in the same place, and I promise once I go back to London we can go back to chatting on the phone or, if you don't want to stay in touch, that's fine too. Whatever you need."

It's almost as though he sees my brain stumbling over what to possibly say in response to that, and I'm grateful when he helps me out.

"Now, come on. I've had a complete change of heart over those cocktails. How about we put the guided tour on hold, go back to the hotel and you let me buy you a ridiculously complicated drink instead?"

forty-one

Kelsey

I WAKE UP THE NEXT MORNING WITH A SORE HEAD AND a smile on my face. Last night ended up being the most fun I've had in a long time. Jakub and I went from sitting in a booth at his hotel bar drinking beautifully presented cocktails, taking sips of each other's as we worked our way through the menu, to taking seats at the bar and chatting to the bar staff after we realised we were the last people in there. It's the first time I've properly been in a group with Jakub, and he was so easy-going, so warm, the bar staff were only too happy to keep serving us drinks way past closing time.

I stay in bed and replay last night, wondering why I've woken up feeling different this morning, why something has shifted in me. I eventually work it out. Last night with Jakub was so easy. Light and easy and fun. Everything else in my life feels weighed down with complications, and the contrast is startling.

I don't think I'd quite appreciated how twisted and tangled mine and Lewis's relationship had become, but I see it now. Finding out about Sam has shaken the foundations I'd built our relationship on ever since I found Lewis in his house, and I can no longer keep standing on them in the hope they'll hold us up. Last night with Jakub didn't make me love Lewis any less, but it did show me how unhappy I've been recently and how it's not fair to me or to Lewis to keep going the way we are.

"You're right to tell him," Joy says, on the video call I have with her and Dessie for moral support before I leave the house. Joy is walking to her first seminar of the day and the path behind her is strewn with students, who she seems oblivious to. Dessie is still in bed, wanting to catch up on her beauty sleep before an audition in the afternoon.

"If you tell him how you feel, you'll be in a better place for what comes next. Go over there, do what you need to do and call us after," Dessie says.

"Yeah, promise you'll call? And if you need us, I'm not working tonight."

"I am," Dessie says. "But that means you can come into Ilk and let me sneak you drinks if you need me to."

"OK," I say. "I promise." I hang up and start to get ready.

* * *

"I've got something I need to tell you," I say, once I'm by Lewis's door. A cold wind whips against my ankles and nips at my face, and I lean into his door to try to escape it.

"Go for it."

I can picture Lewis on the other side, leaning in, a faint smile on his face. Ready to hear something light – another funny story from a bad magazine, like I often bring him. My stomach rolls at the thought of what I'm bringing today. Complete honesty. Last night, telling me how he felt about me, Jakub made it look easy. Then again, it's easier to be open to someone you've only known a short amount of time. If things don't go the way you want them to, you can move forward and the pain of the loss will only leave a small mark on your life. With time, you'll barely notice it. But when you've cared about someone as long as I've cared for Lewis, the pain of that loss is enough to rip your life into shreds.

I'm terrified, but also certain we can't go on as we are.

"These last few months, I've been trying to imagine what it must be like for you not to be able to leave your house," I start, "and I've wanted to do whatever I could to help you."

"You are helping, you know that," he says, kindness making his voice soft. "You went and proved my keeping-you-out-of-my-life-being-a-good-thing theory completely wrong, remember? I was actually thinking about that this morning, and I wanted to say thank you. Since you've been coming round, I've been able to see that there are things I can do to make my life a bit better. I can't leave the house, I'm still way off thinking about that, but I don't feel as trapped any more. You and Lana, you've shown me I can still control how I want my life to look, and that's pretty huge. So, thank you."

I should have just come out and said it. That way, I wouldn't have to deal with the pain in my heart that hearing him say that caused.

"That's good. But the thing is, you're making me sound so much better than I am."

"Go on," he says. His voice is wary, I'm sure he knows exactly what's coming. Perhaps he's been aware of it all along, even more aware than I have been.

"I wish I could say helping you to get better has been my only agenda, but it wouldn't be true. I told you I was fine just being friends, that I knew there was nothing else between us, but that was a lie. As soon as I knew you were here, in Liverpool, so close to me, it made me think that there was still a way for us to end up together. Even though you kept telling me it wasn't possible, that I needed to forget that, and even when I was promising I was fine with just being your friend, it was there. I didn't acknowledge it at first, because I really did want to help you, but this whole time I've been hoping you'll get to a point where you could open the door and fall madly back in love with me."

After a few moments of silence, he says, "Fuck." His reaction is so apt, I almost laugh.

"Yeah. I was sure I was getting somewhere for a while. Once we got used to this set up, it felt like we were getting on better than we had in ages. It was like the old days, only, and I hate to admit this, it was better. It felt like we were becoming everything to each other again. I was waiting for you to see it too, because then you might open the door, let me in, and we'd be together, like I'd been wanting for so long."

He doesn't speak for the longest time, and each minute that passes makes me grow queasier. Sweat pools under my arms and I have to bite my lip to stop saying something to take it back and give him time to put together what he needs to say to me.

"I'm such an idiot," he says eventually, his voice low. "For a while there, I really thought you got it. You telling me to keep the door shut, that was such a huge thing. It felt like a breakthrough, you saying I should go at my own pace. I took it as a sign you were genuinely OK with this. I should have known better."

There's a bite in his words, and I understand it. It's so tempting to stop myself, to go straight to apologies in order to keep him close to me. But I can't do that. I need to get it all out, and that includes letting him understand my own anger for the first time.

"Yeah. And I should have known better too. I should have known that I was only telling myself I was fine with the lies you told me because I wasn't ready to give up on the idea of us. I forgave you so quickly because there didn't seem to be another option. But then I found out about Sam, and now I can't pretend any longer."

"Sam, again," he says. "We've talked about nothing but him since you found out. Honestly, I don't see why that's the bit you can't get over. I keep explaining why I didn't tell you it was him."

"I know, but the thing is I can't make your reasons matter enough. You lied to me."

A cold, humourless laugh escapes from the letterbox. "I'm sorry, after what you just told me, you're turning this back on me? Not sure you're the one who gets to be indignant here, Kels. You knew how much it mattered to me to be in control of my life. No, it more than mattered – it's how I've survived. Every other person in my life spends their time telling me I need to face my fears, that I need to go and get help, but you never did that. I thought you were the one person . . ." He pauses and the sudden upset in his voice nearly breaks me. "You were the one person who was different. You never told me what to do, only accepted me and the situation as it was until I was strong enough to change it. But all along you were trying to control me into becoming the old me, the Lewis you knew and loved before his face got fucked. So, no, Kelsey. You lied to me."

I close my eyes and push myself to keep going, to keep showing him how much he's hurt me too.

"You're right. I have lied. But so have you. Somewhere along the line, you decided not to trust me with everything. You decided I wasn't strong enough for honesty. So, yes, I've let you down. But you've let me down too, Lewis. This whole thing between us is a complete mess."

My throat aches unbearably, and I can't do anything to keep a sob from leaving me. What I've done today has damaged us more than anything that's come before it. For the first time since I found this house, neither of us are pretending, and I know there's no coming back from that. There's no slipping back underneath our blanket of lies and omissions, no matter how comfortable we find it.

"I love you more than anyone else in the world," I tell him when he doesn't reply. "I hate that we've ended up like this."

I lean back against the door and close my eyes, exhausted, despite it only being ten in the morning. My right ear is up against the letterbox, so when he next speaks it's like he's whispering into it.

"This has all been such a mistake. Starting from when I sent you that first message pretending to be in New York. Now we both know that it's time to put a stop to it. We need to stop this. Don't come round again, Kelsey."

forty-two

Lewis

TWENTY-FOUR YEARS OLD

"HOW BAD IS IT?" HIS MUM ASKED WHEN HE CAME downstairs at half one in the afternoon. He didn't need to answer. She got off the couch and went to him, wrapping her arms delicately around him, careful not to press on his still sore ribs.

"Oh, sweetheart. What can I get you? Have you taken the painkillers?"

"Yeah. But they aren't going to do anything, not when it's throbbing like this."

"Don't you think you should set an alarm, that way you can keep topping up rather than sleeping so much and waking up in this much pain?"

He shot her such a sharp look with the eye that wasn't covered in a bandage, she held her hands up and walked into the kitchen.

"Sorry. I know you're right," he shouted after her. In reply she brought him back a cup of tea and a sandwich.

"One day at a time, remember?" she said, as she sat by his side.

"One day at a time," he parroted, but the words that he'd clung to when the doctor first said them, after he'd come round from his operation and had been faced with the awful facts of what had happened to him, were quickly losing their power. It had been three weeks since he was attacked, and the world that had seemed so inviting, so full of opportunity, was now terrifying to him. Aside from living with the pain that was morphing into new forms rather than fading as his body and face got used to his injuries, his hours were spent reliving what had happened to him on repeat. It was getting worse, not better. Every time he revisited those few minutes, he'd add a new detail that would make it even more brutal and humiliating. Sam looming over him, glass in hand, was there waiting for him each time he tried to sleep. The idea that things were going to get better in a matter of days seemed impossible.

His phone beeped, and he asked Melissa to pass it to him from the side table where he'd left it charging the night before. He knew who the message would be from, and knew he had to respond to it.

KELSEY: When are you free to talk? I miss you. Let me know when I can call you. I don't think I can face listening to your voicemail again! xxx

He let the phone fall out of his hand and on to the couch. It had been a week since he first came up with the idea of saying he was in New York rather than letting Kelsey know what had happened to him. He couldn't bear her rushing to his side, having to see the upset on her face as she looked at his. She would do everything in her power to make him feel better, he knew that, but she wouldn't be able to touch the sides of the hurt he was feeling. No one would, and he couldn't even bear for her to try.

This was his journey alone. As soon as he woke up from the operation, he felt a loneliness that he'd never known before – but being with people meant facing up to what happened to him. He didn't want to talk about any of it. He didn't want to pretend to be better than he was. He knew he had to do something to stop Kelsey coming round to the house, stop calling him and Melissa – and so he lied.

Then there was the kiss. He'd planned to tell her the truth, to let her know that, to him, it meant they could only be friends. But then this had happened. And in the messages that had followed since, it was clear the kiss signified something entirely different to her.

He couldn't deal with that right now. He wasn't strong enough to break her heart any more. It would have been easier to just let her go altogether, but he couldn't do that either. She meant too much to him.

"Let me guess. Kelsey again?" Melissa said.

Lewis nodded. "She wants to talk to me."

"That's exactly what you should do. Talk to her, put an end to this New York nonsense and tell her what's happened."

"You know I can't."

"But if she knew—"

"If she knew," Lewis stopped her, "she'd be here in a flash, and she'd try and fix me. I don't want to be fixed by her, Mum."

"So what, you're going to keep lying to her for the rest of your life?"

No. Lewis knew he'd have to stop eventually. He'd have to choose: tell her and let her in, or let her go.

"Not for ever, but for now, yes. Do you really think Kelsey is going to handle this? Going to handle me saying I don't want her around?"

"Maybe not," Melissa admitted. "She'll be devastated. But, if you don't want her around, you'd be better letting go of her completely. If you can't be honest with her – like I really think you should be – tell her you've too much going on to be her friend any more. Tell her anything that lets her move on. Anything that will hurt her less than this."

"I know you're right. It's just I can't imagine my life without her."

"Me neither," Melissa said, reaching for his hand. "But this is a mess, and you need to do something about it."

Melissa left to get them some chocolate from the newsagents. Lewis wanted to go back to sleep. The side of his face was throbbing, but ignoring it for a few seconds more he picked up his phone and brought up Kelsey's last message.

LEWIS: Sorry, Kels. Big meeting coming up at work I need to prepare for, and then I've got a drinks thing in my apartment block tonight. Life in the Big Apple is relentless! Can we talk another time?

His mum was right. This was a complete mess.

forty-three

Kelsey

I ALWAYS THOUGHT WHEN MY HEART BROKE, IT WOULD be this cinematic moment, almost romantic in itself. I would be outside, in a park or by the sea, it would be windy, and I would stand looking out at the horizon, tears flowing down my face before sinking to the ground, my dress billowing prettily around my legs. Or I would be at home, again in a beautiful dress, and there would be candles all around me. I would move through the room blowing out each of them one by one until I was in complete darkness. Or I would be somewhere exotic, in a luxury hotel, and I would move through the grounds like a ghost, my over-sized sunglasses masking the raw red under my eyes. The guests would whisper about me as I passed.

But in reality, my heartbreak is quiet and unremarkable.

I peel myself away from Lewis's doorstep and say, "OK. Bye."

And that's it. I walk away from him and keep going. My tears dry, there's no sinking to the ground, no billowing. If anyone were to look out of their cars and spot me walking on the pavement back towards Allerton, they wouldn't suspect a thing.

I keep moving, replaying the conversation with Lewis again and again as I walk down streets I don't know, past rows of shops that would ordinarily pull me in with the temptation of something sweet or a magazine. Every time I go over what he said, I hear the hurt of his voice as though he's still next to me, whispering it in my ear.

This has all been such a mistake.

It's almost an hour of aimless walking later when I accept the truth lurking underneath what's happened – the truth that I'm heartbroken, but I'm not shocked. This isn't a fresh wound, more like a chronic pain I've been ignoring for a long time that I've given a chance to steadily grow worse before acknowledging its presence. The first time I told Dessie, Joy and Tom about Lewis on a night out, a few weeks after starting at Ilk, Joy asked me if I thought we'd live happily ever after. My out loud answer was obviously yes, and it's the answer I wouldn't let go of while waiting for him to come back. But deep, deep down there was already a part of me that knew that was a lie. Deep, deep down I've known our relationship was never going to end up somewhere as simple as happily ever after. Our friendship was forged on the back of my grief. Lewis became the most important person in my life after I lost the most important person in my life. He came after Dad.

Was it ever going to be any different?

I'm a long way from Lewis's and a long way from home when I finally run out of steam and consider the possibility of doing something other than trying to walk the hurt away. It's cold out, and my throat is dry and sore. I could get on the bus and go back home. Instead, I take a note of where I am, where I'm near, and make a different decision.

I catch the confusion on her face as she steps into the porch and sees her visitor, but she's quick to cover it with a smile.

"Hi, Mum," I say, when she opens the door.

"Hello, you. What are you doing here?" Her face falls suddenly. "Oh God, it's not Gran, is it?"

"No, no. Not Gran," I say. Then, "Can I come in?"

Mum laughs and shakes her head. "Of course you can." She stands to the side so I'm in the house before her, and I'm the one to choose where we go. This is the hallway I spent my childhood rushing through – on the way out to school, Dad already standing by the car telling me to get a move on, or running through after getting home in the afternoon, desperate to get to the kitchen for a snack. This was a place I was rarely still, but I am now, indecision rooting me to the spot as I try and work out which room will be the least painful to be in, which might be the least likely to assault me with memories.

"Let's have a coffee, shall we?" Mum asks, taking the decision from me.

"Sure."

I step into a kitchen that's at once the one held in my memory and also completely new. The layout hasn't changed at all. The sink is still under the window, there are units all along the back wall, and there's a table by the French doors which is slightly too big and means you have to squeeze round it every time you want to go outside. Only, the units on the walls are white now instead of dark oak, there's no longer a red accent wall but grey and yellow floral wallpaper, and the floor is tiled white. The same picture of the three of us hangs on the bit of wall that juts out from where there used to be a utility room before Dad knocked through, but it's in a new chrome frame. Light streams through the windows, reflecting up off the tiles, filling the room with a brightness at odds to the day outside. I'm pretty sure Mum's not changed the sun itself, but it feels so different in here now.

"Wow. I didn't know you'd had work done."

"Last year," she says. "I should have had it done ages ago. Do you like it?"

I look around again before my eyes rest on Mum, who is biting her lip as she waits for my review.

"I love it. You've done a great job."

"Good." She pauses. "I'm sorry I didn't ask you if it was OK to change before I did it. You don't mind?"

"No. It's your house. Why would I mind?"

"Because it's your house too. I wasn't sure if you'd like me altering things. It was in desperate need, though. Let's just say some of your dad's handiwork didn't quite stand the test of time."

Instead of the mention of Dad being painful, when our eyes meet, we both smile. He really was terrible at DIY. I haven't thought about that for the longest time.

"I love it, Mum," I say softly.

"Good. In that case, I'm going to tackle the lounge next. Get rid of some of that awful chipboard."

I take a seat at the table while she busies herself making us cups of coffee from a coffee machine I didn't know she owned. She brings them over and sits opposite me. We sip our frothy drinks in silence and it's a little bit like our weekly mothering hour, only pleasant.

"What's going on, love?" she asks, putting her cup down.

"Lewis," I say, and she nods like she knew this was what I was going to say.

"Go on."

"I told him the truth – that I love him and haven't really been OK with being his friend. And I told him I was hurt by his lying – not just about Sam, but about everything. And now he doesn't want to see me any more."

After I say that, I don't cry, don't break down. It's the worst-case scenario, the thing I've been dreading for so long. But, strangely, I'm OK.

"I'm sorry, Kelsey. Although, I have to say, I'm amazed."

"What's that supposed to mean?"

"I'm amazed you told him that. I worried you would never tell him anything he didn't want to hear. Thank God you did."

Suddenly, with a few words, we're back to how we always are. To Mum judging Lewis, to her disapproval of me being with him.

"Thank God?" I repeat. "You've never liked Lewis, have you? You've always had a problem with him, ever since we became close after *you* sent me to live with him."

She looks at me steadily and takes a long breath before answering me.

"No, that's not true. This isn't about Lewis. Not really. It's the way you were together I didn't like. At first, he was exactly what you needed. He gave you something me and your grandparents couldn't. He gave you an escape, and I was so pleased you had that. But when he left for uni, something shifted. You started to hold on to him in ways that I didn't like. He'd be busy studying or chasing a dream job and you stayed here, never letting yourself grow because you wanted to stay the same for him, worried that if you moved on or changed it would affect your relationship. Your dad dying left such a hole, and I don't think you could bear the thought of Lewis leaving too."

There's so much painful truth in what she's saying. I feel closer to crying now than I have done since I arrived.

"Maybe I have held myself back, maybe Lewis does feel guilty for that, but I love him, Mum. Even after everything. How do I let go of that?"

"I've no doubt you love him, but there has to be a point when you say to yourself it's not enough. You telling Lewis the truth was you saying you're worth more, and I'm proud of you for that."

Our eyes meet and, despite how upsetting it's been listening to her, as we look at each other, the familiar tensions dissipate, until we're the most unusual thing: a mother and a daughter sharing a heartache together in our kitchen. My eyes wander from Mum to the picture of the three of us on the wall. I'm in the middle, smiling a gap-toothed smile straight at the camera, but Mum and Dad are looking at each other, their faces so bright.

"You know, I always thought, of all people, you should understand why I waited for Lewis. You and Dad, you had what we had. You were soulmates. Surely, you'd have waited for Dad and would have fought for him if it was the two of you in this position."

She laughs at that. "Yeah. I would have."

"See."

"But the thing is," she went on. "I lost my soulmate. Your dad was the light of my life, and when he died, for a long time, I thought I was completely in the dark. I couldn't see anything in my future, nothing other than the pain of him not being there. Turns out, though, I wasn't in the dark. I just had my eyes shut for a really long time. When I opened them, I saw you." Tears begin to fall down her face, and she bats them away with the back of her hand. It's been a long time since I've seen her cry. "I saw the friends that had stuck around, Gran and Gramps. I realised I wasn't alone. I won't ever meet another person like your dad, that's for sure, but I've got so many other people I care for, and that makes me know I'm going to be OK. I just wish it hadn't taken me so long to see that. I hate the damage that's done to our relationship."

"It's fine, Mum. We're fine," I say, smiling at her, wiping tears off my cheeks. She's never told me this before, always tried to keep her grief about Dad away from me. I can see that never talking about him, letting me stay with Gramps and Gran, removing herself from my world, have all been ways to protect me from seeing how heartbroken Dad's death left her. But seeing it, sharing it, would have made both our journeys so much easier.

"I hope so. You see, it's not that I don't like Lewis, Kelsey. It's just that I wanted you to find those other people, to discover other soulmates in friends, maybe even in me, so that you weren't putting everything on one person. I know how dangerous that can be." We sit quietly for a moment. "I think, in a lot of ways, we have been the same. I know you lost your soulmate too, when your dad died. You two were so close, and it was so unfair that you had to let him go so soon."

I have to turn away from her to look out into the garden, a garden that's blurred by the tears that are now streaming unchecked down my face. We've never spoken about Dad like this before, and the pain of losing him hits so hard I can barely breathe.

"The difference is, when I was thinking I was all alone, you found Lewis. You had this person who became everything to you. I know it must be terrifying to think that you're going to lose him, but you won't, not if you can find your way back to being friends. You can keep him as a soulmate that way, you can keep him as your person, but you can also move away from him, let him get better. Let go of loving him so much and let yourself live."

"I don't know if I can," I admit, the idea of not being with Lewis, of us going our separate ways, too huge to contemplate.

"Oh, you can, sweetheart. If you let yourself move forward, who knows? You could meet the love of your life. You could find yourself new friends, even new family, eventually. Don't you see? You moving on doesn't mean losing Lewis. You'll still be the soulmates you became when you were teenagers, but you'll also have those other people, so Lewis doesn't need to be everything to you. Your heart broke into pieces when your dad died, and you can't expect only one person to have the power to put it back together for you. You've a much better chance when you've lots of people to love, lots of people to help fill in the gaps your dad left in different ways."

"I don't know," I say again, but this time I feel less uncertain. A tiny, grainy image of a future different to the one I've spent so long dreaming of appears in my mind. It's so small, I can't make out the faces of the people surrounding me. I don't know where it is, if I'm ever going to get to it, but that image gives me a new kind of hope.

"You can," Mum tells me. "It will be the best thing you can do for both of you."

forty-four

Kelsey

SIX WEEKS LATER

"YOU'VE GOT TO TELL LEWIS," TOM SAYS, ONCE I'VE HERDED him, Dessie and Joy outside for a break and told them my plan.

"Not the first thing I thought you'd be saying."

He runs his hand over his new short hair and gives his head a shake. "No, you're right. The first thing I should have said is, I'll be gutted if you leave. You know I will. I don't even want to think about all the glasses that will go unsmashed or the orders that won't go wrong. It will be hell without you." He gives me a playful smile. "But you've got to tell Lewis."

"He's right," Joy says. "Think what it did to you when he disappeared out of your life. You can't do the same to him."

"I don't want to," I tell her. "But it's not the same, is it? We're not even meant to be friends any more."

"No. It's not," Tom agrees with me. "But you still have to tell him."

The knot of nerves in my stomach tightens. I know I have to

go and see Lewis one last time, but I have no idea if he will even speak to me. He hasn't been in touch once since I last walked away from his house, and I haven't tried to get in touch with him either. The time apart has been hard, but it's helped too. I kind of wish I had more of it, but I made my decision last night and I owe it to Lewis to tell him.

"Are you sure?" Jakub said, when I phoned him to say yes. "There's no rush."

"Seriously?" I asked, smiling. "Now you want me to slow down? You've only been trying to convince me every night for a fortnight."

"I have not. I'm fully on board with whatever decision you make, I've simply been pointing out the many, many benefits of you moving down here."

"I know, but the decision is I'm coming. So you better make sure this London is as good as you make it out to be."

"It's going to be even better," he told me.

At first, Jakub's suggestion was practical. His flatmate had just moved out, so he had a spare room. He pointed out that London was overflowing with restaurants gagging for talented waitresses to work in them. If I wanted a change of scene, he said, given the room and the chronic staff shortages, now might be a good time to get one in London. I dismissed it at first, with everything going on with Gran and her recovery from her operation, the upcoming chemotherapy, but the more we spoke on the phone, the harder it became to say no, to turn down a chance for something new and exciting with Jakub by my side. I'd been spending so many hours on the phone to him the last month, enjoying listening to how his day had gone, him sharing the parts of London he'd ventured to that day, the food he'd bought, the people he'd talked to, that me going to live there with him didn't feel like the gigantic step it once would have. When I told Gran, she looked happier than she had in months and told me having an adventure like that would be the best thing I could do for her.

"What if Lewis asks you to stay?" Dessie asks now.

"He won't." I don't mean it to sound so sad, but after I've said it, all three of them reach for me. I get a squeeze of my hand from Dessie, a pat on my leg from Joy and a hug from Tom.

"Right, come on, slackers," Tom says, once he's let me go. "You've three hours of your shifts left, and you can't be spending it out here."

We file back into the restaurant, Dessie and Joy first, Tom and I last. I reach for his elbow just before he walks through the fire exit back into the bustle.

"How will I know if I'm doing the right thing?"

"You won't, but you've got to trust yourself. It's your decision. Listen to your heart. Listen to what it's telling you."

* * *

I never went back to collect the box. It sits there now by Lewis's door, filled with the things I used to take out all the time when I was sitting chatting to him. The blanket, the cushion, the stash of Freddos.

I ring the doorbell, not hiding to the side so he won't know who is here for him when he checks the app on his phone, but standing in full view, a small smile on my face.

"Kelsey?" My name, when he says it, is a question – which I suppose after six long weeks, it would be.

"Hi. Can you come to the door? I need to talk to you."

"Sure," he says, without hesitation.

I sit on my normal perch to get ready for him, but, despite the cold wind that bites the skin between the bottom of my jeans and the top of my boots, I opt to go without the blanket. We're not back to where we were, and it would feel as though we are.

"Hi," he says, once he's opened the letterbox.

"Hi."

"What are you doing here?" he asks, cutting to the point. A ripple of fear courses through my body when I think about what I'm about to say, but at the same time I'm grateful not to have a preamble.

"I came to say I'm sorry. For not respecting you more. You were telling me what you needed, but I wasn't willing to listen. I should have listened properly.'"

I hear Lewis blowing a long stream of air out of his mouth.

"Wow. Thank you." He pauses. "I'm sorry too, for pushing you away like that. For telling you half a truth instead of everything. You weren't the only one who made mistakes. You were right about me making decisions not to trust you – I should never have done that. I owed you the truth about what Sam did to me. It should have always been up to you how you handled it."

I didn't come here expecting any admission of guilt from him, but I'm grateful for it.

"You were right about me not coming around for a while. We needed space. *I* needed space."

"I think we did. But I've been so worried about you," he says.

"You didn't need to be. As well as saying sorry, that's what I'm here to tell you. I'm OK. Really, there's no need for you to worry any more. I can't lie, when I left your house that last time, my heart was broken. I had no idea how I was going to cope without you. But I've been OK. Hurt, upset, but also OK."

He is quiet for a moment, and then says, "That's good?"

"It is. It's amazing, really, given how long I've loved you."

"Oh, Kels—" he starts, but I cut him off.

"No, you need to hear this. It's OK, Lewis. I've been in love with you for years, but I can see now it's not always been the healthiest love. It's been a love that's based on how wonderful you are, how funny and kind and clever – but it's also been a love that's based on fear. You were everything to me, and I couldn't bear the idea of ever losing you. Since I was eighteen, I've dreamt of you as a future boyfriend, a future husband, and I've put those images in front of who you really are, who you've been from the start. You're my best friend, Lewis. I spent so many years thinking that being best friends somehow wasn't enough. But it always was, wasn't it?"

"Yeah, it was," Lewis says, and I'm able to breathe out when I hear his voice isn't angry or upset, but resigned and full of the kindness for me it's always possessed. "It's funny. What you're saying, I could have said to you. I spent the first few years of our friendship imagining you as my girlfriend pretty much non-stop.

I pretended to be OK with you as my friend, when I wasn't really, so I get it. We've been in the exact same positions, only at different times." After a moment, he adds, "Do you know I was going to ask you to the prom?"

I let out a shocked laugh. "You were? I had absolutely no idea."

"Yeah. I'd even bought you flowers. But I realised you needed me as a friend more than you needed me as a date for prom, so I changed my mind. By the time I left for uni, I'd got used to pushing down my feelings, and, when I left, that's what I missed the most. Talking to you, being best mates. I was never sure, though. I never quite got the idea out of my head that we could be more, until that first kiss. It didn't feel right – like we were starting something that might ruin what we had. I guess that's when I realised we were always meant to be friends, nothing more."

It hits me that we've never even talked about that kiss, and how we both felt – everything got so swallowed up in the attack that followed. We stay silent for a few moments, both lost in our own thoughts.

"Should I have told you that?" he asks.

"Yes, you should have. I always want you to tell me the truth."

"We both got pretty good at not being honest, didn't we?" he says.

I smile. "Yeah. Experts in not telling the other how we felt."

"If I could go back, I'd do so many things differently. I'd never have lied to you, for a start."

"Me too. I'd never have forgiven you so easily."

"Fair. I'd never have left you after we kissed. I'd have stayed and talked about what it meant for us."

"I'd never have got pissed and kissed you when I was in such a crappy place in my life. I'd have told you how I was feeling before I laid one on you."

We could go on, but instead, we stop. There's a whole history of wrong turns from being young and in love to reflect on, but I'm not here today to look back. We've got to see what comes next.

"Do you think we can keep any of what we had?" I ask.

"I do," he says. "But I hurt you, and you hid your feelings from me, and us going back to this, to sitting on opposite sides of the door, doesn't feel right any more. If everything stays the same, I don't know how we get past that without one of us having to pretend again."

"That's partly why I'm here. I've got some news I wanted to tell you." This is the bit I'm dreading, and I brace myself for the words. "I'm moving to London. Next week. I've a friend there – Jakub – and he's got a spare room and he's offered it to me. I wasn't sure if it was the right thing, but I figure I've got to try. I want to try."

"What? Kelsey, that's great!"

"Really?" I didn't expect his reaction to be that instant, that positive.

"Of course. I'm so proud of you for doing this. You deserve to have some excitement." The genuine notes of happiness in his voice help unravel the knots in stomach.

"Thanks."

After a pause, Lewis asks, "Jakub? You've never mentioned him before. He's a friend of yours?"

"Yeah. Right now, he's a friend," I tell him honestly. "A good one."

"That's great." I can imagine him smiling on the other side of the door, and I smile too.

"The only thing is, I'm worried about you. I don't like the idea of you being alone."

"Don't you dare worry about me. I'm fine," he says. "I've actually been doing a lot of thinking too, and I don't want to stay behind this door for ever. I've started looking into seeing a counsellor – or video calling a counsellor, at this stage at least – but I've got to do this on my own, at my own pace."

"I know you do," I tell him.

"In the meantime, I do have *some* company . . ."

I know who he's talking about at once, and I start to smile. "Lana."

"Yeah. She's been coming round a fair bit. Makes no sense to me. I've told her I've nothing to offer her, but she keeps sitting where you are, and all I know is I'm happy about it."

"Oh, I know exactly why she's coming over. She's realised how brilliant and funny and wonderful you are. Good on her." I'm laughing with relief as I stand to leave. Lewis won't be alone, after all. "I guess this is goodbye, then."

Lewis doesn't respond. I hear some shuffles, some sniffles. I sit back down when I hear him.

"Sh-it," he says, the word coming out wobbly, not under his control. He coughs and tries again. "Shit. I'm going to miss you so much. I can't imagine—"

"You're going to be fine," I tell him firmly.

"Yeah," he says. "We're both going to be fine."

His hand shoots out from the gap in the door, his fingers reaching out for me. I take them in mine and squeeze hard. He squeezes back.

We sit like that for a long time.

forty-five

Kelsey

TWO YEARS LATER

"WHAT'S THE PLAN NOW?" GRAN ASKS.

I sit back in my chair. "Well, I don't know about you lot, but my plan is to go to sleep for the rest of the day. Honestly, I'm the most full I've ever been."

"Same here," Gramps says, his already tight white shirt pulling even tighter across his stomach than it was this morning. "I can't remember the last time I worked my way through four courses for lunch, especially when three of them were bread-based. And we've got the cake to get through when we get home."

"You're joking, aren't you?" Mum asks. "Didn't I specifically say not to make a fuss?"

"Yes, and didn't I specifically tell you to stop talking nonsense? It's not every day my daughter graduates with first-class honours."

Gran rolls her eyes at the same time as putting her hand on Gramps's arm. "Honestly, Kelsey, it's like a bloody wedding cake. You should see the icing. He's been working on it for weeks."

I grin. "Can't wait. Shall we go then?"

"Oh, go on," Mum says. "I suppose there's always room for cake."

I have to practically roll myself upright to get off my chair, like I'm back in yoga class, coming out of a pose. Gran, Gramps and Mum head outside Grantas, the swish Italian restaurant I booked us near the university, for some fresh air while I wait by the welcome desk until the waitress comes out with my suitcase from the back. I'd come straight up from London on the earliest train I could book to be at the graduation and hadn't had time to go to the bungalow before.

Gramps takes the suitcase from me when I join them on the pavement and leads the way to the car. I link arms with Mum, and we follow after.

"Are you sure you're really all right? I didn't want to ask too much over lunch, but you do look a bit tired, love."

"I'm fine. Really, I am. Lots of late nights at work, that's all."

"And Jakub?"

"He's fine, Mum. Just busy and going away for his annual boys' holiday next week."

"That's good. And everything's OK between you?"

"More than OK," I tell her, giving her a kiss on the cheek before getting in the car.

When we get back to the bungalow, Mum and I are greeted not only by an exquisite gold and cream graduation cake that looks so professional it's hard to believe Gramps hasn't had it made by a winner of *Bake Off*, but by a full spread too, laid out in my old room, which is now the dining room it was always supposed to be. The bungalow is decorated with black and gold balloons and banners, and, to top it off, as soon as we walk in Gran, goes to the fridge and pulls out a bottle of Moët.

"This is too much," Mum says quietly, her eyes filled with tears. "I can't believe you did this."

"It's not too much at all," Gran says fiercely. "You've been a rock to me these last couple of years, and to Kelsey, all the while working your bum off to get your degree. We are so, so incredibly proud of you."

Gran hasn't managed to keep the tears in her eyes, and they stream down her face, cutting lines through her carefully applied blusher. She covers Mum in a hug and the two of them stand like that for so long, I move forward to take the Moët out of Gran's hands in case she drops it. I put it on the side before wrapping my arms around both of them. From my position, I spot Gramps watching us from the doorway. We catch each other's eye, and he gives me a wink. I wink right back.

After the delicious cake and the mini scotch eggs that I couldn't imagine putting in my mouth but ended up eating three of, we sit down in the lounge. Within minutes, Gramps and Gran are asleep.

"Why don't you go now? I'll stay here and have a tidy round," Mum says quietly from beside me on the couch.

"Go where?"

"You know where. You're only here for a couple of days, and you're out with the girls and Tom tomorrow night. You should take your chance and go now."

Since moving to London, I've been coming home every few

months, whenever I could get a weekend off working at Laverne, the new restaurant in Soho I got a job at when it opened, that happened to become a celebrity hotspot from its first weekend, and therefore one of the busiest restaurants in London. At first, my family presumed part of the reason I came back was to see him too, but I never did. After the first few visits, I told them to stop asking me.

Apart from a few messages every now and again to check in with each other, Lewis and I haven't spoken. I know snippets about his life from what Mum has told me after she's met up with Melissa a few times, but, other than that, I don't know anything about Lewis's life. Now two whole years have passed, Mum's only saying out loud what I was thinking the whole train journey back. Two whole years in which I've never stopped missing him, but have fitted in missing him alongside new experiences, like falling in love, making new friends, taking yoga classes, developing an interest in baking to ease the pain of not living with Gramps and Gran any longer, becoming an excellent teacher in Zoom so I could see my family while not being with them to celebrate Gran's all clear after her chemo the night she found out, becoming a supervisor at work, learning to take pride in my job. Gradually making him a part of my experience instead of the whole. All those other times I came home, I wasn't ready to see him. I was scared I'd fall backwards; I'd stop being this new person who was doing great on her own.

Lewis felt the same. A few months after I moved, he called me. He wanted to let me know that if he was quiet, it didn't mean that he wasn't thinking about me, only that he wanted to give me space in my new life, and for him to have space in his. I told him it was fine, and I wanted to do the same for him. Without saying it, we agreed we would both know when it was the right time to see each other again.

Now, it's time.

* * *

There's a whole lot different about Ellcott Avenue, two years later. The raw newness of the estate has been covered by trees maturing, borders that have been planted along the strips of grass, autumn leaves brushed into little mounds in regular intervals along the road. A few families must have moved in, because there are three bikes propped up against the fence at number twenty and a basketball hoop facing out to the road in front of the corner house. There's even a knitted cover for the post box at the entrance of the road.

Lewis's house has remained almost the same. Still no car in the driveway, no new shrubbery or flowers planted, no further outward signs of life spilling out of the house itself. But there are two differences I spot immediately. My blue box has gone. Someone has moved it, so the pathway up to the front door is clear. And the door is open.

Slowly, I walk towards it. I can't hear anything from inside – no voices or movement, no clues about who is inside or what might be going on. My first thought is that this might not even be his house any more. Maybe Lewis's door is open because Lewis isn't here now.

I get to the doorway and am offered my first uninterrupted view of the hallway, which doesn't look as dark and cavernous as it did through the letterbox now it's suffused with the soft afternoon light that's seeping through the entrance. I take an uncertain step inside, and then another. Part of me knows I should call out, but I'm compelled to keep moving.

I make it as far as the kitchen before I stop dead. There's a man inside, his back to me, in the process of unloading groceries on his kitchen worktop. He's tall and slim, wearing a hoodie and a dark grey beanie hat. He whistles softly as he carries out his task. When he turns to put a four-pint bottle of milk into the chrome fridge behind him, he spots me and the milk drops from his hand, spilling all over the floor.

I haven't seen his face in over three years. His hair is the same unruly style I remember, his eyes are that deep shade of hazel I always loved. As well as all the pieces of him I remember, there are two thick scars across the right side of his face – one reaching to the outer corner of his eye, another running from his ear to his chin – as well as a spider's web of smaller ones, and he's wearing a pair of tinted glasses his perfect vision hadn't required him to wear before.

"Hi," I say. The boy I have loved since I was a teenager is standing right in front of me, the familiarity of him after all this time taking my breath away.

The milk spreads over the kitchen floor as we remain frozen, staring at each other.

"I'm sorry, I didn't mean to barge in," I say.

He holds his hands up, as if to tell me it's fine, and begins to smile, that same beautiful smile that pulled me through the hardest time in my life.

"Hi."

I hear steps on the stairs then, and turn to find Lana coming down, her hair wet, a brush in her hand. "Oh, Kelsey! I can't believe it's you." She runs to me and covers me in a hug.

"You're here," I say, looking between the two of them. "I'm so pleased."

Lana blushes before looking over at Lewis. They're beaming at each other.

"I hope this isn't too weird," Lana says.

"No, no, not at all. It's great." It is weird, but it's also wonderful. I can't help looking at Lewis's face, his happiness shining through.

Lana, noticing the mess around Lewis, sets about cleaning up the milk and sends Lewis off to put on new socks. They share a smile full of so much warmth for each other, it makes my heart swell.

She talks the whole time he's gone, telling me about Lewis's therapy, about how he slowly got the help he needed, how it started by opening the door for a minute, then five, then ten, then stepping outside for ten seconds, then walking to the end of the drive, then to the end of the road. How one day she opened her front door to find Lewis standing there, asking if he could come in for a cuppa.

When Lewis returns, Lana goes back upstairs to dry her hair, squeezing Lewis's arm and smiling at me as she goes.

"Are you sure this is OK, me being here?" I ask, wanting to be totally sure.

To answer, he takes a step forwards, and then another. In a few strides, he's in front of me and pulling me into his arms.

"I'm so proud of you," I whisper, my throat thickening. I hug him tightly, amazed at how wonderful it feels to be with him again.

"Not as proud as I am of you," he says.

Lewis is the first to pull away, and he looks down at me, smiling, a little sheepish.

"Do you, maybe, want to stay for a while? Have a drink? If you have time, that is. If not . . ."

I reach out and place a hand on his arm. I smile. "I've got some time."

acknowledgements

THIS BOOK IS THE RESULT OF MONTHS OF UNWAVERING support, insight and editing wizardry from my wonderful agent, Maddalena. I'm always in awe of the care and consideration you give to my writing and can't thank you enough for all of your work on this and every other idea I throw your way. Thank you!

Thank you to Hazel Holmes for backing this story and taking such good care of it throughout the publishing process. Working with UCLan Publishing has been a dream experience, and I'm so grateful to be one of the first adult fiction titles on your list.

Editing isn't my usual favourite activity, but editing with Jasmine Dove has been a joy. Thank you so much, Jasmine. Thank you, Kathy, for your spot-on copyedits, and to Poppy Loughtman and Becky Chilcott for designing the fabulous cover. My appreciation and thanks to everyone at UCLan who has worked on this book.

To the #VWG – thank you always for being the most wonderful writing group. All these years on, and I still can't believe my luck at finding my way to such a talented, kind and hilarious group of people. To Carolyn O'Brien, your support and enthusiasm means the world. Thank you for the walks, mystery wine and tapas!

To my friends, thank you for all the encouragement and for

your excitement about my books, which always makes me smile. Special mention to Fernanda, who must have single-handedly been responsible for more than half of the sales of my debut novel! You've been amazing.

Thank you to my lovely colleagues for your enthusiasm and support. It's meant so much.

To my family, thank you for everything you do and for all the good memories I can steal and use in my books. To Mark, Max and Sophie, thank you for putting up with me always being on my laptop. You're the best, and I love you lots. Thank you to Poppy, too!

To everyone who has read this book, thank you, thank you, thank you. I hope you enjoyed it.